Diary of a Codependent

2nd Edition:
Reclaiming SMITH

KISHANA SMITH

ISBN: 978-1-5356-1614-0

Preface

In writing this piece of literature, my primary purpose was to have a place to release and process the emotions that I was feeling. Self-healing was my primary motivation. As this piece of work approached conclusion, I no longer wanted to keep it to myself. I wanted to share my truth in hopes that it may empower, motivate, and validate another survivor. I also hope that this book will elevate awareness about abuse. No two stories are the same. I encourage you to tell yours.

This book is fiction, based on a true story. Certain characters and locations have been altered to maintain confidentiality. This book contains profanity and a few graphic scenes. Throughout my journey of growing and healing, my values have shifted. I no longer hold on to my old ways and perceptions, nor do I conduct myself as I did during those years. However, in hopes of giving my reader the true experience of my incarceration and abuse, I did not want to amend those aspects of my story.

Some scenes in this book may provoke your own memories, whether you are a survivor or know one that has experienced Domestic Violence. I encourage you to take time to take care of yourself, however that feels best for you. If you would like to seek confidential hotline support, three resources that I have found helpful are: Codependency Hotline 1-855-315-4766, The Domestic Violence Hotline 1-800-799-7233, and The National Sexual Assault Hotline 1-800-656-HOPE. The abuse could be a past or present situation. These resources also offer support to individuals who are currently supporting or seeking to support someone else. There is great strength and power in your voice.

Dedication

This book is dedicated to:

Audrey Morrison (Aunty)- A brave and selfless woman who has sacrificed her own dignity and confidentiality for the publication of this book. Thank you for having the courage to accept the fact that the abuse I endured was not your fault. I hope that one day I am fortunate enough to be half the woman that you are. Due to my experience of abuse, you have acquired secondary trauma. Together, we will heal!

My siblings, *Leighton John-yarde* and *Kylie Salmon*. Kylie, your playful pickiness has taught me resilience and independence. Leighton, your unconditional love, forgiveness, support, and willingness to believe in my dreams have helped me become who I am today. You opened your home- and heart- which enabled me to publish this book. Thank you.

Anthonina Fenelon- Since the day we met at the bus stop, as eleven- year-olds, you have cheered me on. You were always the first friend to believe in me and walk beside me through it all. Do you remember all the after-school activities you joined for my sake? Even then, while you were unaware of what was going on, you kept me safe and never left me alone. If I could ask for many wishes, one would be for every individual to have a friend like you; the greatest gift of all. You, along with *Rea Shqepa* and *Claudia Gomez*, have contributed countless hours of tears, advice, revisions, and support to the publication of this book. I thank you all for loving this project and caring for its vision, as if it were your own.

This book is also dedicated to the sincere hugs that I have received, along with the warm smiles and encouraging words. Also, the endless conversations that have made me feel that I could touch the SKY and those that tried to break me. I have learned to believe in myself!

Finally, this book is dedicated to all those who have experienced abuse, to those who have lost hope, to the invalidated ones, the invisibles, the voiceless who want to be heard, to those that have witnessed injustice in an unfair world, and to those whose dreams and innocence were stolen from them. May your pain be less, and your spirit be strong. This book is for you!

Contents

Chapter One 1

Chapter Two 9

Chapter Three 17

Chapter Four 27

Chapter Five 41

Chapter Six 51

Chapter Seven 61

Chapter Eight 73

Chapter Nine 83

Chapter Ten 101

Chapter Eleven 113

Chapter Twelve 127

Chapter Thirteen 139

Chapter Fourteen 153

Chapter Fifteen 163

Chapter Sixteen 173

Chapter Seventeen 191

Chapter Eighteen 201

Chapter Nineteen 209

Reclaiming SMITH **221**

Preface II 223

Boston 225

Good, Better, Best 241

Sigma Kappa Psi 249

Bibliography 261

About the Author 263

Chapter One

May of 2009
Richmond, Virginia

I could feel my black Nokia cell phone vibrating next to me as I slept on Aunty Sidney's living room floor; I had two cell phones. The black Nokia was my work phone, so I knew what the vibration meant. I looked at the blue screen to see a text message, which read, "Ready to play?" It was Latoya, my friend from high school and my partner in this game.

I got up from the eggshell-colored carpet to see Aunty grabbing her purse to leave for work. When I had gone out the day before, she had told me to come home at a reasonable hour. The birds were starting to sing when I, at last, came home. I could tell by the look on her face that she was still upset with me for the decision I made the night before, regardless of her concerns.

Aunty was always well dressed when she left for work and this morning was no different. She wore a navy-blue business suit, with gray heels and silver accessories. As she left the apartment, she said "I love you."

I hurried to get dressed in my game clothes. Today, I would execute my plan! This plan would be my way out and I knew I couldn't do it alone. I had known Toya since middle school and we'd been close, like sisters. For a long time, it had been Toya and myself against the rest of the world. Until very recently, she had understood me, and I had understood her. We had always trusted each other, *so I had thought!*

We'd met Ronan the year before, in high school. Ronan and Latoya, or Toya as we liked to call her, had been dating for the last six months. Through much of our dialogues, inserted with many variations of sentiment, I learned that I was viewed as their 'confident' friend; the one that knew what she wanted and wasn't afraid to go after it. Despite their relationship, and our friendship, I had a nagging feeling not to trust him, a feeling that I often ignored.

I had gone over the rules of the plan several times with both of them. Each of us knew what we would do, the goal was to get it done without overthinking. Toya would be the driver while Ronan and I would have to get in, play, and get out — in less than two minutes. I didn't want Ronan *grandstanding* and Toya had to be ready to meet us, immediately, when we got out.

I put on my baggy blue jeans, dark colored sneakers, a navy-blue V-neck T-shirt, and my big black hoodie. Leaving the apartment, there was no need for me to grab the items, as they were already in the trunk of my car, packed two days ago.

I jogged, with purpose, through the burgundy-painted apartment building's main door, as the spring breeze awakened my senses, reminding me of what was to come. I started walking faster toward my shinny sliver- all back interior, Mercury coupe, parked in the apartment lot. Several times, unsuccessfully, I tried to unlock the car door, sabotaged by my shaking hands. I blamed this on everything: my nervousness, the weather, fatigue. Blaming it on everything but the truth, which was that I felt afraid of the uncertainty and the unknown, I was fighting the urge to not go back into the apartment.

With every mile getting shorter and heavier, I'm not exactly sure how I drove to our meeting place. I was constantly fighting the urge to turn around and return to what I knew. The intended destination was fifteen minutes away. The ride was filled with stoplights, shopping centers, and yards of cornfield. As I waited for the lights to turn green, I looked at the people in the shopping centers, envying their smiles and what seemed like carefree attitude. If only they knew what I was about to do. Would they see the pain in my eyes? Would they read my words and sense my fear? Would they offer a helping hand, a kind word, a warm smile? Would they see their daughter, sister, cousin, friend in me? Would they protect me? It's too late to matter now, too late to turn back…

When I pulled into the park, Toya and Ronan were already there. I popped my trunk open and grabbed my high heels, along with my bag of equipment, and got in the front seat of Toya's 2007 burgundy Toyota Scion. She was chewing on her bruised lower lip and avoided looking at me, at all cost, even when I talked to her. I was the leader of our game, the mastermind, so I had to wear a strong face, for myself and for them. I tried to maneuver confidently, to seem as though I was capable of carrying out what we called this game. But, I would argue, that this was far different from the games I had been used to. I was so nervous and scared. If someone had said, "Let's do something else," I would have agreed. My stomach was in knots. And I was fighting what felt like the onset of massive diarrhea. I looked at Toya, gave her a slight nod, and said, "Let's play!" "Where to?" she said.

"The one on Fitzgerald Road."

As we started driving, I turned and looked at Ronan, who sat in the back seat, not saying a word. Silence was not a common thing when Ronan was around. He possessed a huge sense of humor and would frequently spout ridiculous jokes to make us smile. Ronan was extremely tall, about 6'2", with bean- shaped, warm eyes, and we called him the gentle giant. He played basketball for his community college, driven by his aspirations to one day, make it to the NBA. He felt that if the NBA didn't work out for him, at least he would have gained a college degree. Today, he looked terrified and far from his usual self. He planned to use the money from the robbery to get his mom an apartment in a safer area. The crime rate was rising in his hometown of Baltimore City and he no longer felt safe at school knowing his mom was in danger.

The silence amongst us felt heavy and imprisoning. I thought back to those nights when it felt like eternity would not be enough for Toya and I to share our dreams and secrets. Those days were precious, in comparison to now, when it feels like Toya has turned into a stranger, sitting beside me, whose thoughts I could not read. *What was she thinking? Was she afraid?*

Toya drove rather quickly towards our destination, which was about thirty minutes away. I looked out the window as our route took us out into the country, while Pleasure P flowed through the car speakers singing, "*Boyfriend Number Two,*" which was our favorite R&B song at the time. If we had the strength, maybe we would have been dancing. But, the three of us were so tense I could feel it, and none of us had the vision or forethought to say, "*Different game, please.*" Toya slowly drove us past the Kentburg Bank. It was about 9:15 in the morning, and there were only five cars in the parking lot. From my prior research, I knew that three of those cars belonged to employees. "*It's a slow Thursday morning,*" I thought.

"Toya, let's circle again and wait for those customers to leave."

I had researched criminal cases that were related to bank robbery. I used the knowledge from those findings to build a plan and to choose what I thought would be the most appropriate bank. Toya turned left and drove up the ramp to the shopping center next to the bank. "Are you guys ready?" Toya barely mumbled.

We reluctantly shook our heads.

"Okay. 'Cause I'm going to circle once more. Then, I'm pulling into the bank, and its *game* time, regardless of whether there are customers. I don't want the camera or neighboring businesses to catch my plate driving around and around this bank!" She pulled out of the shopping center lot and down the ramp. I quickly removed my sneakers and slid my feet into the high heels.

As the radio continued to play, I knew Toya enough to understand that she was aggravated. My mind was in *game* mode. I was concentrating on what was about to happen. My adrenaline began to pump and I could vividly read the sign, "Kentburg Bank." Toya drove into the parking lot and I pulled the hoody over my head and zipped it all the way up past my forehead, disguising my face. The hoodie was an example of an urban fashion trend at the time. There was an image of a bug-like creature, with mesh eyes on part the of the zipped hoodie that covered my face. The mesh enabled me to see out of the hoody while my eyes were hidden. I wore long baggy pants and high spike heels to make me look taller than I was. Toya slowed down, right in front of the door. Whether I was ready or not, nothing was going to ever be the same again.

I pressed the button on my stopwatch and I jumped out of the car. Hoody up and face masked, my eyes focused on what was visible: Kentburg Bank. As I approached the bank entrance, I felt puzzled by the lack of noise around me: I didn't hear any commotion behind me. I turned around and saw that Ronan had not followed me. *Seriously?* My mind argued with itself that I had to continue with the plan because I was sure that the camera had already caught my image. Needless to say, I did have a choice, I still had time to turn around. I still had time to say, "No! This is not how the story goes!" My body was physically moving faster than my thoughts, and within seconds, I was on the other side of the double doors and in the bank, alone.

The bank was dim and the only lights that registered with my eyes where those located to the left side of the bank, which seemed to serve as lighting for the teller stations. The teller line was occupied by three individuals, possibly all identifying as female. I yelled, in a stern, deep voice, "Hands in the air! Away from the counter. Press the button and I'll shoot everyone in here."

Three petite- built, elderly ladies stood behind the counter. I quickly and carefully, scanned the bank lobby, as I instructed the customers to sit, back-to- back, on the lobby floor. I kept my 99mm pointed towards the customers, just in case anyone wanted to play 'hero.' I could hear the tellers screaming as I jumped over the counter. The sense of fright trumped the tone in the space, and it felt clear that the tellers were being compliant, at least for that moment. I didn't want anyone to get physically hurt. I ran across the teller line, going from drawer to drawer, four in all, loading my bag with their tainted currency. After I cleared those drawers out, I jumped back over the counter to make my way out of the front door.

On my way out of the door, I sprayed the pepper spray that Toya often carried in her purse for protection. I wanted the fumes from the spray to cloud the vision of everyone inside the back. The robbery would have been smoother if Ronan had come in. However, I had executed my plan. I looked at my stop watch — 1 min. 39 sec. Less than two minutes — just the way I'd wanted it.

I got out of the bank and prepared to jump into the car. My eyes searched the entire parking lot and didn't see Toya's car.

"Where the fuck is she?" I wasn't surprised that Ronan had betrayed me.

But I expected that Toya would still be here. I searched for my cell phone.

"Yo. Where you at?"

"I pulled off. I thought I heard sirens."

"What?" My heart fell to my stomach.

"I'll be right back."

"I gotta keep moving. The cops will be here in less than two more minutes!

I'll be on the side of the highway."

I ran towards the cornfield. My vision was blurred and my eyes were burning from the massive amounts of pepper spray that I had sprayed minutes before. I had run in heels, several times before, so I was used to them, which meant that running through the cornfield wasn't necessarily difficult. What was difficult, though, was hearing the sirens getting closer and the realization that there will always be consequences when playing the *game*. I looked over to the busy highway and saw Toya drive past me. I nodded at her, which meant to go straight to plan B — get the cops off my ass by any means necessary. She shook her head no. Now, it was time to panic. My heart rate instantly increased, and I could feel the effects manifesting in my stomach. Fuck, everything was falling apart. I dropped to the ground and crawled under the nearest bush.

From the bush, I saw three cop cars rush to a stop on the side of the cornfield. A white female officer jumped out of her cruiser. Three other cop cars followed. I could see them running all through the cornfield. I was crawling in the dirt, headed in the opposite direction of where I saw most of the cops. As soon as it looked safe, I would get up and run. To my surprise, in this tiny speck on the map town, I saw a helicopter almost directly above me. I pierced my body even closer to the ground and eased my way underneath another bush. There was so much noise from the helicopter, I could barely hear the cop voices and walkie talkies getting closer.

The female officer walked past the bush in which I was under. The officer paused. I hoped with everything within me, that the officer would keep walking. Instead, she kicked my heel, and jumped back. "Stand up! Put your hands in the air! Drop your bags, the phone, and the gun."

She had seen my fucking blue high heels that wouldn't camouflage against the brownish green bush. *I wish if I could shoot myself; but my hands were not responding to my thoughts. Once again, I reject the act of suicide.* I crept out from under the bush and raised my hands as soon as I was on my feet.

"You are under arrest. You have the right to remain silent. Anything you say or do can be used against you in a court of law." She just had to remember my Miranda Rights! Her partner cuffed my hands behind my back and threw me in the back of their cruiser. They took me straight to the station. Every time they whizzed around a corner, I was slammed from one side of the seat to the other, with no way to sit upright, or brace myself so I wouldn't fall over. The bank that I had just robbed resembled a house, which made me feel more monstrous. My thoughts raced... *Toya just had to fold under pressure. If I'd really been on top of things, I would have seen that neither of them were built for this....*

Chapter Two

We pulled up in front of a building that resembled a house, a brick building with a cement porch across the front. There was even a shade tree in the front yard. The building looked like a lot of the other houses in the neighborhood, except for the large blue and gold sign that announced this was the local police station. The two cops duck-walked me out of the car and into the building, where I could smell the potent aroma of coffee. The officers pushed me past the front desk and down to the end of a long hallway, where there were three holding cells. They were old- fashioned cells with steel bars. When we arrived to the last cell along the path, we jolted to an abrupt stop, in front of the cell entrance. The officers un-cuffed my hands and shoved me into the cell, the slam, loudly confirming their hierarchy. The taller officer of the two told me to remove my heels, pants, and hoodie, ordering me to slide them through the bars. He then tossed them on the floor at the end of the hallway, where I could see them. He looked at me with his face expressing disgust and said, "Heels, you crazy bitch?

"Well, why not?" I shot back at him, with a smirk.

I stood there, in the cold cell, wearing only my panties and a blue, v-neck T-shirt. Minutes later he came back with a big, black, wool blanket. He told me to move to the wall at the back of the cell.

"Stand there. And don't move." He ordered.

The officer opened the cell door, glared at me as though I were a disgusting sort of insect, and threw the blanket at me. If looks could kill, I would have been dying a slow, agonizing death. *Yes, I thought, I came to your peaceful town to cause chaos.*

I stood up and stood against the back wall. He threw a heavy wool blanket at me so hard it about knocked me over. The horrendous smell smacked me in my face, prompting me to wonder if the blanket had ever been washed. I didn't dare move a muscle till he'd locked the door to the cage again. Then I picked up the blanket and shook it out. It smelled musty, but I wasn't in a position to wonder how clean it was, --I needed to shield myself. I wrapped it around my shoulders and curled up on the cell room cot. At least that blanket was big enough to hang down past my knees when I stood up.

I sat in the cold, dimly lit cell for what felt like three hours. There wasn't much to look at in the cell and, what was there, was designed to intimidate. A metal toilet, with no toilet tissue. A metal shelf of a bedframe, with no mattress. I glanced outside the cell at my pile of clothes. *Aunty is going to kill me,* I thought. Escape was the first thing on my mind. Could I overpower the officers and get hold of the keys? *That only works in the movies.* Stuck the way I was, barefoot and in my underwear, I didn't feel as though I could overpower much more than my shadow. Toya would get a piece of my mind when I saw her again. The next thing I thought about was what I would say during questioning. *My family can't afford a lawyer. Imma get a public defender. They're 'posed to have my best interest at heart, but really they defending the State. Toya and Ronan are both still out there. Damn.*

I wonder what they would tell the officials if they are ever questioned. Think, Giselle. Think. But my thoughts only went around in circles, always coming back to the same place — I was cooked.

Another heavy-set officer came to get me out of the holding cell. He was came to the cell with a snack bar, of some sort. *Would it have been that unbearable to leave the snack at his desk for five minutes?*

What do they do all day in this town — just sit around and eat?

"Put your hands through the slot." There was a pie hole near the lock on the bars. He placed a set of handcuffs on me, then opened the cell. We proceeded back down the same hallway to a door on my right-hand side. Inside, there was a long white table and two chairs. There were two piles of papers and a detective sitting at one end with his hands resting on top of one of the piles. I looked towards the ceiling of the room and saw an old fashioned gray camera with a red flashing light.

"I'm detective James Strouss. Let's cut straight to the chase." *I refused to let the detective see how miserable I felt.*

"So, tell me why you robbed the bank?"

"Why are you a detective?"

"Ma'am are you on drugs?"

"I don't do drugs."

"So, you are telling me that you are sober."

"Don't I look sober?" I sat up straight in the chair and wrapped the blanket tight around me.

"Do you want a bottle of soda?"

"No."

"All right. Answer these questions. Name?"

"Giselle Greene."

"Age?"

"Nineteen."

"Occupation?"

"Student at Virginia State University." "Tell me how everything happened." Silence.

"Where is the driver?" Silence.

"I know that there is another person. There's no public transportation in this area. You didn't get all the way out there on foot."

"Well, since you know everything, why don't you tell me where the driver is?"

He purposefully assembled his papers, got up, and left the room. I guess he was frustrated by the fact that I did not want to answer is most important question. They took me outside to a blue cop car, still barefoot, and clutching the blanket with my cuffed hands.

*　*　*

Central Booking read the large blue letters painted on the wall. My mind was racing a mile a minute, as my bare feet slapped against the cold concrete. I still had no shoes and barely had any clothes on, under the blanket. The cops claimed they had taken my clothes for evidence.

I was shoved into a room which had a toilet and a concrete bench. The sign on the door read D- Block. A female that looked to be Hispanic lay sprawled out on the concrete bench. She was stoically shivering. That cell was kept colder than it needed to be — maybe on purpose. Minutes later, I was cold too. The Hispanic girl asked me what I was there for. I didn't feel like talking. I was still numb over the shock of being picked up and under arrest. Only criminals go to jail, and I wasn't a criminal. I was just a chick who was so angry I had to strike out somehow. If the rules of the game would have been different, I would have been at home, counting my money.

I had my commit papers crumpled in my fist. I unrolled the pages and read through them again. None of the words made any sense to me. I was about to roll the pages back up, when the Rican chick tugged them out of my hand.

The Hispanic girl let out a long, low whistle. "You robbed a bank? Damn!

None of that petty stuff for you, girl."

A tall black male officer walked into the holding cell and threw me some blue pants that had PRJ on the leg.

"What the fuck is PRJ?" I said.

The Hispanic girl turned to me and said, "Pamunkey Regional Jail, the Hanover county jail, and that's where we both about to go. You ever been locked up?"

"Nope."

"How old are you?"

I didn't answer her. We sat on that bench for at least two more hours. The big, bold blue door opened, and I anxiously looked up, thinking that maybe they would call my name. Instead, two Asian females were pushed in. They looked to be in their thirties. Both of them were nicely dressed in skimpy, casual clothes. They both had long black hair, and their nails were well done. They sat down, looking confused and scared. As soon as they sat, the Hispanic chick began to pick on them.

"Why are you here?" she said.

The first Asian lady shook her head. "Why are you here?" She shook her head again.

"What? You don't speak English?"

Minutes later, the door opened again. In walked another Asian female.

This one was really young. She looked like she wasn't even hitting twenty. She had a mini skirt on and orange heels. She joined us on the bench, looking scared. The door opened again. An elderly Asian woman walked in. Now, I really had to sit up on the concrete bench, as there was no room to lie down.

"What's going on?" I said.

The nosey Hispanic jumped up. "Oh, I know. This is a salon raid. They raided the salon for prostitution." She told the elderly lady to hand over her commit papers, and began to read the charges. "Misdemeanor Prostitution. I knew it! That's a damn shame!" She continued reading. "You dumb ass. Told a cop that he could receive a full package for sixty dollars, after they'd been observing your salon for nine months."

The oldest Asian lady bowed her head and slouched down beside me onto the concrete bench. She looked as though she'd been working for sixteen hours straight. There was a language barrier, but body language was universal, and I could see the shame written all over her. Shame is an emotion that I could definitely relate to. But damn! She was old enough to be someone's grand-mom. She should leave this life to the young folks and go sit down somewhere. I looked over at the Hispanic chick. "Yo. What's your name?"

"Valarie."

"I'm Giselle."

"Imma call you GiGi."

"I gotta pee. Ain't no tissue."

"You betta drip dry. He really ain't gonna bring us no toilet tissue, girl," she said, pointing to the sign hanging above the toilet, "This is a holding cell. Not the Holiday Inn."

The big, bold-looking door opened again. "Greene, Giselle..."

I jumped up and gripped the waist of the pants they had given me earlier. There was barely anything left of the elastic that was supposed to be holding them up. The pant legs dragged on the floor. I walked out towards the officer. He walked me about two doors down the hall to a small cluttered room. I looked up and saw a television screen showing an old, white, red-headed judge sitting behind a desk. I sat in a metal folding chair, which was located in front of the screen. The judge read off my charges — too many to count. But, a few things stood out: Armed Robbery, Felony One, Possession of an Instrument of Crime. The judge set bail at a two hundred thousand dollars. My heart dropped to my ass and my body suddenly felt heavy, like it could sink through the floor. The officer who was escorting me walked me to the room next door. He took my mug shot from every angle, along with fingerprints. That was when it hit me; *this shit is real!*

When I was brought back to the holding cell, I felt numb. I didn't speak. I sat on the cement bench, numb and empty. I felt as though I had just heard my death sentence. Life as I had known it was over. The hours went by. I couldn't see a clock, and the police had taken my watch. We were all bone weary, but we were too frightened to think about relaxing, and there was no place to sleep, even if we wanted to do that. I should have been hungry, but after hearing the amount of bail set to my name, food didn't mean anything to me. Six of us sat in that cell, sweating and frightened. If any one of us had to use the toilet, the rest of us formed a line around her, to give her a bit of privacy from the leering officer. The heavy door clanged open and closed over and over, until everyone had been processed.

Three officers then entered with long chains, and more cuffs, to shackle our feet, and ran chains from handcuff to handcuff, and foot shackle to foot shackle, so that we stood in a line, one in front of the other; tall, short, skinny, black, Asian, Hispanic, like a line of dogs. Or, should I say, lost sheep. I tightly gripped my commit papers. If they were to fall, there would have been no possible way for me to pick them up.

The officers led us out of the cell, around the corner, and down a short hall to a locked exit door. The officer in front made a show of punching in the code to open the door. It opened with the clang of steel meeting steel. They lead us through a brightly-lit garage where two police cars were parked. Just beyond, the door was raised to reveal a blue and white van, or paddy wagon, that would cart us to the Hanover County Jail. It was big, more like a truck than a van.

It was still dark out. One of the officers said it was three in the morning. The Asian girls were in front of me. I watched them each take her turn leaping into the wagon. When the youngest girl went to leap, her flip-flop fell off her foot and she fell backwards on top of the rest of us. I looked over at the officer. He didn't show a bit of concern. I guess this sort of thing had happened many times before. When my turn came, I held my breath and made the leap, landing sprawled on the floor of the paddy wagon. My chains nearly knocked the woman behind me down, but that didn't mean anything to the officers.

I have heard it said that on the human chessboard all moves are possible. But I had landed in check mate, and could see no moves to get out of that. I looked around at these women: murderers, rapists, thieves, prostitutes, and drug dealers. I could not bring myself to feel as though I should fit in, even though I was sitting there with a robbery charge. I could not come to terms with the fact that I was being charged a thief. As a result of my escape plan, I was faced with spending years in prison. *Damn, Toya, why did you leave?*

Chapter Three

The ride down to the county jail was cold and dark. When the van drove down a bumpy road, we shook and rattled like marbles in a cigar box. When the van turned a corner, we slid from one side to the other, landing on top of each other.

I was experiencing the feeling of chills throughout my body. Later, I came to realize it was my fear, my sense of intense loss, that had me feeling cold. I sat immersed in my thoughts. So this was really check-mate. It was as though the black knights and bishops had my white king surrounded on all sides, and all I could do was sit in that police van and shiver, huddled with the other five women. I don't know what they were thinking and feeling. We were all quiet — probably too upset to say much.

When I looked over at Valarie, I swear she looked bored, like she'd seen it all before. I recalled those movies of prison life that I had seen, *The Birdman of Alcatraz*, and *The Shawshank Redemption*, and I wondered if I would be spending the next lo-o-o-ong stretch of my life encased in chains, like the ones I wore in that van. Tears and snot dribbled down my face. I tried to wipe them away, but chains aren't very good for that.

While the six of us sat along the two sides of that van, clanking and rattling our way to the county jail, I was reminded of the era of slavery. I felt like property, being exported to a destination. When we arrived at the jail, our officers lined us up and each of us, in turn, took a flying leap off the van, chains and all. That was the first part of our introduction to life at the county jail. We clanked our way down a long hall, with an armed officer in front, another officer, just like him, in back, and two more armed officers, one on each side of us. I had never seen so much firepower lined up against six helpless women. They marched us down a long hall, turned us to the right, where a heavy, polished steel door stood. It shone like silver in the artificial light. The door was massive, and as solid as the door on a bank vault. It opened electronically, then closed behind us with a heavy, ominous clank.

As far as I could see, I was still in check-mate. I could see no way to get out of the situation, or even to make it better. When your king is cornered, and any move you make would lead to his death, all you can do is hold still till your opponent tells you what your fate will be.

The officers led us in a line into a cell, and there removed our chains. Then, one by one, they led us through the intake process. They took from us anything that might be considered valuable, any cash, jewelry, identification, even the clothes we had on. In exchange, we were each given a number, along with the standard-issued prison garb. That consisted of a loose fitting pair of pants with the letters PRJ down the side, a blue, short-sleeved shirt, a pair of blue slip-on sneakers, and three sets of underwear.

From there we were led to new holding cells. A better term for them might be quarantine cells. The prison authorities held us in those cells, two at a time, for a full week. Each of those cells measured less than ten feet by ten feet. They did this so that the prison doctor could have blood work drawn and other lab work done, to make sure none of us were carrying anything that could turn into an epidemic among the other prisoners.

Valarie and I shared a cell for those seven days. The officers let us have one shower during that time. Otherwise, we were cooped up in that cell together. We didn't get any time out for exercise or fresh air. They brought our meals to us, three times a day, like clockwork. Oatmeal and a banana for breakfast. The oatmeal was generally cold and gummy by the time it was brought up from the kitchen for us. For lunch, they might give us a hot dog on a bun, or macaroni and cheese. For supper, they often gave us meatloaf and mashed potato. They might give us a vegetable with that, like broccoli. The food tasted stale. Sometimes, it was even green with mold. Usually, it all tasted as though it had been sitting around for the last month — or more. Some nights, it was all I could do to keep from throwing up. Though at that time, food didn't mean much to me. I felt as though my life was over.

I cried a lot. Whenever I think of that first week, I'm glad that Valarie was there. She was only a couple years older than me, but she had been through the system before, and she knew what to expect. We were trapped in a tiny little room, with no sunlight and no fresh air, and no privacy from the leering officers. We had nothing to look at except each other and the ugly gray walls, which were all too close for comfort. After sitting in that cell for seven days straight, neither of us looked too pretty.

But Valarie was special. She would help me buck up when I was feeling down, and I helped her keep her spirits up when she was feeling like nothing in this world would ever be nice for her again.

Every day that week, we watched the other prisoners in their blue prison garb, walking back and forth between their cells and the cafeteria, or their cells and the common area, or sometimes going off on one work detail or another. I couldn't accept that this was where I would have to be. I hadn't been arraigned yet, and I had not met the guy who would be my lawyer, so my life was on hold. Before I was arrested, I had been going to college, studying criminal justice. I had been counting on college being my ticket away from Alton. I had liked going to school. I had always done pretty well with classroom stuff and homework--I guess because it helped keep my mind off of what was emotionally going on with me.

Some of the officers really did look scary. I didn't know if it would be hard to stay out of trouble with them, or what would happen if I did something they decided was wrong. The prisoners I saw, some of them swaggered, like they were super tough, and no one better mess with them. Some of them just looked plain scared. But we all know that a cornered dog that is scared is the last thing you need to face alone. Yeah, I knew how to act tough and smart. I used to think I could do that with the best of them. In some parts of town, it's the only way to survive. But this was a different world. I wondered if I would survive in it.

That week tested both Valarie and me, but instead of fighting each other, we became allies. We weren't permitted much of anything by way of entertainment. We couldn't go to the common area to watch television, or talk with the other inmates. We couldn't play music, though we did sometimes sing. We didn't have access to books, but we didn't have much interest in reading at that point.

We did manage to keep in our possession a pad of paper and a pen. Valarie came up with the idea of making a deck of cards out of the paper. Playing cards would be a change from twiddling our thumbs, so we set to work drawing up the number cards, and making pictures of kings and queens for the picture cards. We used a half sheet of paper to make each card. We played by the hour — mostly Spades. At least the officers did not object to our using paper and pen that way.

While being in quarantine and waiting for our medical exams to clear, if we weren't playing cards, talking, or sleeping, we were filling out paperwork. The amount of paperwork felt overwhelming. There was a phone authorization list; it was painful and difficult to think of phone numbers. With the technology that

I became accustomed to, it seemed there was no eminent need to memorize phone numbers. There was a visitation form; at that point the last thing I wanted was for someone to see me under those conditions. But, I placed people's names on list anyway. I strongly did not want to put Alton's name on the list. But, I knew that the lack of doing so would raise many questions from Aunty. I also filled out a form, which was like a mini application to work on the 'fast-line.'

It wasn't all terrible, and the week did come to an end. Valarie and I were at last led out of the cell. Leaving that cell felt weird. I had been in that cramped little space for so long that I was afraid to step out of it. I had spent so much time just looking at, and not taking part in the life around me, that I was afraid to join it. If the officer hadn't been there to prod us along, I might have headed back to the quarantine cell. At least I knew what to expect in there.

He marched us down the hall, and ushered Valarie into a cell at the end of the bottom tier. She appeared to settle right in, heading straight for the empty bunk, and depositing her small cache of belongings on top of it. The officer led me up a flight of stairs and down to the far end of the top tier. I looked at the row of blue doors, each with its tiny window, reminiscent of the doors on classrooms. If I didn't listen to the sounds, or stop to think about where I was, I might have expected to find a teacher behind each door, poised and ready for class to begin.

The officer stopped at the last door along that side of the tier, pulled a key out of his pocket that was nearly as big as his hand and opened the cell door. I didn't know what to expect, when he more or less pushed me in. As I said, I had seen some pretty tough looking females going up and down the hall. I hadn't heard them talk much. I had only seen how they looked. Judging by their body language, it would not be a good idea to get on the bad side of any of them. *Just who were they putting me in with?* The woman who stood in the center of the cell was probably just as apprehensive as I was. She was older, maybe even in her forties.

"Hi, I'm Candy."

"Hi, I'm Giselle." I said as I hoped she would not notice how badly I was shaking. After we introduced ourselves, Candy talked and talked for hours. Within the first few hours, I learned that Candy like to talk and she liked playing mama to me. She was happy that I was young and basically friendly, and she wanted to explain everything to me. She even told me she was sentenced for life.

"Things aren't so bad in here that you can't get used to it. Just don't get comfortable. Do your time wisely and get up outa here, young buck."

"Why do you have to do so much time?" I said, eager to hear the answer. Anyone's story had to be more interesting than mine and, I think that unconsciously, I felt that understanding why people were in prison would help me figure out how to survive it.

Candy put her hand on her hip and started strutting back and forth, like an officer or a warden, "Yes, Ms. Greene. Continue to tell us about County jail. I want you to give us the line of events leading up to today. That's a question you shouldn't ask around here. But I'll tell you."

"I met a man about six years ago and fell in love. His name's Ace. He on C- Block. We met in my hometown, the thorough streets of Harlem. He moved me out here to take over this town. Took all the customers from this other dude and his crew. We were pushing crack/cocaine, then moved on to dope." "What's dope?" I interrupted her again.

"Heroin. I was in college in New York. Then I dropped out, after meeting this nigga. I didn't see the purpose in going to school or working. College graduates can hardly find a job, now-a-days, and they be in debt till they die. Why work a nine to five and bring home a check of couple hundred when I could make that in one night?"

"Me and him were doing all right out here. Then I started doing drugs. We flip our supply all night. That's when you make the most money. Being high helped me stay up. One night we got into some foul shit. He always had his eye on this one chick. Shorty had a body and a pretty face. It seemed like she had a lot going for herself. She was a college girl. After a while, she became one of our regulars. A dope fiend. I could see the spark in his eyes when he looked at her. It was more than lust. He told me that if I had her looks and my demeanor, I would be the perfect chick. He digged my street smarts and my loyalty. But in his eyes, I wasn't blessed with the best of looks."

"One night, I was feeling real sick. This was after I found out that I was pregnant with his kid. So he left me at the crib to go serve Lee — that be the chick's name. My woman's intuition told me to get in my car and follow him. When he pulled up to her spot, I saw a gray Chevy parked in the alley. It looked familiar. It belonged to couple a' niggas who were tryna redo us a few weeks before. I sat in my car and watched. No one was in the Chevy. I walked to her back door, my pistol cocked, looked through the kitchen window and saw this bitch suckin' my man's dick. I kicked down the door and shot at her, but them otha niggas must'a thought I come after them. They were in the crib, getting ready to rob Ace. Everybody started shooting. The bitch and another nigga ended up dead. They gave me life for her body, and Ace got twenty to forty for self-defense."

"Life," I said quietly, and shook my head. It kinda looked to me like that Ace fella wasn't worth shooting — he would have been pretty good at getting himself shot without Candy's help.

Candy sat back down on her bunk. "Yeah. I'm in this county, waiting to see what comes of my appeal."

I climbed up onto the top bunk, while Candy continued to talk. I couldn't imagine spending the rest of my life in prison; it would be too much like dying.

Every day I read through my papers, knowing that my preliminary hearing would be in a couple of weeks, though at that moment, two weeks felt like a long time. Tears fell from my eyes, so I tried to cry in silence. I began to mumble the Bible verses that I had always heard my mom and grandma, and later my Aunt Audrey recite.

The Lord is my shepherd, I shall not want. He maketh me to lie down in green pastures. He leadeth me beside the still waters. He restoreth my soul. Ye, though I walk through the valley of the shadow of Death, I shall fear no evil, for thou art with me. Thy rod and thy staff, they comfort me.

"It cracks me up, how people come to jail and find religion," Candy yelled from her bunk.

"No, Ms! I've always known religion. God didn't leave me, I left God."

"I'm cool with that. I love God and I don't like when people play with religion. That's why I came at you like that. You gonna need God to get you through this. Especially looking so young and pretty as you are. I know you saw them vultures looking at you and making them comments."

Candy rolled over and went to sleep, and I lay on my bunk thinking about stuff, till I decided to pull out my letter pad from under the mattress.

Dear Diary,

I feel so out of place at times. I still go into shock mode. I've been in this county jail for a week, now. I spent it in what they call observation. It's a bunch of isolated cells, for observations and various medical exams. Those days were rough. That's when I got my first phone call to Aunty. My heart rate sped up when I heard her voice and she accepted the call. We both cried. She said that she saw me on the news. She had put out a missing person's report, because she didn't know where I was for a couple of days. All I can think of is how hurt and embarrassed she must be. I wonder how she feels going to work at the bank, where she had worked for years. Aunty had always been proud of what she did. She had done her work well and she had the respect of the people who worked with her, but I am certain her coworkers are looking at her with suspicion. Her birthday was yesterday. She raised me the best she could since I was really little, and this is the gift that I give her! I can't believe this is real. Prior to being here, I was screaming for help, but no one heard.

Valarie did this county several times before, so she's been helping me a lot. There is a big black lady with dreads, keeps flirting with me. When I leave my cell, I try to avoid eye contact with her. I don't want her to get the notion that I'm interested in whatever it is she thinks she wants.

This county prison is not exactly what I expected jail to look like. There are two tiers. The rooms are in a rectangular layout, going all around each tier. The rooms all have navy blue doors with a rectangular glass window, five inches by four. Each room measured about eight by ten feet, with a bunk bed, a desk, a porcelain toilet and a sink. Talk about feeling like a caged animal! Candy is a talker. I've never been much of a talker. I hope I get a good lawyer. Still waiting for mail.

–Me.

I shoved the letter pad back under my bunk, wrapped my black wool blanket tight around me and rolled over to face the wall, all in one motion.

Chapter Four

"Greene, you have a visitor." I looked up at my cell door and saw Mrs. Officer Santos through the window. It had been so long since I had seen anyone from the outside, I could not believe what she said.

"Yes, visit! Greene. Hurry." She said to me again.

I nodded, and pushed my sloppy joe to the corner of the rusty metal desk.

The sandwich wasn't so appetizing that I regretted leaving it behind. Then I got up and peered into the mirror over the sink. That mirror was a plate of somewhat polished steel. The authorities would not permit glass in a jail cell, as we prisoners could use the broken pieces of it to commit suicide, or to attack each other, or maybe even dig our way out of there. The steel was stained and rusted, and if you looked into it really carefully, you might be able to tell whether or not you had a nose. But I still wanted to get a look at myself before I faced whoever was here to visit me. I ran my hands over the six cornrows that I had braided to the back of my head. I wanted to look at least somewhat presentable. Six cornrows aren't many, but it still took about an hour to get them lined up evenly around my head. I felt better when I took the time to keep as clean and neat as it was possible to be, even though I was in jail.

That one moment I had taken to glance in the mirror was too much for Mrs. Santos. She kicked my door with her steel-toed boot, making it clang, and gave me a venomous look, pointing her thumb out to the hallway.

"I'm ready." I said with a nervous nod.

She opened my cell door with her large, heavy looking master key and walked me across the hall, where she opened a white painted door. It was the first door I had seen in that complex that didn't look as though it was part of a jail — much. The first thing I noticed when I entered was the smell of mildew and rusting metal. Four plastic chairs were lined up in front of a long, bullet proof plate glass window, which served as a dividing wall between the prisoners and their visitors. There were four big telephones bolted into the glass. Officer Santos escorted me down to the third chair and phone. I guess they thought this was the safest way to communicate during visits at the county jail. I looked through the glass and saw three very familiar faces. It was Aunty, Alton, and my cousin Molly. She was my Aunty's daughter, and she lived up in New York. She didn't come down to visit much, though she did try to be nice to me when she came. I was glad she was there, because I thought she would be a comfort to Aunty. My heart sank when I saw Alton. Why did he have to be there? Molly was OK. She had always tried to be nice to me.

As soon as she saw me come in, Aunty picked up the phone on her side of the partition, then sat staring at it as though she had never seen such an object before.

When I pulled my chair closer to the phone, I could see how filthy the room was with dust and grime. The thick glass window was covered with graffiti. I guess doodling on windows was a therapeutic activity for some of the prisoners and their visitors. I wondered where the prisoners had got the markers to make that mess. No one had bothered to clean that window on either side, so I had to peer through an assortment of 'motherfuckers' and other swear words in order to see my family.

I picked up the phone on my side, and watched as Aunty's eyes filled with tears. None of us were able to speak those first few moments. We simply stared at each another. At last, Aunty said, "Hi." Her face trembled with emotion, and she swallowed several times, trying to hold back her tears. Her voice came across squeaky and tinny, as though through a bad connection.

Molly was the strongest of us all. She would be the one to break the ice and set the tone of the visit. She plucked the receiver from Aunty's hand to ask the first questions. "How are you doing?"

It was obvious that I wasn't doing too well, but the only thing I could say was, "I'm OK."

"What?" Molly shouted back to me.

I finally had to shout at the top of my lungs, the way the other three prisoners were, "I'm OK!" for Molly to be able to hear me.

"Why did you do it, Giselle?" Molly shouted back.

I could still taste the sour meat from the sloppy joe in my mouth, and any words I might have said seemed to get stuck in the grease from it. "Can we talk about that later?" I knew that later wasn't a nice thing to say, after Aunty and Molly had gone to so much trouble to come see me, but I didn't want to say anything in front of Alton. I thought I would explode if I had to talk to him. If I decided to talk about it with anyone, I wanted it to be only with Aunty. Maybe, if I had been in a better head-space, I could have explained why I had robbed the bank. But the honest truth was if I had been in a better head space, I would not have robbed it. Besides, that visiting room was not a good place for confessions. Everyone in that room was doing his best to shout over everyone else. I had to shout just to hear myself speak. I could hear all the other loud conversations around me. There was no such thing as privacy in this place.

But I guess part of the problem that led to my being in jail was that I had spent so much energy trying to keep things private out of fear over what others would say or think. Fear of seeking help.

Aunty took the receiver back from Molly and changed the subject. "They asked us for identification, they checked if we were on the visitors list. They put our purses through a metal detector and then each of us followed through the detector. They made me take my jewelry off and take it back to the car."

"Thank you so much for coming. Thank you all for going through the hassle to see me." I shouted, "I have my preliminary hearing next week. Will you be able to make it?"

"Where will it be?" Aunty called back.

"I think it's at the Hanover County Courthouse."

Aunty changed the subject again. "Toya and Ronan turned themselves in."

"Really?"

"Yeah, Toya ran to Delaware for a couple of days and then her mom talked her into turning herself in. When her and Ronan when to the station, Toya was charged and released to fight the case from the streets. Ronan was taken into custody because they discovered that he had another case pending in Maryland. He is in this same jail, with you. I've been in contact with Toya's mother. Mainly, we are trying to figure out what was going through your heads prior to all this. Why didn't you just tell me that you were in need of money? Why didn't you tell me anything?"

In need of money? *I hadn't done it for the money*. Yeah, you don't do anything dumb like rob a bank if you haven't hyped yourself up to believe that you really could get away with it. I didn't know if I could ever talk to anyone about what really happened. I stared into my Aunty's sad eyes, and all I could do was burst into tears — again.

Alton glared at me.

Aunty continued, "A couple of your friends said that they called up here to ask about you. They were told that you were on suicide watch."

Suicide watch? The officers told us it was a quarantine. We didn't have any razor blades, and we couldn't sneak drugs into those cells, so our options for suicide were limited. Maybe the officers were watching to make sure we didn't kill ourselves by sticking our heads in the toilets — or saving medication that none of us were there long enough to receive. "No Aunty," I quickly shot back. "I was in something called quarantine. It's an observation cell that a new inmate has to stay in until their medical exams are complete. Which usually takes a couple of days."

I tried to change the subject. "Aunty, I signed up to be a line worker."

I could see Aunty saying something to Molly on the other side, the Molly grabbed the receiver from Aunty and shouted, "What is that?"

I began to explain, "I will work with about six other females to serve food on the chow line, clean the showers, sweep and mop the floor of the common area."

"Oh." Neither of them knew how limited my options were in that jail, and there was no way I could explain that to them. Aunty took the receiver back from Molly and asked, "What's the common area?"

"It has chairs, couches and television sets. It's where everyone gets to be twice a day, to play cards, braid hair, make phone calls, watch TV, or just talk."

I am sure Aunty wondered why I would take a job like that. It's a dirty job in this very grimy jail and it doesn't even pay. But the line workers are out of their cells and in living areas for a large part of the day and they are allowed extra food, along with a few extra privileges. The prisoners are allowed one shower a week. The line workers can get two or three, and that makes a big difference in a place like this. But most importantly, it would make the days go by a little quicker. Aunty had never been in jail, so there was no way she could understand any of that.

Alton grabbed the phone from Aunty's hands. As far as I was concerned, his being there was an interruption to a visit I had really wanted. "How can I send money?" I began to answer but was distracted by the look of lust in his eyes and the smirk on his face. So I looked at Aunty and said, "You can set up an account and put money on the account so that I can call you. To send money, you would have to get a money order and send it to a designated address. I will write the address to you. But Aunty I know that you have a lot going on. If you can't afford it, I really understand. I will figure it out," I explained.

Alton shouted into the receiver, "I will send you money next week." He had obviously been in a prison setting before, or he knew guys who had, so he understood my situation. I wished that he had not, and that my aunty had been the one to understand.

An officer opened the door, which creaked on hinges that belonged in a Grade-B horror flick "Johnson, your visit is up in five minutes. Greene, time for you to wrap up."

"All right." I looked at Aunty, Molly, and Alton through the glass, and again, began to tear up. They stared back at me. Our visit had been too short for us to say half the things we wanted to say. Aunty and Molly looked so sad, and Alton was his usual smirking self. It was the same shitty grin that I had seen many times before. *I love you*, I heard three different voices say. *I love you too.* I put my hand on the glass, palm flat. Aunty pressed her palm on the other side of the glass, as close as she could get to my hand. I longed to hug her, and to feel her holding me in her arms, the way she did when I was little. I was desperate

to feel her touch. I exited the visiting area and walked the short journey back to my cell. It was so noisy but I couldn't make out what anyone was saying. I was still mentally and emotionally stuck on my visit.

When I got back to the cell, Candy was sitting on the bottom bunk, wiggling her feet and thumbing through a book. "How was your visit, young buck?"

"It was okay." I didn't feel ready to talk about it, so I climbed onto the top bunk. I shoved my head in my very flat pillow and began to think. My thoughts ran a mile a minute, and I needed to sort through them, before I fell deeper into depression. So, I pulled out my letter pad and began to write,

Dear Diary,

Wow. A taste of home just came to see me. Aunty looked very stressed out. She looked like she hadn't eaten in days; kinda like me. I've just been picking at food, only because I know that I need to survive. I haven't seen Aunty cry in years, but she cried as soon as I sat down in front of her. The sadness is literally making my body hurt. I could throw up right now, I'm so hurt. Candy said that the first visit would be the hardest. But I didn't feel THIS horrible yesterday when Terrance came to visit me.

Molly didn't say much to me. I wonder what's going through her head. I'm happy that she came over from New Jersey to see me. One thing that I worry the most about is that Aunty doesn't really have much support, since she moved. I fear for her well-being during this time. I hope Molly will visit often to give her comfort.

I wonder if Aunty's co-workers know what's going on. Will they lose trust in her? The news and newspapers describe me to seem like this dangerous gangster who deserves to be locked up with the key thrown away. Will her boss at the bank think Aunty's just like me? Or worse, that she taught me how to rob banks? Will she lose her job? That would add to the long list of things I already feel guilty about. Suicide watch? I could only imagine all the other stories people have come up with. I wish I didn't care what everyone thought. My body instantly became hot when Aunty told me they thought I was on suicide watch. In brief moments, I do think of killing myself. But, that's not something I would want other people to know… And Alton can take his money and shove it up his ass.

-Me.

My sadness morphed to anger. I knew me and I knew that the emotions that I was feeling weren't safe. I knew that a nap would help me to not feel, at least for a little while. There wasn't much else to do but sleep, anyway. Tears ran down my face and onto my letter pad.

* * *

Clang! Clang! Bang! The racket startled me out of a sound sleep. Candy was repeatedly banging on my bunk.

"Don't you hear the door clicking?" she said. I could hear the irritation in her voice.

"NO! Why is the door clicking?" My head spun from being awakened so suddenly.

"They're clicking the door for you to go downstairs and work. It's chow time. That's a sound you better get used to."

"Well, can you not bang on the bunk! If you have to wake me, tap my shoulder, or say my name. I'll hear you." I gripped the railing on the right side of my bed and turned over. My eyes still closed. I put my feet into my blue, surprisingly comfortable, slip-ons. I grabbed my toothbrush.

"Girl, you don't got time to brush. If you don't hurry down there, they gonna go on to the next name on the list and leave you behind," Candy shouted at me.

I sighed and leaped out the door. The top tier was quiet for the first time all day. As I walked down the concrete steps, I could see all the other ladies standing at their locked doors, staring at me through their small windows. I could hear the commotion on the bottom floor.

"Greene, you're working tonight. You and Jameson can meet the guys at the first door to bring in the food cart.

"Okay." I hadn't seen this officer before and could barely read her name tag on her grey corrections uniform. She was short — I don't think she came all the way up to my shoulders — slender, and white. And, she didn't look as though she was any older than I was. Yet, there she was, ordering me around. She clicked four more cell doors, and five ladies joined us to work. Most of them looked older than me — tougher and more experienced. I might have been the youngest girl there, except for another girl, who was white and had an athletic build. She wore her hair in two Pippi Longstocking braids.

I walked towards the double doors with the elderly lady, and Jameson, the girl with the two braids, leaped in front of me, cut me off, and headed straight for the food cart. I wasn't ready to be bold just yet, so I let her by. The older woman and Jameson pushed the cart and I held the door. We walked down the long hallway that I remembered from the first day when I came in.

I could see two guys, one was dark skinned who may have been about thirty, and the other was a chubby white guy. They were both tall, and they wore the same blue uniforms that we had on, except, they also wore some silly looking white hair nets.

They both smiled. I could see Pippy Long-stocking slip the black guy a note on orange paper. The cart was big enough to block the view from the officer and the camera. When she turned to help Jameson push the cart. The dark-skinned guy, winked and blew me a kiss.

I could smell stale bologna, as they pushed the cart past me. They walked it to the middle of the common, and the rest of us followed behind. By then, almost every cell window was occupied by a face staring back at us. We opened the steel cart door and began to line the trays out on a wooden table. I looked in each of the trays, one by one. Bologna, cheese, and carrots. There was also a tray with about twelve loaves of bread and two small containers, one mayo, one mustard.

The little officer turned to me and said, "Greene, since you're new, you are going to hand out the bread. Four slices to each person. If I catch you giving more, I will send you back to your cell and you won't work this line anymore."

I nodded — as if the work was anything I would have cared about doing outside the jail — as if they were paying me anything to do it.

"Cho-o-o-ow ti-i-i-me," the little officer shouted out. She sounded as though she was calling the pigs to come to the hog wallow. No. If I'd been a pig, I would have left the farm when she let loose with that shout.

All the top tier doors clicked open. The ladies marched down the stairs, holding their plastic cups as if they had been trained many times before to come down for chow in an orderly manner, like a troop of Pavlovian dogs. It reminded me of the boys holding out their bowls for gruel, in the Oliver Twist movie I had seen. I watched the lady beside me hand two pieces of slimy bologna to each person. I turned to her and asked, "Do we usually have bologna for dinner?"

"We have bologna about three times a week."

By the look of the meat, I figured that somewhere back in the kitchen, they had large batches of bologna sitting out, for a couple of days, ready to be served to us. I wondered who they had in charge over there. In about fifteen minutes we had served both tiers, over a hundred women. When we were done, I took my tray of food and walked upstairs to my room. I opened the door to see Candy on the toilet, legs spread wide and her huge white cotton panties at her knees. The room smelled like an outhouse.

She must have noticed my staring at her, sort of open-mouthed. "You never seen someone take a shit?"

I closed the cell door and thought to myself, *I haven't. Not in the same room that I have to eat my food.* I sat at the desk and began to put my two sandwiches together. I could see from the corner of my eye that Candy was undoing her braids while doing her business. I hoped she didn't think I would do her hair, at least not while she was doing her business on the john. She ran her fingers through it and said, "I can't wait for common room so I can get in the shower and wash my hair… Twenty more minutes."

I swallowed about half my sandwich. I had no desire to chew and taste.

The meat smelled freezer burnt, like it had been in the kitchen for months. And I didn't like raw carrots. When the doors clicked for common room, the housing unit sounded like a busy stadium. I heard people shouting to each other across the tiers. Someone turned the TV on and I could see Bow Wow and his co-host on "106 and Park." I reached under the bed for my dark brown plastic bin. I opened it and grabbed soap, my wash rag, and some underwear. Candy was already out of the cell, heading for the shower line.

Lil' Wayne's *A Milli* was playing loudly on the TV. I didn't mind the loud entertainment while I waited for my turn in the shower. As, I stood on the top tier, I could see people eating their snacks, the ones they'd purchased from the commissary. I saw others using the big blue phones that where drilled to the wall. Four on the button tier, and four on the top tier. They looked exactly like pay phones. There was only one person ahead of me when Valarie approached.

"When you done in the shower, come downstairs so we can play Spades. I saw that you had a visit, tell me about it when you come down."

"I'm coming down when I'm done."

This would be my first shower since released from quarantine. While in quarantine, we were given two showers which were in a single- person shower unit. So I experienced what every first- time inmate has to go through — shower shock. I gripped my stuff as entered the shower room. The walls were moldy cement and the floors were slimy cement. I wish I could compare the smell to a high school gym locker, but this was infinitely worse. Ripe? No, it, whatever it was, had died a long time ago. Two steps into the room, the floor sloped down and my feet disappeared into the ankle-deep, murky water. I clutched my shower shoes tight with my toes, hoping I wouldn't lose them in the swamp.

Three other naked ladies were in there with me — an Asian woman and two black women. "Eww," I said, and hoped nobody heard it. I really didn't want to look like a wimp. I put my dry things down on a nearby chair and began to soap up my wash rag. Then I looked over at the Asian lady. There was blood dripping down her leg and into the oozing water. Hay! I had gone in there to get clean, not pick up someone else's dirt, skin infection, or bacteria. This was something else no one on the outside would ever understand.

"Oh my God, is that your period blood?" I asked while I quickly reached outside the shower to grab my clothes. Within seconds, I was dressed, and out of the shower, racing back to my cell, dripping wet.

"What's wrong? What happened?" Candy said to me when I entered the cell.

"I was just in the shower, with someone's period blood touching my feet. That's some unsanitary shit."

"If you wanted a private shower you should have stayed home."

Chapter Five

I awoke from my sleep to the sound of banging and loud calls. The darkness at the narrow window that faced outside confirmed that it was not yet breakfast time. Maybe the sound was from the officers changing shift. Eager to find out what was happening, I climbed from my bunk and went to the cell door. From the small window I could see six men dressed in heavy khaki green army uniforms. They were so loaded with riot gear, padding, and shields, they looked like ninja turtles. Their entrance onto our unit may have been discrete, but, they had brought three leashed K-9 dogs, which were loudly barking in the common room. Adding to the sound of menace, was the sound of heavy boots clomping on the concrete floors. The men stood in a rectangular formation in the center of the common room, dog leashes in hand. The correctional officers standing by them. Their stance demanded our respect, as if they wanted us to know that the big guys were on the block. It wasn't long before the entire female unit was wide awake. The large clock in the common area read five in the morning. Candy hopped off her bunk and joined me to see what would happen next. We stood, taking turns peering through the window.

"Why are they here?" I asked Candy.

"That's the search team. They're looking for drugs. Marijuana, crack/ cocaine. Weapons, any contraband."

"What's contraband?"

"Anything that we are not allowed to have. Altered prison property."

The unit officers, opened the cells, three at a time. I stood at my door, looking down at the bottom tier. A female officer stood at the front of each cell as she stripped down the two inmates inside. I saw them hand her articles of clothing, one by one. She shook each item separately. I couldn't quite make out what she was saying to the ladies but I saw one girl turn around and separate her butt cheeks. "What?" Then her cellie did the same. Did the officer not realize that people on the top tier could see directly into those cells? Didn't they think to ask these ladies to step to the back of their cells? Maybe the officer didn't care. *Oh yeah, there's no such thing as privacy in jail.* I saw the officer cuff the ladies and hold each of them by their arms, while the ninja turtles entered the cells with the dogs. I saw a variety of things flying around the cell: papers, white underclothes, snacks. And then, the ninjas were in the next cell.

Little did I know; this would last more than three hours. I should have been nervous at the sight of these huge men, and the fact that they had large, aggressive dogs with them. I was a bit excited for the entertainment this meant for me. I wasn't watching people play cards or listening to their war stories, I was witnessing something that I had never seen before. I impatiently waited my turn to get a closer look at the ninja turtles. My adrenaline was up. I was likely feeling the same sort of excitement soldiers feel when they walk into a combat zone. However, my excitement disappeared when I realized that those officers were about to see me naked. Their voices grew louder as they approached our cell.

When Officer Santos stood in front of our door and inserted her key in the lock, it sounded louder than it had before. The door creaked and groaned — an excellent sound effect for a horror movie. "Greene and Casey, strip down. Hand your clothes to me one at a time." Candy seemed to have no problem with this request. I guess it's something one can get used to after doing it enough times. She stood at the end of the bunk, beside the toilet. I stood behind her, trying to shield myself from some of the exposure. Candy took her blue top off first then her blue, worn out pants. Mimicking Candy's moves, I took my bra off next. It was less stressful to simply follow Candy than to have the officer shouting demands to me of what item they wanted me to strip next. When completely naked, I heard the same voice at the door, "Lift your arms high, and shake your breast. Put your head down, and run your fingers through your hair, turn your head left, then turn it right, so that I can see inside your ears. Okay ladies, stick your tongues out and say, AWEEE! Turn around, spread your butt cheeks, and cough." My feet were cold on the concrete floor and I kept thinking how embarrassed I was. Not exactly about the officer seeing my body. She had just seen about ninety others before mine. I was more embarrassed that Candy had seen me naked, as I still considered her a stranger.

"Put your clothes on and cuff up."

Candy and I stepped out of the cell and stood next to officer Santos. The ninja turtles then went storming in. I will never forget the sound of their heavy boots. They didn't say a word as they ripped our cell apart. Our grey wool blankets went flying off he bed as they flipped our plastic mattresses over. White sheets fell off the bed and onto the floor. The edge of my sheet almost went inside the toilet. Underneath my mattress was my letter pad diary. The ninja that found it, slowed down and began to read the contents. *Please don't throw it away*, I thought to myself. With little to no interest in what I had written, he threw it onto the desk. They then pulled out our grey bins, going through mine rather quickly. I didn't have much. One ninja took a seat at the desk, leaned over and slowly began to go through Candy's bin.

"Casey, are you a state inmate?" he asked her with a very stern voice.

"Yes, sir."

"I don't know who approved some of these things to come in. But, you're not supposed to have hair rollers."

"I have my property sheet, sir. It shows all the items that I came in and the signature of the officer who approved them."

"Are you trying to be a smart aleck? Cause I can throw all this shit out, no questions asked."

"No, sir."

I had never seen big, bad, tough Candy act so cowardly. I would say it was the fact the at this very moment she was reminded that she was powerless and in a position of oppression. Actually, if I were to back track to her story. I would say that choosing to be in the streets with Ace over education was pretty cowardly too. However, who am I to judge? I don't know the full details of her life and judging her would indirectly say that it's okay for people to hurt me. It was at that very moment I received my first revelation on what would be a very long journey.

The ninjas exited our room, slamming the door behind them. A very deafening sound confirmed that the cell was locked. Candy and I sat for about twenty minutes in silence. The face of a black female officer then appeared at our door. She opened the slot of our door and held two brown paper bags in her hand.

"Wassup, Officer Moore?" Candy said with a sudden excitement in her voice.

"I'm here. Nothing much new with me. You cool in dere?"

"I'm chillin', the search team just tried to get me for my shit."

"You know that's how they do."

"Yo, this search has been going on for about three hours. When they letting us out?

"Probably not until Chapel tonight."

"All right."

I opened my bag to find a small container of Cheerios and a box of milk. I thought of what Officer Moore had said about us having Chapel tonight and felt comforted. Valarie had told me that we leave the unit for Chapel and walk to the other side of the jail. She said it looks like a real church. And volunteers come to conduct the service. I hadn't been to church in such a long time. Being away at college, I was always on the move and there were no churches around my school. I sat up on my bed, eating my cereal, and began to think that if a church was closer to my college, I probably wouldn't have gone anyhow. The last time that I was in a church was about a year ago, and I couldn't stop crying. The people at church who were seated around me, probably thought that I was crying out of pure conviction or that or that I was crying tears of joy from being in the presence of God. But I cried because I had a love-hate relationship with God. I loved him because he had blessed me with some wonderful things. But I could never understand why he allowed so many horrible things to happen. I talked to him all the time about this but, he never seemed to be listening to me. And then many people often argue the point of free will. That is where it all gets confusing for me. I no longer cared. All I know is that I have been carrying around this deep pain and the only prayer he had answered was my latest prayer.

Hours crawled by. The day felt endless, as we were confined to our cells. Candy didn't talk much that day. She sat at the desk, reading a book, and looking over her legal work. She was reading a book by Stephen King, called *The Long Walk*. She said it was really good. I bet it was, 'cause I could hear her rubbing her crusty feet together as she turned the pages. Reading was her idea of relaxation on a Wednesday afternoon.

Officer Moore, came by our cell, pointed to me, and signaled for me to leave my bunk and come to the cell door. When I did, she whispered that one of the kitchen workers asked her if an inmate named "Greene" was on the female block. She said he told her that he knew Ronan and he had a kite for me from Ronan and that he would be cleaning the hallway by the chapel tonight. When I asked her what a kite was, she looked at me as if I were stupid, and explained that a kite was a note. He wanted me to follow his cue so that I could get it.

"Chapel, ladies. Chapel!" A male officer yelled from the bottom tier, followed by the clicking noise of our door.

"If you're not going to Chapel, close your doors." The officer yelled.

Candy grabbed her Bible and began to leap through the door. For a heavy lady, she moved quickly. She turned around when she got to the door, waving her Bible in the air and said with a smile, "You can't go to war without your sword."

I chuckled at her excitement and followed behind her. I didn't have a Bible, as I hadn't been in the jail long enough to order one. When we got to the bottom of the steps, I realized that almost the entire unit was lined up to go to Chapel. The line was twisted around the stairwell. Candy saw that I had a question in my eyes. She said to my softly, "A lot of these ladies do turn to God in here. But, the rest only go to the Chapel to spend time with their girlfriends."

The line began to move along, as each female stepped up to sign out and to get pat searched. Some ladies even got their Bibles checked. We proceeded to walk through the double doors and into the main hallway of the jail. I saw big windows along one side of the hall. The view outside showed a few trees coming into bud, with the spring. The sight made me long even more for a breath of fresh air. The lawn around the jail was not well kept but it was refreshing to be able to get a look outside. We passed some jail employees who were dressed in different uniforms.

Not gray like the ones the ones on the female unit. These were khaki-colored uniforms and I saw a guy dressed in a white shirt, black pants, and what looked like a captain's hat. We turned left and walked down another long hallway. This hallway didn't have concrete floors like the rest of the jail. Instead these floors were well-polished stained wood. To my left, there were two rooms that looked like classrooms, with chalk-boards along one wall. As we approached the Chapel, I saw a black guy standing in the corner, with a bright yellow mop bucket. As I walked closer, still in line behind Candy, I recognized him as the same black guy who had winked at me when he brought the food cart in. He was silently mouthing something. I began to read his lips. *When you go in the Chapel, ask to go to the bathroom,* they read. I slightly nodded my head to let him know that I had understood. I had learned how to read lips and understand complex sentences because mouthing words was one of several ways that Alton used to communicate with me. When he and I were often in public or at the dinner table accompanied by other people, he would 'mouth' words to me, forcing me to learn how to read his lips, a skill that I disliked, yet perfected.

The Chapel was beautiful, with ornately gilded walls, hung with historic paintings. We tramped down plush burgundy carpets to the benches, while staring in front at the amazingly designed alter. The officers directed us to sit down in rows. A lady introduced herself as Ms. Betty Jones and said that her ministry came every third Wednesday to conduct services. The smell of grape juice was appealing to my nose. I guessed that it would be used instead of wine for communion. I saw officer Moore standing at the end of the pew I was seating in. I walked past two ladies flipping through the song books, and over to Ms. Moore so that I could ask if I could go to the bathroom. She nodded as if this sort of thing happened every day. I walked past Betty Jones and down three small steps. I was still a few steps away from the big door that separated the chapel form the jail hallways, when I felt the strong grip on my arm. I looked around to see the same guy who had been in the hallway with the yellow mop bucket. He shuffled me down two steps to a dark corner that appeared to lead to the basement under the chapel. "You Ronan's friend, right?" I nodded.

"I have mail for you." He bent down and lifted his pant leg. It looked like the note might have been hidden in his sock, so I quickly approached him, until my eyes caught the glint of steel; I froze! He immediately stood up from his squat position and with his left hand he quickly grabbed a hold of my mouth. He held a knife at my neck with his other hand. I could taste his sweat and smell the remains of cleaning products on his hand with the callouses of his hands scratching my lips.

"If you scream, I'll kill you right here in this hallway."

I didn't scream. I froze. What made me think it was safe coming here? Why did I fail to listen, again, to that God- given gut feeling that danger was lingering in that dimly lit hallway? I really believed that Ronan was trying to communicate with me, in a quest to protect each other; executors of the same crime, prisoners of the same world. I was wrong!

Using the hand that held the knife, he tugged his pants down. I faintly begged, "Please don't do this. Please don't do this to me." I didn't dare cry out, not for lack of tears, but presence of fear--fear of being caught. Ironically, in a prison filled with cameras and officers, we were invisible. Or probably purposely so. I could feel my heart beating a thousand miles an hour and my body was shivering with cold sweats. I don't remember breathing. He used his erected penis in a motion to ease my baggy waistband. Ultimately, he succeeded in shoving my pants down. I stiffened and I kicked backwards, hoping that his knee would buckle. This just made him grip my mouth harder, and he poked me with his knife to remind me that it was still in his hand. I could hear the women upstairs singing *Amazing Grace* as he shoved his penis inside me, slamming it in and out, four hard, slow times. While God was being worshipped upstairs, I found hell on the steps of the Chapel basement. I felt his grip on my mouth loosen, so I used that opportunity to elbow him in his stomach and pulled my pants up. It took all my energy to race up the stairs and run towards the illusion of safety.

The signing was becoming stronger, as I heard, "Twas grace that taught my heart to fear…" I knew exactly what I had to do. I felt a different kind of fear. But, I knew that this, too, would save me. I put on a brave face, expressionless eyes, and unreadable lips. Once again, I became a ghost of myself, conveying to the world that I was okay. Did they even care?

I felt invisible as I entered the Chapel, sat down, and took my place. I was finally safe from being caught and punished for roaming the hallways, like I hadn't been punished enough. Officer Moore glanced at me, as our eyes met. I understood that we both knew the truth. She smiled at me. I was so furious that I wanted to strangle her and watch her suffer. Instead, I had to sit still and say nothing, as the hour-long service dragged on. I wanted to run up to Ms. Betty Jones, whom I had just met, so I could curl up and cry on her lap while she would hug me. I wanted to die. But instead, I just sat there, barely breathing, trying to pick up whatever pieces of me that were still left alive.

When the officers marched us back to the housing unit, I felt disconnected from my body. It was walking, it was following orders, but I was somewhere else. A very familiar place, that I had been to so many times before…

Dear Diary,

Why is my life so painful? I feel like I will never escape these acts of evil. I feel dirty. I am dirty, disgusted, and ashamed. I'm scared. Why could I be so damn stupid. I wonder if Moore knew that this was gonna happen? Did she plan this? Did they plan this? Did Ronan plan this? Does he want revenge against me? But, I didn't do anything to him. That guy must have known ahead of time that he was going to do this. How does he know this jail so well? How were there no cameras back there? I fucking hate this place. I hate people. No one can be trusted. Why would God let this happen to me? Haven't I had enough? I know I was doing something wrong, but I don't think I deserve what happened. I don't even care, anymore, about what Ronan is going to say in court. I shouldn't have cared in the first place. I hope the guy who raped me will one day rot in hell. I hope he didn't give me anything. I hope that I won't get pregnant. If I get pregnant in here what will happen to me in here? I don't even know if I could tell anyone. The officers may just look at me like it doesn't even matter. I'm just another inmate. Or, I may get in trouble. They may think that I wanted it. They may think that I'm just looking for a reason to sue the jail. They may isolate me in an observation cell. I won't be able to get visits. Everyone is going to think that I'm dirty. I will have to just deal with this alone. I'm so sorry that I went into that corner. I have to put my big girl face on, I have my preliminary hearing in the morning.

~Me.

Chapter Six

"My name is Mr. Henderson. I will be your public defender. I am here to represent you in the case *Commonwealth of Virginia vs. Giselle Greene.* This will be your arraignment hearing. In a few minutes, we will go before the judge and ask him to modify your bail."

I was staggered. I had never seen the man before. He certainly could not know me. How could he possibly represent me, or my best interests, and what was I supposed to say or do in front of the judge? "In a few minutes? With all due respect sir, I've been seeing lawyers come to the jail to meet with their clients before a hearing. You don't know anything about me or the case, other than what you have read. How are you going to properly represent me?"

"Client? Well you're not exactly my client. I'm paid by the state and I have a large case load. If you want personal attention, you can hire a lawyer, and then you will be someone's client."

Looking around the cold holding cell. I was reminded of D-Block, and my first night of being in jail. I felt despair and panic. I was losing the little hope that I had left. He was a slender white male with red hair, almost balding, and had slightly freckled face. He carried a very tattered chocolate brown brief case. He stood in the holding cell with me and the other inmates. While he shuffled through his papers, I looked around at everyone else. Three men in orange jump suits, one male in pale yellow, and two dressed in navy blue, like myself.

None of them had traveled from the county jail with me.

I had been awake and dressed since seven-thirty that morning. Before I was escorted from the cell, one of the officers handcuffed my hands and shackled my legs. I believe the primary reason for leg shackles is to make the prisoner feel less human and more helpless than he or she had before. It is like wearing a brand. Being bound up that way causes many people to panic. Sitting still was all I could do to keep from vomiting. I was escorted from the county by two men who, by the way were dressed, appeared to be court officers. They put me in the back seat of a white car marked *Hanover County Prison*. Inside, it was just like any other police car. The back seat was slippery molded plastic, with a space between the back rest and the bench seat to accommodate a prisoner's hands when they were cuffed behind him. The two officers sat in front, protected from their angry or panicky passengers by a bullet proof glass shield.

Then they drove me through what must have been miles and miles of farmland — mostly cornfields. I'd been trapped in a cornfield when the officers first arrested me. There was nothing comforting about the sight of all that corn. I don't even like corn. The hay fields and pasture land we passed just didn't look safe to me, if you know what I mean.

When we arrived at the courthouse, I was escorted to a prisoner's waiting room, where several other inmates were waiting, with their lawyers, to see the judge. Judging by the uniforms they wore, those inmates, most of them guys, were from other jails. The lawyer who had been appointed to my case was there, and I've already told you about him.

My shackles and I shuffled into the courtroom and I saw Aunty sitting in the back row. Two rows in front of her, I saw the two ladies who had been working in the bank the day we robbed it. They had come in with a lot of other people, their friends and family, I guess, and they were all chattering and pointing.

I bowed my head when I saw the camera, as I didn't want any more pictures of me in the media. More than that, though, I was ashamed to face Aunty. Yes, I had asked her to be there. Yes, I wanted her support. But, still I was overwhelmed with shame. Along with that, the bank tellers would now get to see me, unmasked, undisguised, and shackled for what I and done to them. They may have felt a sense of closure knowing that the system of justice was in motion. I would have loved to be sitting where they were, watching the system work in my favor for all the harm Alton had done to me. If only the injustice done to me was not hidden. I could also be entirely wrong.

On the other hand, those women may not have been satisfied at all. They may have been filled with anger, and rage, and would have wanted to take matters into their own hands. I felt about as welcome as a cockroach.

One of the court officers told me to sit in the front row of the courtroom, where seven other inmates were already sitting. We waited for what may have been ten minutes, when the bailiff announced, "All rise. The honorable Judge Crenshaw presiding. Court is now in session."

The judge, a short white man, walked up to a huge black leather seat at the front of the courtroom. The proceedings might have been fascinating had I not been so frightened. The ceremony and pomp with which people's lives are almost nonchalantly destroyed is noteworthy.

"Please be seated."

I watched as the judge took cases from other inmates who were only present on a television screen. It looked as though the officers had set up a live camera from a meeting room in the jail. The judge took three cases in that manner. They were all very brief. Then I watched as he proceeded to the cases with the inmates in the courtroom. The judge called two other cases prior to mine. I was trembling and nauseated and too busy trying to hide my face from the camera, as well as the women sitting in front of Aunty, that I paid no attention at all to the decisions passed on those two prisoners. I experienced a sense of shock when the judge announced my docket number.

"Docket number, 09-CR-37802. *The Commonwealth of Virginia vs Giselle Greene.*"

The officer signaled for me and my public defender to stand before the judge. I faced the judge with my lackadaisical public defender standing to my left. The prosecutor was on my right. The judge asked the defense if he wanted to "waive the reading."

"Yes, your Honor." I heard Mr. Henderson say.

The judge then shuffled through the papers that were before him. He then asked the prosecutor to make a statement in regards to bail.

"Your Honor, I believe that the bail of $200,000.00, should remain the same. It should not be reduced because Ms. Greene has committed a serious crime, a felony robbery. And Ms. Greene has family members in Jamaica and several US states, she is a flight risk."

The judge shook his head, almost as if he was validating the prosecutor's argument. He then asked the Defense for a response.

"Your Honor, I do ask that you consider the reduction of bail regarding Ms. Greene. She is a young lady who is enrolled in college. She has no prior criminal record." *At least he said something in my defense.*

My stomach was in knots and my throat was extremely dry, as I watched and waited. The judge shoveled through more papers before he looked up to give us an answer.

"In the case of *The Commonwealth of Virginia vs. Greene* bail remains the same. The next court date is set for June 30, 2014."

Honestly, I was surprised that the prosecutor knew so much about me. I was really counting on a bail reduction. As I was escorted from the courtroom, I looked to Aunty, and hoped that she could understand. I was telling her good-bye, and thanks for coming, all in one.

Back at the county jail I sat in the holding cell waiting to be brought back to my housing unit. The experience of being in a courtroom for the first time was very alarming. It was as though, up until the hearing, I had been dangling from the top of a sky scraper, gamely holding on with the fingernails of both hands — that was until someone gave the fingers of my right hand a crushing blow with a sledgehammer. That was what the arraignment felt like. At that moment, I did not know how I would be able to hang onto sanity.

It made me realize the seriousness of what I had gotten myself into. Seeing the bank tellers and their family members illustrated how badly they wanted to make sure that I would pay for my actions--and pay the maximum price. They say that when victims show up to court it shows the judge that they really feel harmed by the injustice that was done to them and they want to see… justice. I could feel all the eyes piercing my back. I was in a daze. What would it mean for me if the judge did reduce my bail? I did not feel at all comfortable with the public defender who had been assigned to me. But, at least the state had given me something — I mean someone.

The hearing was over. Now, it was up to me to assimilate it and to make sense out of it. I shuffled out to the same white car that had carried me to the courthouse, and had to see the same dreary scenes going back to the jail that I had seen leaving it for the courthouse. The officer who drove me that long dreadful ride back to the jail walked me towards the holding cell. I watched as he methodically sorted out the keys he would need to unlock the very heavy chains I was wearing.

He walked me back to the housing unit. The halls were quiet and I could see a huge clock that read 11:05. When I got back onto F-Block, the common room was packed and blasting with sound.

"GiGi!" someone shouted.

I looked over to the far corner and saw Valarie waving me over to join her.

"How was court?"

"It was okay; my Aunty was there."

"You weren't able to talk to her, right?"

"Nah, but I felt that we said a few words just by looking at each other."

"Yo, that woman named Diamond asked me about you." "What woman?"

"The big dark skinned broad what has the dreads."

"Oh you mean Lady? She looks like she about fifty."

Valarie let out a chuckle. "You right, Lady. Her name Diamond. She said she tryin' to see what up with you."

"Nothing is up with me."

"If she interested, which she is, you should hop on that. She got money. She good wit Commissary."

"I'm good. Not interested."

"Alright. What do you want me to tell her?

"Tell her I'm not interested."

"Nah, I'm not gonna tell her that, she gonna think you stuck up. That could be bad for you in here. Diamond get what she wants. She been coming here for years; she got crazy pull. Imma tell her you got a boyfriend at home that you loyal to."

"Okay. Whatever."

"G — RR — EE-NNN-EEE you have a visit!"

I leaped from the chair and over to the female officer who'd announced my visitor. She and I walked up the stairs to the second tier. I knew exactly which door lead to my unexpected visitor. I walked about two steps ahead of the officer and I was surprised she didn't stop me. When we arrived at the door, I paused to let her to open it. Not because I felt that doors should be opened for me but because I didn't want to be reprimanded for jumping the gun. When she opened the door I could see Aunty through the glass partition. I stepped right up, eager to see her after the court hearing this morning. She had the phone receiver in her hand, ready to talk as soon as I sat down.

"Aunty, thank you so much for coming. I didn't expect that you would drive such a long way here, after leaving court."

"It only made sense since I already took the day off."

"Aunty, it seems like my bail is staying the same. I was really hoping that it would get dropped so possibly I could be released."

"I know."

"I wonder how they know that my mom lives in Jamaica? Oh yeah, they have access to whatever information they need to figure out. I wouldn't run off to Jamaica."

"When I left the courthouse, I went to a bail bondsman across the street. He asked if I have any assets that we could put up for your bail. I'm going to make some calls to see if that's possible. Now I see how serious this is, I'm going to talk to your mom and the rest of the family to see if we can put money together to get you a lawyer."

"Aunty, please do! I met my public defender today before we came into the main courtroom. He isn't a nice guy at all. He said that he was going to try to get the bail reduced. He could not have cared less whether he was successful or not. Did you notice all of those people who were sitting around you? They were the tellers from the bank."

"Oh, that makes sense, I could hear all the bad things they said — I couldn't even begin to tell you. But, that's not what's important right now. How are you holding up?"

"The best that I can. Seeing you helps me feel better. More important, how are you? I'm so sorry, Aunty. I really am."

"I know you are. I can't stay. I just wanted you to know that I'm working on things. I love you." Aunty motioned to put her hands on the glass. I did the same. "I love you too."

We ended the visit before the time was up. There was no officer waiting to shuffle me out of the visiting room. So I walked to my cell. The door was already open because common room was still in motion. I eased my feet out of my shoes, and climbed the ladder to my bunk. I felt so emotionally drained and my vagina was still in tremendous pain from that guy forcing himself into me the day I went to chapel. I didn't ever want to go near that chapel again.

I really needed a nap, so, I climbed up onto my bunk and lay down. I didn't know anything more until Candy shook me awake. "Yo, wake up."

I felt a rough, aggressive shake pulling me out of sleep. "What?"

"You was just screaming 'SKY! SKY!' Are you all right? Why were you screaming that? Were you having a dream? Yo, you got tears in ya eyes, you cool?"

"Yeah, I guess I'm cool. I don't remember screaming anything. But, thanks for waking me up."

"I gotcha. Don't go back to sleep, though. They gonna call you to work the fast line pretty soon. It's almost dinner time."

"Okay." I slept most of the day. I jumped off my bunk and reached into my grey bin for my toothbrush to brush my teeth. I still felt strange when I woke up here. It was as though I needed a moment to figure out where I was. I guess that while sleeping, I would forget that I was in jail. The reality of being in jail would hit me hard again, when I woke up.

When my teeth were brushed, I sat at the table waiting for the door to be clicked for me to start working. I then thought that maybe I should try to find a book to read--getting lost in a plot could take me far away from here. I watched from the table as Candy half lay on her bunk with her book, oblivious to everything around her, and thought that I should try reading something.

CLICK - CLICK - CLICK

"Fast line workers, come on down!"

In a daze, I hopped out of the cell, and headed for the fast line. I served bread, and cleaned up without emotion or thought. I was just going through the motions. I was doing all I could to numb the pain; I didn't want to feel anything. After we served dinner, it was time for common room. I opted to stay in my cell. I didn't want to shower. I didn't want to feel clean. I just wanted to lay in my bed. Like I mostly did. I was happy that Valarie didn't come to check on me. I lay waiting for common room to end. Then I would be called to clean the showers while the other fast line workers either swept and mopped the floors, or cleaned the tables. My thoughts wouldn't leave me alone. I pulled out my journal and began to write.

*   *   *

Dear Diary,

When they called me down this evening to work the fast line for dinner, I made sure not to go close to the door. I didn't want to see that awful guy who had raped me. If I had, I don't know what I would have done. Maybe I would have run into the hallway, not caring about any repercussions.

Maybe I would have tried to fight him. Or maybe I would have asked him why he did that to me. Avoiding him was the only way I could deal with my fear. I also was beginning to feel that I deserved to be in prison and treated like dirt. It's hard to navigate this world and act like I'm okay. Truly I'm not. Court was very unfriendly this morning. The judge didn't look at me. It was as though I was not worth his consideration.

I dread cleaning the showers at night. I love to clean. But, I dislike the officers who work the second shift. They make this jail feel like hell on earth. One officer in particular, Ms. Bush, talks to me like we are back in the 1850's, and I'm a slave on her plantation. I don't believe that what she does is for the welfare of the jail and the justice system. I believe that it's a matter of her personal gratification.

~Me.

Chapter Seven

November of 2009
County Jail

I t's been one hundred and eighty-one days since I've been behind bars, and two more days until I go to court again. Yes, I have been counting the days.

And if boredom allows, I may start counting the hours. These days may not necessarily seem long to someone with a huge imagination. I've tried to train my mind to think that I am at a summer camp and I will be going home at the end of the summer. But the summer ended two months ago. Additionally, it's hard to stay in imagination mode when I keep receiving deceptive sprinkles of hope from the court system. My court dates have now been postponed four times.

Within these past five months of being isolated from the world, not much has happened, on my end at least. The kitchen staff that prepares our meals have been rotating the same items on the menu. If I have to eat another hot dog, I may throw up. I keep reminding myself that I should be grateful, because a meal is a meal regardless of what it is. I haven't received any more visits from Terrance. In regards to this judicial process, he told my aunt that he was unable to help.

I speak to Aunty over the phone at least once a week. She has been sacrificing so much for me during this period of time. She made an account through the telephone system that connects inmate calls. Every week, she puts forty dollars of her hard earned money, towards the account so that we can talk.

She found me a lawyer, Thomas Scott. Aunty and a couple of other family members contributed to the deposit to retain this lawyer. Mr. Scott is known to be the second best criminal defense lawyer in the state. Mr. Scott has been up to the jail twice to visit me. I feel comfortable with him representing me.

Mr. Scott informed me that DA has offered a sentence of five to fifteen years for a guilty plea. I don't want to take the plea because I feel that I may be able to get less than five years. It's hard for my mind to accept five years, when a couple of months ago, I thought I may only be serving a few months. I asked Mr. Scott if I can go with an open plea or take my case to trial and he said the decision to do so would be a horrible mistake. During my most recent visit with Mr. Scott, he brought my discovery packet along with him. I was oblivious as to what exactly made up a discovery packet. He placed a big white package on the table. The package looked like it weighed no less than twenty pounds. I guess they had a heavy case against me, no pun intended. He said, "This right here is the reason why you don't want to go to trial, my friend. In this package is all the images captured from the cameras in the bank. There are also images caught from cameras that were located at surrounding businesses. There are statements from all of the bank tellers, statements from all of the bystanders. And of course, statements from Ronan and Toya. I have the interview between the detective and yourself from the first day you were questioned. There are pictures of all the clothing you wore, pictures of all the evidence from your car, illustrating that this was a premeditated crime."

"How is it okay for them to take pictures of things in my car? I still don't understand why my car was even impounded. It wasn't used to commit the crime. My car was parked at the park near my house, this crime was committed almost thirty minutes and many miles from where my car was parked."

"Exactly! The car was not parked at your house. That's the reason it's considered to be a part of the robbery. You drove it to the park. Toya picked you up from the park; it's a part of the crime. Go ahead, open the package."

I opened the top of the package and slid my hand inside. The pile of papers was too big to fit into my hand, so I removed them in small increments. One paper was had a black and white image. I paused, trying to recognize what it was until I realized that it was my mugshot. My heart beat sped up and my body felt a sudden rush of heat. I could visibly see my hand shaking as I held this piece of paper. It was hard to see such a disturbing image of myself. It was excruciating to know that this would be the image that the rest of the world was seeing. This image would influence their perception of me for the rest of our lives. Not wanting to deal with these emotions, I quickly shoved the picture back in unison with the pile, foolishly expecting that it would disappear, like a lot of things in my life.

"When will I see you again, Mr. Scott?"

"I will not see you again until the next time that you will appear in court.

You should consider taking the plea. There was a firearm involved in this crime. And a firearm carries a mandatory minimum sentence of five years. I will be in contact with your Aunt to obtain character reference letters from people in the community. You should contact any mentors that you may have had — any professors or coaches that would be willing to write a letter of reference on your behalf."

"Okay. Thanks."

I signaled to the officer that the visit between Mr. Scott and I was complete. I got up and exited the meeting room. I began to walk towards the housing unit, side by side, the male officer. If I took the public defender's advice and hired the second best attorney in the state, then why was I still left with important unanswered questions? How responsible was I to advocate for myself in this situation? Could I trust Mr. Scott just like I had trusted others in the past? Will he, too, be one of them?

Upon entering the cell, in disbelief, I watched Candy gathering her things. In my absence, they had called her to bunk and junk, and she too, was leaving me. It felt like I was being hit over and over again. I had been with her since the beginning, it had been six months since my incarceration and friendship with her. One by one, she neatly arranged her books, the ones that were displayed on our metal desk, and placed them in her gray chest. She didn't have a cheap gray bin like myself. Mine was county issued. Candy's was ordered from a state prison catalog. Her chest was manufactured well, good quality and strong enough to last for years. Which made perfect sense since most inmates in the State prison are there for years. She stripped the bottom bunk of the tattered, white sheets, and bundled them up to be returned to the prison officer. She strategically arranged her belongings so that everything would fit in the chest. I knew that she wasn't exactly pleased with the outcome of this trip. She came back to the county jail in hopes of a judge reducing her time. However, her time was not overturned and she would be returning to the State prison with the same amount of time that she left there with: a life sentence!

I didn't know how to react to this "bunk and junk" call. I didn't know how to react to Candy leaving. I tried to not make any eye contact with Candy until she tugged my blanket and began to speak, "This is where I leave you. Keep your head up and don't lose that smile. You will have dark days in here but don't let those days transform your soul. You're young and whatever the outcome is at sentencing, you still have your entire life ahead of you. It was a pleasure to share these past months with you. When they do the next trip up to the State prison, I hope to not see you departing from that bus. I love you, young buck."

"I love you too, Candy. Don't stop trying to appeal your case. I will never forget you."

"One more thing, keep your sword close."

I climbed from my bunk to give her a hug. We tightly embraced each other. It was the first hug that I had received in months. I didn't want her to leave. I was feeling a great sense of loss. Although I spent most of my days in silence and bottling my thoughts and feelings, I would often confide in Candy. It was comforting knowing that if I ever needed to talk or had a question, she and I were in the same room. I wondered who would be placed in this cell with me. I wondered if there were any more questions that I needed answered before going to court. I watched as the cell door closed behind Candy. I knew that someone new would be placed in the cell with me. I hoped that it wouldn't be someone who was much of a talker. I've always been an introvert and enjoyed this aspect of my personality. Also, I wasn't in a good space to do a lot of conversing. My mind was filled with thoughts regarding court and my heart was filled with pain. I lay on my back and stared at the ceiling, trying to think of a college memory to pass the time.

I was in a college Criminology class. This was a morning class in which most of my classmates were half asleep as they stumbled in. My professor was a man of color who looked as if he might have been in his late fifties. He had a stern personality and was very unapproachable. I was early for class this particular morning. I woke up really early and showered before the dorm bathrooms were occupied. I remember putting on one of my favorite sweaters. On my way to class that morning, I couldn't figure out why everyone else smelled so awful. Everywhere I turned, it smelled like the person next to me had not showered in weeks. It smelled like a dead rat and spoiled milk, combined. When I arrived to class, I sat in the middle row. I watched as the professor walked down the aisles handing out our graded exams. He stood about two rows ahead of me and stopped. He looked around, and with an awful expression on his face, blurted out, "It smells like shit!" The entire class, that was still half asleep, burst into laughter. I laughed so uncontrollably, I felt my eyes tearing up. And the smell seemed to be getting stronger.

"I can't teach like this. Did someone pass a skunk? Is everyone okay with us leaving the class, one by one, so that we can figure out where the smell is coming from." We all agreed and began to exit the class. When I passed him, I felt his hand tap my shoulder, "Ms. Greene, I think the smell is coming from you." I chuckled and said, "That can't be, Mr. Terry."

"Do you want to check the bottom of your shoe or you book-bag?" I opened my book-bag and to my surprise the smell erupted, even stronger than it had been. I nervously shuffled through the contents inside to see what the smell could have been. When I unzipped a small inner pocket, I found a steak and cheese sandwich wrapped in foil paper; my left over lunch from last week. That would have made perfectly good sense — I hadn't used that book-bag since the prior week. When I removed the sandwich, I heard a combination of laughter and slurs.

"This is what happens when you're rushed to consume your lunch," I replied with a smirk. I wasn't embarrassed. I had seen worse results of forgetfulness during my stay with other college students.

I spent so much energy thinking that the smell was coming from someone else, and frowning my nose at whoever thought it was okay to smell that way. All along, the smell was coming from me. It was then that I remembered the saying that my grandmother would always recite, "Why do you look at the speck of sawdust in your brother's eye, and pay no attention to the plank in your own eye?" (Matthew 7:3)

Snapped back into reality, by the clicking noise of my cell door, I sat up on my bunk. When I looked towards the door, I saw Layla approaching the cell, kicking her gray bin towards the cell entrance. I knew Layla. Not on a personal level but we'd had vague interactions. I braided her hair a couple of times, during common room, in exchange for commissary items. I wasn't excited or upset that she was about to be my new cellie. I guess my feelings were neutral.

"Hi Layla. Do you need help?"

"No Sweets, I'm good."

Sweets? I ignored my discomfort and uncertainty with her choice of word, only because I could hear the officers announcing the start of common room. I walked past Layla and out of the cell. I wanted to be one of the first to get to common room so that I could reserve a table. Earlier that day, Valarie and I discussed playing Spades during night common room. In regards to reserving a table, I guess Valarie and I were thinking along the same lines because, I could see her dashing to the table in the center of the common room with her deck of cards in hand.

"The same two girls are gonna join us tonight," Valarie said to me.

Honestly, I didn't care who played against us. Lately, I had been engaging in the game of Spades quite frequently to occupy my mind. Valarie was consistently my partner in this game and we were beginning to learn each other's technique. We won most of the time. Prior to coming to this jail, I hadn't played much cards. When I was younger, my grandmother and I would play Chinese checkers or a Jamaican card game called, three-a-cards. That was the closest experience that I had with cards. But, I was beginning to love spades.

At the circular table, all four of us took our seats. There was a lot of noise around us, as usual. I could hear people arguing about what television channel should be viewed. People were rushing to the showers. But none of these insignificant details held my attention. I was anxious to speak with Valarie about us going to court. She and I had upcoming court hearings that were set to occur on the same day.

"Valarie, what do you think is going to happen when you go to court?" I asked.

"More than likely Imma get released. If I have to do more time, probably six more months, county time. They're not gonna send me Upstate for such a petty assault," she said, while she dealt the cards.

"Your case might work out good. You don't have a prior criminal record," Valarie continued.

I didn't respond. The truth was, I had no idea how things would turn out and it made me sick to my stomach every time I thought too much about the possibilities. I don't know why I kept asking the same questions--maybe just a way to cope with my nervousness.

"Let's bid, y'all know common room never last as long as it's supposed to," I heard coming from the girl sitting to my left.

"I have four and a possible," Valarie said.

After scanning my cards, again, I raised my head up to confirm that I had five and a possible to contribute to Valarie's four. *A really good hand.*

"I have five and a possible," I began to say until I was interrupted by the loud sound of a crashing noise. "Valarie, MOVE!"

Straight across the table, and behind Valarie, I could see a red plastic chair as it flew into the air. Diamond, the girl that was sitting in the chair, was now sprawled out on the floor. I watched as one woman, an older Latina, and Diamond, a middle aged black lady, argued at the top of their lungs. Diamond struggled to her feet and grabbed her bowl of cereal that sat on the common room table. Cereal and milk went flying towards where the other lady stood. Red chair in hand, the Latina began to continuously hit Diamond back to the floor. Hit after hit. Each hit with great rage. Uproar and loud chanting came from the other inmates. I could see instant swelling on Diamond's face. *Where are the officers?* As she lay on the floor, Diamond, slipped a shank from her sleeve. She then stabbed the other lady in her ankle. I heard a horrific scream of pain that echoed the room. Blood went gushing onto the floor. When the lady fell next to Diamond, she began banging Diamond's head on the concrete floor. "Oh shit," I heard Valarie say. I ran up the steps to the top tier. I heard keys jumping and rattling from the waist of the officers as they ran towards the scene.

I could feel the cold, blue railing, against my hands as I stood from the top tier, watching the commotion. "Lock it in! Go to your cells and lock the doors! NOW!" I heard the officers screaming this demand. I watched as the other inmates slowly scattered, heads turned, watching as the officers tried to restrain the two ladies.

I walked to my cell and locked the door behind me. I was greeted by Leyla's voice, "I'm glad I was still unpacking and didn't get a chance to go down there. If Diamond saw me down there, she would have expected me to jump in and help her. I'm not going to the hole anymore for Diamond's bullshit."

"That fight was serious," I responded.

"Yea, they usually are. The officers' bout to take them to the hole right now. They'll be released from the hole in about sixty days. They might even get another charge, aggravated assault, and have to go back to court. Diamond still hasn't learned anything. I use to date her back in the day--she gets easily pissed off and resorts to violence. I'm pretty sure that's not the first time she put her hands on Patty."

"Oh, Patty is the name of the other lady?"

"Yeah, I guess she had enough of Diamond abusing her, and she just snapped."

I nodded and climbed up to my bunk. I could still hear commotion outside the cell. I could also hear the medical crew. I didn't want to stand at the door and watch. I wanted to get out of this place. I pulled my blanket to cover myself and rolled over in bed to face the wall. I then began to drift in and out of sleep. I knew that the night wasn't over for me. Later, I would be called to clean the showers. I could lightly hear Layla arranging her things. I could hear people yelling slurs towards the officers because the officers would not reopen common room. In the midst of my drifting, I heard something slide underneath the cell door.

"Babygirl, you got mail," I heard Layla say to me.

I was filled with instant happiness and wondered who had sent me a letter or even a card. Layla handed me two envelopes. One envelope read, Damien lever, the other, Alton Benjamin.

Wow! This letter from my brother, Damien, would be the first one from him since being incarcerated. For the past six years, my brother and I have lived in different states. Due to the age difference, we weren't very close when we lived together in Boston. He and I are ten years apart in age but there are some memories that I hold dear to my heart. I remember that he would often put me in the back seat of his very long, grey station wagon car. It was handed down to him from our grandfather. He would drive me to the McDonald's on American Legion Highway and then take me to the Mattahunt, where I would sit on the sidelines and watch him play basketball.

I know that the day of my arrest must have been very hard for him. We had made plans for me to come to Massachusetts that day. I would have been spending that weekend with him. Instead, I decided to go through with my other plan. And I didn't call him to cancel. If I would have called him that morning, he would have sensed that something was wrong with me. He would have then attempted to pry me for information and talk me out of what I was going to do. I do hold a lot of guilt for the decision that I made but I knew that it was the best decision for me.

Receiving a letter from my brother today was quite emotional. He expressed his anger and disappointment. Both complex emotions rooted to the fact that he felt betrayed. He couldn't understand that I didn't have the courage to tell him the truth about the things that I was internalizing. Also, he couldn't understand how I came to the conclusion that robbing a bank was easier than confiding in him.

Along with Damien's letter, I received a letter from Alton. Alton's letter, in particular, made me sick to my stomach.

Dear Giselle,

I hope that this letter will reach you in good spirts. May the Lord continue to keep you under his wing. May his angels protect you. I think of you all the time. And I dream of you all the time. I cannot believe that the best thing that has ever happened to be, has been taken away from me. Our son is becoming a big boy. He is getting so tall and is saying complete sentences. Along with this letter, I have sent some recent pictures of him. I hope that you are happy with the money that

I have sent to you. I will send more as soon as I am caught up with my bills. I am wondering what was going through your head when you robbed the bank. Why didn't you come to me and tell me that you needed financial help? I would have helped you, Baby. Why don't you write me any letters? I put money on the phone, please give me a call? I miss you. I miss hearing your voice. I can't wait for you to come home so that we can get married. We can move far away from your family and no one has to know that we are together. Love Always, A.

My eyes filled with tears. I grabbed my diary because I didn't know what else to do.

Dear Diary,

I hope the next time he dreams of me; he awakes from his sleep in a cold sweat. Relived that he's awake from the thought that he just escaped death. I don't like to think of myself as evil. Evil I know I am not! But, sometimes these evil thoughts I cannot suppress. When I think of how much this man has influenced my depression. I thought that these walls would create distance between us. But, distance has only been created on a physical level. He still haunts me, and he still wishes to haunt me. I hope that I will be fine when I stop opening his mail. What God is he serving? What religion? Excuse me if I'm wrong. But, regardless of the religion, don't they all teach principles of peace and love. Actually, don't excuse me, correct me if I'm wrong.

~Me

Chapter Eight

"All rise, court is in session. The honorable Jefferson Presley presiding." I saw a guy dressed in an olive green colored suit announcing the entrance of our judge. His suit resembled the uniform of a police officer or a correctional officer. As individuals began to stand at his request, I heard the sound of wood screeching, followed by silence. I could see over my shoulders, that everyone in the courtroom, including myself, was standing. The courtroom was jam-packed with court officials, law enforcement, inmates, and people waiting to hear the outcomes of several cases.

A male judge entered the courtroom. I watched as he climbed a few steps and proceeded to sit in his black leather seat, which was located behind a raised desk. This courtroom seemed more official than the one that I went to for my bail hearing, or arraignment as its properly called. The American flag was strategically arranged at the right hand side of where Judge Presley was seated. Judge Presley was a man that could have been in his late fifties or early sixties. He stood at about five feet, six inches. His demeanor appeared cold and conservative. However, I knew that it wasn't wise to judge a book by its cover, and hoped that my fate was in the hands of a judge that was liberal and open-minded, one that would bring forth justice, yes. Justice and leniency.

"Good afternoon, please be seated." I watched as Judge Presley nodded to the individuals standing to my right. That nod must have been a sign of clearance that the representatives of that state were now allowed to address the court, which seemed a bit informal.

"Your honor, I am Richard McCoy, attorney for the state. This case is the *Commonwealth of Virginia vs. Giselle Greene.* Docket number 09-CR-37802. The defendant is charged with felony robbery and possession of an instrument of crime. On May 14, 2009, Ms. Greene entered the Kentburg Bank on Kutztown Road. On that day, she carried a gun which was displayed with an intent to inflict fear on the persons inside the bank. Ms. Greene implemented the use of pepper spray as she robbed the bank. Mary Grumbly, Shannon Keller, and Susan Shepardsburg were the tellers in the bank on that day. Since the actions of that day, these women have expressed feelings of anxiety and fear."

I felt the goosebumps on my arms as the attorney voiced my actions that took place on the morning of May 14. My lawyer was standing beside me and I hoped that he had prepared a well-thought out rebuttal. I saw a lady seated a little bit below where the judge was seated. She was busy typing everything that was being said in the courtroom. I believe she may have been using a typewriter because the sound of the keys was exceedingly loud.

After a long pause, the state attorney continued, "At this time, we ask the court to find the defendant guilty of robbery and possession of an instrument of crime. For punishment, we ask for the mandatory sentencing and a fine of $10,000.00 dollars."

"Ms. Greene, may you please state your true name for the record."

"Giselle Greene."

"Ms. Greene, defendant, to the charges of robbery and possession of an instrument of crime, how do you plead? Guilty or not guilty?"

I'm so confused. When I read my discovery packet, I saw that I had about fourteen charges. Now, I'm only being charged for two things. Maybe this could be working in my favor.

"Your honor, my name is Thomas Scott. I represent the defendant, Giselle Greene. Giselle Greene pleads guilty to both charges."

"Let the record show that defendant Giselle Greene has made pleas of guilty on both charges, robbery and possession of an instrument of crime. Now, Ms. Greene, has your lawyer advised you of your rights?"

"Yes."

"Do you understand your rights?"

"Yes."

"Have you and your lawyer discussed your rights and options?"

"Yes."

"Is there anything that you would like to state for the record, Ms. Greene?"

I heard my lawyer interject again. "Your honor, I would like to ask for leniency in the sentencing of Ms. Greene."

I watched as the judge looked over to the attorney of the state. "Does the prosecutor have any objections?"

"The state has no objections, your honor."

"You may proceed."

"Thank you. Your honor, my client, Giselle Greene, has no prior criminal record. We have provided a variety of letters from members of the community which illustrate that Ms. Greene is a scholar and a cheerleader.

She had displayed a high degree of ambition, kindness, and dependability. She is a member of many organizations including the S.I.F.E team. She recently traveled to Florida and Philadelphia to represent her University. I do believe that Ms. Greene made a bad decision. Ms. Greene has illustrated good behavior during these past months in the County Jail. I ask for your consideration of leniency in sentencing."

A court official walked over and handed the judge what looked to be my character reference letters. I thought he would have received and read them before this moment. He scrambled through the letters, showing no interest. His eyes made such brief contact with the letters, I doubt he even read one line. The court, silent.

Judge Presley began to speak. "The court has considered the nature and circumstance of the offense. I have considered the aggravating factors brought forth by the district attorney. I have considered those factors in arriving at a sentence for Ms. Greene. The crime was especially cruel and senseless. The offense was committed with two deadly weapons, a gun and pepper spray. The court has also considered the emotional harm imposed on the victims and their families. Also, the harm inflicted on the community. As mitigation, the court finds that the defendant has no prior criminal history, the defendant has family and community support, the defendant has no mental health issues. What makes this situation even worse was that Ms. Greene was not under the influence of drugs or alcohol. Ms. Greene, I have a daughter your age. She is currently in college. I could never picture her doing what you did. You are ungrateful to have given up a college education for something so senseless and I will make an example out of you."

"It is ordered that the defendant shall be incarcerated in the Department of Corrections, under maximum custody, for at least five calendar years and up to fifteen calendar years, with the possibility of parole. The sentence will begin today. The defendant will receive credit for one hundred and eighty-three days. It is ordered that the defendant will pay retribution of $10,000.00

dollars. You have twenty days from today to file a notice of appeal. You have the right to be represented by an attorney. If you cannot afford an attorney one will be appointed to you." Silence.

I could feel my knees go numb, as is they were about to buckle. I wanted to faint. But I knew that I had to appear strong for Aunty. I heard the judge's voice again.

"Counsel, is there anything else for the record?"

"No, your honor."

I felt two officers as they approached me and grabbed my arms. One on my right arm, one on my left. They began to escort me out of the courtroom. My vision was blurry and I remember my lawyer saying final words to me. I couldn't make out any of the words, nor did I care to.

I looked back at Aunty. She was accompanied by two of my really good friends; one friend that I had known since high school and one friend from college. I saw the tears rolling from Aunty's eyes and I could only imagine all the things that she must have been feeling or thinking. I felt like a true disappointment and that feeling was one of the worse feelings in the world. In that moment, there was nothing that I could do to console her. I nodded to her as a sign of good-bye. There was nothing that I could do to assure her that everything would be all right. I didn't know if I would make it out to freedom in five years. I couldn't even wrap my head around the thought of five years.

The immediate moments after sentencing, I felt that I was carrying a ton of bricks on my shoulders. I felt heavy. I felt drained. And I also felt numb. I knew that I was feeling many different emotions and I wasn't sure that I would be able to carry this load and not shatter. I was silent for hours--so silent that I felt the top of my mouth stuck to my tongue. My jaw locked. I didn't say anything mainly because I didn't know what to say or how to express what I was feeling. Also, because I was still in a state of disbelief. I knew that my body was physically moving because I had to walk out of the courtroom and to a holding cell. But I didn't feel in sync with my body. I felt like I was somewhere else, watching the events from today unfold. I couldn't wait to return to the jail where I planned to go into my cell and completely strip myself of this mask and come to grips with what was happening.

The ride back to Hanover County Jail was tough. I was seated next to Valarie, just like I had been on the ride to court. However, on the ride to court, we were both anxious to know the outcome of our situations. Now, Valarie was anxious to be released. The judge gave her case a ruling of 'time served.' Which meant that in a few hours, she would be set free. Her time served in county, as she awaited sentencing, was sufficient to cover the punishment for the crime she committed. She was riding back to the jail to 'bunk and junk.' Valarie was bursting with excitement and was talking about all the things she wanted to do once she arrived home. She also talked about all the foods that she couldn't wait to eat. As she described these foods in great detail, I tried to be excited for her. I tried to be present which was requiring an amount of energy that I didn't have. I thought back to the day that we meet, in Central Booking. I also thought of how great of a support Valarie had been to me. I was glad that she would be able to see her daughter. I was also overwhelmed with sadness that I had many more years to serve.

Back at the jail, the fast line workers were serving dinner. I walked by the tables where food was lined out, I walked by the other inmates who were being served, and went straight to my cell. When I tried to close the door behind me, it was resisted by Layla. She was trying to enter the cell with her dinner tray in hand.

"How was court?" She asked as she placed her tray on the desk.

"The judge gave me five to fifteen."

"Months?"

"No. Years."

"Damn, I'm so sorry."

I began to sob.

"I know this is not what you want to hear. But, upstate is way betta than the county. You can go to school. You can work and get paid. They got more freedom up there. The food is way betta. The commissary is betta too."

"Hmm..mm."

"They still serving dinner. It's burgers. You should get it before they clear it out."

"No thanks. I'm not hungry."

"I know ya sad. I get it and you have the right to be. That sentence is not an easy pill to swallow. But you will have better days. I've seen you around here. You carry yourself well and ya gonna be fine. Ya not a trouble maker. Ya family come to visit you here. I'm sure they will come there too. Visits in the state prison don't have a thick glass separating you from ya family. It's contact visits. And they can buy you things from the vending machine. You can even take pictures with them."

"I hear you. I realized that of all the things that I was charged with, there was only two charges mentioned in court."

"Yea. They do that. Although you are initially charged with a bunch of things, for sentencing, they narrow the charges down to that are most significant. The ones that will actually stick."

"Okay."

"Most likely, they gonna send you on the next trip."

"Is it like the movies, when you get off the bus and everyone is lined out at the fence watching you?"

"Ya funny girl. No. Maybe at other state prisons. When you get to Fluvanna, the bus is going to enter through a big clearance gate. The bus then drives to the back end of the prison campus where there is an intake office. Usually the other inmates are at work or in their housing unit. Even if the inmates were all out in the yard, they wouldn't see you because of where the intake office is located."

"Okay." The cell door began to click. I ignored it.

"They calling for you to clean the showers or clean up dinner, something like that."

"I'm not going!"

"If you don't go, they gonna fire you."

"I don't care."

Minutes passed and the cell stopped clicking. And I didn't hear any officer screaming my name. I guess they got the message.

"Valarie Gonzalez, BUNK AND JUUUUUNNNNNNKKKK!"

Echoed loudly as if it were being announced through a sound system. I heard people banging on their cell doors as Valarie exited her cell. I heard a combination of 'good-byes' and 'don't come backs.' I even heard someone say, 'smoke a cigarette fa me.' I didn't know if I should stand at my window to watch her leave or stay on bunk to pretend it wasn't happened. I could see Valarie running to my door.

"I'm happy for you, Valarie," I said to her through the window, and I meant it.

"Hold ya head. I found a friend and Imma miss you. I know I'm not all smooth around the edges. But, I'm good peoples so don't forget me. Be careful who you be around when you get upstate. Use caution with people that don't got nothing to lose." I watched her as she walked down the steps.

Dear Diary,

Valarie just bunked and junked. I guess I should try not to grow attached to anyone in here. Or I should get familiar

80

with goodbyes. Today I was sentenced. I will be going to the state prison. I hope to get another visit from Aunty before I leave for upstate. The state prison is about two hours from here. Which is about two and a half hours from home. I dread the hour and the minute when my mom is informed of the court hearing. She has bad stomach ulcers. I'm no doctor. But, over the years, I've observed that they usually erupt when her stress levels are at a high. She has been involved with supporting me throughout this time. So involved, that many would think that she lives in the United States. I can guess that she will be calling Aunty before the end of the night to receive an update. If she gets sick as a result of the news, it would add to the difficulty level of me doing this sentence. This is an indescribable feeling. I'm crying as I'm writing this. I can't stop crying. My face is swollen, my pillow and my shirt are both soaked. Five to fifteen years to be served in a State prison.

Honestly, I knew that this outcome was a strong possibility. I just don't know how to accept it. I have been crying and throwing up. I'm in so much emotional pain, my body hurts. I don't know if I can make it through five years. Is five years even a guarantee? I feel like Aunty wasted her money to get me a lawyer. I feel that I let everyone down. The judge didn't even look at the letters. I don't think that he even cares that they were provided. I feel that he knew the sentence that he was going to give me, before he entered the courtroom.

Everything happened so quickly.

I didn't speak up for myself because I had nothing to say. What was I going to say, I apologize? In that moment, I don't think an apology would have meant much to the people that were in the bank that day. Their statements, that I found in my discovery packet, made it very clear that they hated me. One day when I'm released, I will tell my side of the story. If I don't make it out of here, I hope that someone will find and release this diary. I hope that the words from this diary will be interpreted as an apology to them. I want them to know that my true intent was not to harm them. I would also want them to know that I had to follow through with my plan. I would want them to heal from the injustice that I did to them. I would also want them to try to dig within their hearts and understand that I had options, but none of them were good options. It was either a robbery, a homicide, or a suicide. All of which were wrong. I picked the lesser of all evils. Hurt people, hurt people. Which is not a justification, just trying to be understood. If I would have apologized or verbalized any of this in front of the courts, they would truly think that I'm senseless, irrational, or even delusional. Maybe I am. Maybe my circumstances made me this way.

It bothers me that the judge compared me to his daughter. What a horrible comparison. I'm pretty sure that my nineteen years on this earth have been fractured by experiences that his daughter couldn't even begin to fathom.

Or if she could begin to fathom or identify with any of these experiences, her privileges definitely set her aside from me. It's fine that he thinks he made an example of me. I plan to make an example of myself.

-Me.

Chapter Nine

April of 2011
State Prison

Dear Diary,

    I haven't written to you in such a long time because I've been in a program called the Y.A.O. It's a program for young adult offenders. Anyone who is sentenced to this state prison who is under the age of twenty-one, must stay in this program until their twenty-first birthday. If someone enters the program and then turns twenty-one before ten months of being in the program, they still have to complete at least ten months. I guess it's a safety issue. The youngest girl in this program is sixteen. This program is very strict and similar to a hard core boot camp. Each morning, our cells are thoroughly searched. If this diary would have been found, it would have been confiscated and read in front of the entire housing unit. When I arrived here, I mailed the first half of my diary home. I've decided to start the second half of this diary because I have completed the Y.A.O., and I will be released from this program tomorrow. I learned, very quickly, that the acronym C.O's and the word officer were used interchangeably in the state prison, when describing or calling a correctional officer. The C.O's in the Y.A.O.

speak to us with a more respect than the officers in county. But, I'm not excited to see if that also applies to the officers in general population.

Being in the state prison is very different from the county jail. This prison is huge. Behind these tall wired fences are acres of land. This prison was once a college campus. There are many buildings. Each building has a different name with different housing units. The Y.A.O. program is located in the R.H.U., Restricted Housing Unit. This building also houses the death row inmates and inmates who are sent to 'the hole' which is a slang term used for solitary confinement where inmates are sent when they violate prison regulations. Currently, this prison has three women who are on death row. The hole is a prison inside this prison. Although we are separated from them, by many steel doors, it baffles my mind that us Y.A.O. inmates would be housed in this unit.

Our state uniforms are also different from county uniforms. These uniforms, which consist of pants and a buttoned down shirt, are called 'browns.' My guess is that this clever name was consequential to the fact that the uniforms were supposed to be the color brown. Rather, the uniforms favor a very dull burgundy or deep red wine. Accompanied by poorly constructed brown shoes that are stiff and hard, which make my feet hurt. I don't feel the need to be fashionable in here, but, there is no valid reason why the shoes have to be so damn ugly.; los zapatos aqui son muy feos!

I've tried a lot of new food dishes in the past year, not by choice. Sometimes being here makes me feel the effects of culture shock. I was shocked to learn the names of different foods, like subs are called hoagies and I often made a chip dishes called chichi. These were made with crushed potato chips or cheese puffs and Ramen noodle soup. Though it sounds odd, the food here is tolerable. And sometimes quite enjoyable. Once every couple of months, we are served an incentive meal. It's usually a meal with a greater portion than normal. And the meal is frequently a dish that most people like. I guess the meal serves as a motivation to hurry home. Our most recent incentive meal was turkey and cheese subs, with French fries and cake.

The cells are about the same size as the cells in the county, 6x8. Except these cells are cleaner. When I was in county, I thought that the purpose of the small window in our cell doors, was for us inmates to look out. Now that I am in state prison, I've realized that the purpose of the small windows is for us inmates to be observed by the officers. These officers do rounds about every twenty minutes.

There is one officer who does his rounds very invasively. I feel like he conveniently does a round every time my roommate or I exit the shower. Glancing in is not sufficient for him. This man stares at our naked bodies, as if it's legal to do so. There are two tiers on this unit with the cells arranged like a circle. Often times the officer will sit centered, in the middle of the circle within the common room, to easily see inside the cells. This is when the inmates on the top tier, like myself, have a bit of an advantage to our privacy.

My roommate, Trisha, and I have become very close. We've grown together since the program which forces us to do. But she's cool. She has a great singing voice. She often sings at night, which helps us to mentally escape this place for a while. She's Dominicana! So she teaches me different Spanish words. We even dance silently to the Bachata music playing in our heads. I'm glad to have met her. Our friendship has definitely grown and it saddens my heart that her sentence is double the amount of time that I have.

The officers let us out of our cells for 'common room' in the Y.A.O. housing unit, twice a day. During common room, either in the morning or night, we are allowed 'free time' as we once did in grade school — where we have the choice to play cards, play basketball, watch television, talk to other inmates, do our hair, and just chill. Every Sunday, we are able to go to the Chapel for church service. The service is beautiful in content and in appearance. Since the Y.A.O. is segregated from the rest of the prison population, we are seated in the balcony which overlooks the Chapel. Every pew in the Chapel is usually packed. I don't say this to glorify the fact that the prison is full. But I love the sight of looking down at the bold D.O.C. acronyms stamped on the back of everyone's uniform. Once service starts and people begin to surrender themselves, there it is great beauty in witnessing inmates dance and praise their God. For that moment of worship, the officers aren't in charge. The positive energy takes charge, illustrating that pain is temporary and we do have control of our joy.

This prison offers a wealth of vocational courses and courses for a high school diploma. I've taken a difficult course called Machine shop where I learned blueprint reading, structure of metals, basics of the Manual Mill and Engine Lathe, Mechanics of CNC Machining and CNC turning. My instructor said that most people usually take years to complete the course. I completed the course in ten months, because while I'm here, I want to learn as many trades as I can. I want to have a couple of options to lean on when I get home. My instructor said that there are two valedictorian awards given each year. One for the high school diploma side of the school and the Lisa Wagner Award, which is for the trade side of the school. This semester of the program the two Award recipients are from the Y.A.O. My friend is receiving the valedictorian award for her high school diploma and I was chosen to be the recipient for the Lisa Wagner Award. There are hundreds of us graduating today. This is probably the only time the Y.A.O. graduates will be mixed with the general population graduates. I'm pretty excited. Our cap and gowns are a pretty royal blue which will cover our 'browns.' My graduation is in a few hours. I am expecting Aunty to attend as she said she'd make it with a friend.

Amalia, my best friend since middle school, has been by my side throughout this sentence. Since I've been in the Y.A.O., I've received over thirty letters from her. We stay connected through mail, which is commendable on her behalf being that she is a college student and has a lot going on in her life. Although it's nice to receive mail in here, I know it's hard for the average working adult to sit down and write a letter. I don't expect mail; I know that I put myself here. Being upstate has taught me the intimacy of mail and the power that it has to connect people on a deeper level.

A few months ago, while on a visit with Aunty, she told me that Toya and Ronan where now sentenced. Toya was charged with conspiracy to robbery and received a one-year sentence. I was also told that she would not be coming to Fluvanna Correctional because her and I were not allowed to be housed in the same prison. Instead, she would be serving her one-year sentence at the other State prison for women in Virginia. Ronan was also charged with conspiracy. However, he would be serving three years in a state prison for the additional charges from another case.

A lady named Mrs. Henry visits our housing unit, Monday through Friday, to run support groups. She is in her sixties and has been incarcerated for over thirty years. She is doing a life sentence and refers to herself as a 'lifer.' While incarcerated here, she completed her college degree in Psychology. She runs groups on Anger Management, Narcotics Anonymous, codependency, and Distorted Thinking. There was something about Mrs. Henry's strength and resilience, despite her life sentence, that stood out to me. It was only a matter of time until I adopted her as my mentor. Out of all the support groups, I have found the one on codependency to be the most helpful. Prior to being here, I didn't know what the word codependency meant and now it's a word that I will never forget.

Mrs. Henry explained codependency as complex traits that are shown in one's personality. Codependency has many shapes and layers. It is understood as a pattern of painful dependence on others to create meaning, value, and identity for one's self. These traits are usually developed in people who have loved ones who are addicts or children who have experienced neglect or any childhood trauma. As a result of trauma, these folks develop social and emotional habits that no longer work in adulthood. However, these are not the only factors that cause codependency. Codependents illustrate survival behaviors like compulsive caretaking of others, people-pleasing, scapegoating, martyring, approval-seeking and control. I learned all of these in just a matter of a few months and hadn't realized how applicable these traits are to the way that people behave. For many people, it's an unconscious action that they can't name, but Mrs. Henry has given me the tools to apply these meaning that is so valuable. Listen...

Compulsive caretaking of others can be a strong trait seen in those who have been caretakers of their parents with an illness or folks whom have loved who are classified as addicts. When a caretaker or someone bears witness to the trauma of someone else, they themselves can be traumatized by this experience. Ms. Henry explained this is a secondary trauma. A young child who has become the caretaker of their parents is often referred to as the parental child. This is a relationship in which the roles are reversed. The parent either has an illness or is an addict, therefore illustrating childlike behaviors. The child then takes on the role of the parent in order to care for their parent. Most people who have lived this experience will unknowingly carry caretaking traits throughout life. They tend to find friendships or intimate relationships in which someone is in need of their care. It is amazing to have someone who is willing to be a caretaker. However, codependents with this trait compulsively care take. Unknowingly doing so to feel needed and add a sense of value to their lives.

People-pleasing in association with codependency is allowing expectations, resentment, and willingness to say 'yes' instead of 'no' run their life. People-pleasers are set on being perfect and nice. They put the needs and wants of someone else above their own. They will agree to do things, even if deep down they don't want to. People that have this characteristic will avoid saying no because they feel that doing so will make someone upset with them. People-pleasers are often referred to as doormats and will reason with themselves that what they are doing is acceptable but do not realize they have a "disease to please."

Scapegoating is the willingness to take the blame for the wrongdoings, mistakes or the faults of others. Some people may do this because they don't want punishment inflicted on the person that has done wrong. Or they feel that they are a better candidate to endure the punishment. Someone may even be prone to scapegoating because they fear the person who has done them wrong. Extreme codependency can be deadly.

The term martyring is to suffer greatly or to die for a cause. In regards to codependency, martyring means sacrificing too much or choosing to suffer for a cause. This trait is often illustrated in one's career or their field of work.

Approval-seeking could be as simple as changing the way you say something, altering your appearance, or giving in to a choice of meal to make someone else happy. Or it may be as complex as altering your entire life around someone else's wishes or expectations because their approval makes you happy. People with this trait often do things to obtain compliments. Approval-seeking causes a lot of pain and stress to those doing it. Many people are approval seekers without even realizing it.

Controlling. This is where it gets tricky. Referring to codependency, the term controlling does not mean controlling others, it means controlling oneself. I've learned that most codependents don't have full control of their lives, they will try to find small areas in their life that they can control. Even if this means controlling something that's negative. The example that Mrs. Henry used was someone who is a compulsive caretaker may not control the fact that their entire life is consumed with caring for someone so they will purposely take control of their eating habits. Whether this may mean eating too much or too little.

Codependency creates stress and leads to painful emotions. Shame and low self-esteem create anxiety and fear about being judged, rejected or abandoned; making mistakes; being a failure; feeling trapped by being close or being alone. The other symptoms lead to feeling anger, resentment, depression, hopelessness, and despair. When the feelings are too much, you can feel numb. I really appreciate these past months of being in Ms. Henry's support group. I have realized that I am codependent. Tomorrow, Ms. Henry has set time aside to do a one-on one session with me before I am released to general population. It will be my last session, which is a bit scary knowing that I have so many codependent traits and Ms. Henry has not yet taught us every aspect of codependency.

The officer just announced that the cells are now being opened for all graduates to line up.

I gotta go. It was nice touching base with you.

It has been well overdue.

-Me.

As I walked into the Chapel with my head held high, I was feeling proud. For the first time in a long time, I didn't feel like I was incarcerated. My blue gown flowed side to side, as I approached my designated pew. I looked over to the visitor's section and saw Aunty and Ms. Craine staring back at me. I smiled. I hoped that she was proud of me. The Chapel was beautifully decorated with yellow and turquoise flowers. I saw all of the instructors dressed in formal attire. When we were all seated, Superintendent Brown addressed the crowd. Although a graduation program wasn't created, I knew exactly how things would go. After the superintendent's address, the graduates would sing, my friend would do her speech, and my speech would follow. I sat in my seat overflowing with excitement, nervousness and my joy, which froze once I heard my name announced. It was time for me to address the crowd!

"I am honored to be the recipient of the Lisa Wagner Award and would like to welcome the Wagner family. It's a pleasure to have you attend this ceremony. I have been told that Ms. Wagner was an exceptional woman who was dedicated to helping others better themselves. Unfortunately, I never had the pleasure of meeting her. However, I would like to thank her for making a difference.

My journey has been filled with lots of ups and downs. Prior to my arrest, I was a Virginia State University student, majoring in Criminal Justice. I was a cheerleader and an active member of many organizations. My life changed in an instant and the feeling was so unreal. I remember the day of my sentencing. That day will always be vivid in my memory. The judge looked down at me and said, "You are sentenced to five to fifteen years, to be served in a state prison." It was a cloudy day. It's a bit ironic because I felt that the sun would never shine in my world again. When I turned around, I saw my aunt and friend in tears.

The tears, the hurt, the embarrassment and the guilt, not only for myself, but for all those who loved and cared about me--that broke my heart more than the sentence itself. I would have to somehow turn their pain into joy. When I was in high school, I wanted to be the valedictorian. Maybe I would have achieved that if I were hungry enough. Being here has made me more determined to be successful. Since I have returned to my relationship with God, I have discovered that positive opportunities can come out of this unfortunate situation. I consider this an investment in my future.

That is why this graduation is such a blessing.

Although I came to this prison with a positive outlook, after a while, I felt that my growth was at a standstill. Actually, I felt that I was going backwards. I began to dwell on the past. Also, I began to think about what everyone at home was doing. All of my friends are in college. When I get home, they will be starting their careers. What about me? Those thoughts became very overwhelming and discouraging. I soon felt completely drained.

Look around you! We each have a different story and a different purpose.

So don't measure your success by the success of someone else. Success has

many different meanings. After I came to that conclusion, I began to focus on the here and now and what I would like to accomplish in the future. Life is life, regardless of where I am. And life is very precious.

When I was younger, I had a huge imagination. I was a dreamer. As the years went by, I got caught up in day-to day life. Dreaming was no longer second nature. When I came here, I began to dream again. And believe me, I had big dreams. Dreaming has given me a different state of mind. I began to make short term and long term goals for myself. It was at this institution that I learned pay value and began to set deadlines. Whenever I'm having a bad day or whenever I feel like giving up, I remind myself that I have a deadline. Being a dreamer has rebuilt my confidence. If you can do something once, then you can do it again. I was successful in my dreams. I can definitely turn my dreams into reality and again be successful. With that confidence, I have been able to tell myself that I can achieve anything that I set my mind to. Many people expect the worst and hope for the best. I, on the other hand, expect the best at all times. That mindset has resulted in tremendous achievements for me.

I encourage you to dream, have confidence and do the things necessary to accomplish your dreams. We are individuals capable of great things. I congratulate all of you because being in this Chapel today is an accomplishment. Let your accomplishments be the motivation to push you toward future successes. I would like to share with you a poem that I wrote for the Y.A.O. talent show. It's entitled, 'Big Dreams.'

When I was a little girl, I had Big Dreams.
A doctor, that wasn't good enough for me; I had to be higher.
A solider, that wasn't good enough for me;
I would have to command the whole army. A hairstylist, only if I had my own salon.

Mommy, Aunty, my brother; they always told me, "The Sky is the Limit."
Biggie Smalls said it too.
"The Sky is the Limit."
And that would be the motivation for everything that I do.
So I took the steps necessary to be all that I could be. Graduated from high school, went on to college, But... I got caught up.
I had to stop, think, make a decision;
A or B, A or B, A or B,
B! I went with a decision that many would consider quite contrary.

When I was a little girl, I had Big Dreams.
A doctor, that wasn't good enough for me; I had to be higher.
A solider, that wasn't good enough for me;
I would have to command the whole army. A hairstylist, only if I had my own salon.

It's ridiculous how one decision could change your life forever.

I choose B and caught myself a case.

The D.A. indirectly took all my Big Dreams, and put them in my discovery.

Man, that discovery!

It was a cloudy day in November when he said,

"A felony, we want the mandatory!" But, every morning when I wake up, I have A or B, A or B, A or B.

A, I look out my prison window and still the 'Sky is the Limit.' I will be all that I can be!

Are you listening to me?

Are you listening to me?

Because all my life I've felt like no one has been listening to me.

Yes, I said it!

I will be all that I can be.

Because this right here is not good enough for me.

I don't like waking up on a hard mattress and to a cold tray.

This will never be good enough for me. Because when I was a little girl, I had Big Dreams.

After writing that poem, I realized that the sky is not the limit. It is only the view. So, my possibilities are limitless. I am living out my dreams every day. I am thankful for the help that I have received from God, my family, and friends. Through all of my court appearances, they were there. Today, as I look into the audience, once again, you are here. Your support means the world to me. I love you. I would like to take this time to express my appreciation for all the help that I have received here at Fluvanna Correctional, and for selecting me to be the Lisa Wagner Award recipient.

In conclusion, I have learned things here that Virginia State University could have never taught me. Sometimes we have to hit rock bottom to bring out the best in us. I have evolved from some of my darkest times and there will be more obstacles in the future. But, I will believe in myself. Success will be the end result, if you remember to believe in yourself. Thank you."

open up your [...]
Soul. ACCEPT Him AS your [...]
SAVIOUR. HE NEVER FAIL. (I DREAM of MARRYING
you all the time. I only WISH MY DREAM could
come thru. Stay Sweet. FAST FOR DELIVERANCE
in OUR life. I MISS you. MISS you. SAME

Graduation

State Correctional Institution

at

Fluvanna

April 20, 2011

TO BE WITH you. I WILL NOT CARE WHAT
PEOPLE MAY SAY OR DO. I LOVE you. AT
TIME THERE ARE THINGS I WOULD LIKE TO
SAY TO you. but WORDS GET IN THE WAY.
you ARE MY LADY. you ARE EVERYTHING I
NEED MOST. you ARE ALL I AM LIVING FOR

I am sitting here in Illinois, staring in the darkness across the miles thinking of you. If I could only come home to you, it would have mean everything. I really miss you. Honey, whenever I am with you I will cherish every moment. I will love you faithfully. You will be the one and only. I just want to give you some serious loving. please tell me you feel the same. being alone with you just me and you in our world. I have a good feelings its going to be good. Honestly I am thinking, and to make our choice right with God. I am really really thinking of marrying you at some point of

UNIVERSAL LOVE. CHERISH YOUR LOVE, ENCLOSE ARE PHOTO (3) I DO hope you LIKE THEM. I DO THE Picture FOR YOU SO YOU CAN BE REMINDED OF YOUR HANDSOME FUTURISTIC. (emiter). I DID MAKE THAT WORD.

Temperature is rising, can you smell your perfume, your body is my playground let me lick you up And down, I am going to make you feel so good. and I will be good to you. So you dont have to worry. I see you in my dream all the time, baby girl you so fine. You are a American Queen, I am a Jamaican King. do everything Just for me, you dont

standard of our relationship. Fathers Day I was
thinking deep and picturing you as the
expected mother of my child. It is so
natural I must want to hold you, look

I never thought
about anymore me.
9. Smile, Keep smili
9, Keep things "tight" !!
you. Soon

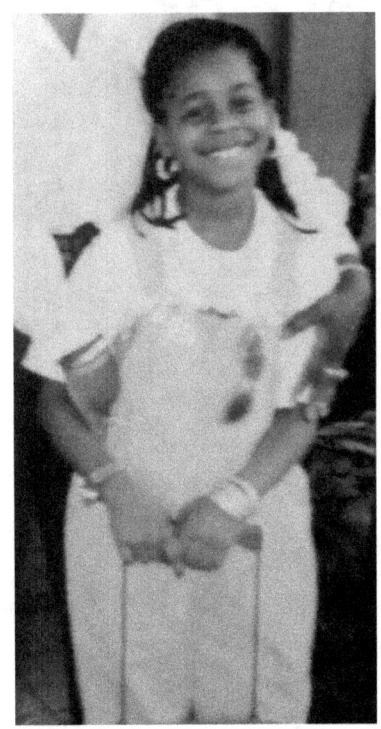

Hi

I HAVE RECIEVE YOUR LETTER
today AND was HAPPY Seeing your
mail. After reading the contents
I was sad heading all what
you have to say. I appreciated
your feeling and also I respect
it. I would love to be THAT FATHER
THAT YOU NEVER HAD. I DONT
Know now if you would HONOR my
visit also if you WANT me to
Continue send you CASH.
I am speechless right now. Dont
Know how to express myself. So enclose
is a picture of your little BROTHER
JAYDEN I Know you will love it.

Chapter Ten

"SKY, SKY.....Uhh." Tears.

"Gi.Gi, wake up! Are you okay? You were screaming sky really loudly in your sleep. Why? It scared me because I could hear you crying."

"Thanks for waking me up. I'm fine. I don't know why I was screaming that. I have strange dreams quite frequently."

"Oh okay. Me too. Sometimes I dream of my life before prison. Sometimes, I dream about the day my house was raided, it haunts me in my sleep."

"COUNT TIME, LADIES...COUNT TIME. AT YOUR DOORS, LIGHTS ON, PROPERLY DRESSED AND QUIET," Officer Cedric screamed at the top of his lungs, as he usually did every morning around that time.

We walked over to stand by our locked cell doors. I could see across the tier and down at the bottom tier, that every cell was occupied by young, sleepy faces. Count time wasn't anything new to me. Count was done three times a day; once at 6 a.m., again at 12 noon and finally at 9 p.m. I've also been told that night shift does a non-standing count at 3 a.m. But, I've never been awake to witness it. We've been trained to stand silently for count time because noise may disrupt the officer and result in an inaccurate count. The consequence of that would be a misconduct for the inmate who does so. Misconducts can easily lead to being sent to 'the hole,' a high level disciplinary method used to punish inmates inside the prison.

I recall one time 'count' took about two hours to clear. Trisha and I were getting antsy as we stood waiting in our cell. It was lunch time and we would not be served until this afternoon count was cleared. We were starving. As they were trying to figure out if someone had escaped, I could only think about my grilled cheese that was being served for lunch that day. I was happy to hear that Trisha had a few commissary items for us to snack on because they counted us three times within the two-hour wait. Finally, they figured out an inmate was off grounds at a hospital trip and this information had not been properly recorded.

For me, the morning count was the most uncomfortable process of them all. An officer would scream to wake us up causing me to have an intense headache, then my 'cellie' and I would have to stand in a cramped doorway without haven removed the morning crust from between our eyes or brushed our teeth. I'm thankful count required silence because I wouldn't have wanted to have a conversation while smelling morning breathe with my cellie. I watched as Officer Cedric and Officer Toole did their round, carefully recording numbers on their clipboards. I really liked the way Officer Cedric interacted with us. His all-white beard reminded me of Santa Claus. And the way that he reprimanded us was like that of a wise grandfather. He didn't yell or punish us, instead he would talk things through, with the goal of us learning a lesson.

Each morning when he searched our cell, he would run his finger over the light panel, in search of dust. Our cell search would be scored on a point system. At the end of the week our points were calculated, determining whether or not we could advance to the next phase. At first, many inmates rumored he was mean and picky. I will never forget when he said, 'If someone cannot clean and care for a 6X8 cell, how can they be trusted to clean an apartment or a house. Many people do not realize that the way you keep your place of residence will carry over to the way you present yourself to the world.' I truly feel that he is one of the only officers that actually cared.

"Twenty-six inmates on Delta pod. Copy?" I heard Mr. Cedrick dispatch on his radio. Yep, twenty- six, soon to be twenty-five, when I'm released to general population in a few hours.

We had about fifteen minutes before count would be cleared, which meant we had to quickly get things in order. I walked away from the cell door and proceeded to brush my teeth with the awful tasting, knock-off Colgate toothpaste I purchased from commissary and Trisha was doing the same. Within that time, we would have to be properly dressed in our browns – shirts tucked in and ready for the day. This amount of time also included cells to be cleaned and beds made. That particular morning would be a bit different for me. My belongings were neatly packed in two cardboard boxes, waiting by the door for my release to be announced. My diary was strategically packed at the button of the box. I hoped Mr. Cedric would not go through my already packed things.

"I'm gonna miss you, GiGi."

"I'm gonna miss you too. I wish you wouldn't have gotten caught kissing Kelly. You and I would have been on the same phase and leaving this program together."

"Yea, it's cool. I'm just glad I didn't get really caught. Officer Toole only thought she saw us kissing. She set me back because of her own doubt. But I'm glad she wasn't sure whether or not we were kissing, because I would have been sent to the hole with a hefty misconduct."

"True. Well I can't wait until you're out there with me. Did you decide whether or not ya coming to the program I'm going to?"

"Nah, I may not come. I'm not ready to tackle those emotions yet. I have too much going on at home. Too many things on my mind. The last thing I need is to dig up that can of worms."

"I hear you. I'm going to the Chapel this Sunday, I will turn around and look up into the balcony so that I could see you. And don't stop going to Ms.

Henry's groups."

"Yea. Imma go. Nowadays all I want do is sit in this cell and cry. It's hard knowing that mi abuela just got diagnosed with cancer and I can't even be there for her."

"CHOW TIME LADIES…CHOW!"

I gave Trisha a hug. "I hear you, my love. I could only imagine how hard that is. I don't know what else to say. But, I'm here for you."

I slipped my feet into the shoes and hurried to tie the laces. I could see that Trisha was still styling her hair and leaned over to grab her mascara.

"Hurry girl, you know we only have five minutes to get down there."

"Yea, but I can't have Kelly see me like this. She's been eyeing the new girl that just came in two days ago."

I chuckled. "Okay."

I walked down the steps and over to Officer Toole who handed me a breakfast tray. She told me to sit at table six. I was happy when I realized we were having cornflakes and a banana. When I sat down, Sabrina was already seated at the table. Minutes later, I saw Andrea walking over to join us.

"Morning, Sexy. So is today the end of us?" Andrea said within the same breath.

"I saw that you got a visit yesterday. Was it your sister?" I quickly asked while emptying the milk carton into my cereal.

"Nah. That was my spiritual adviser. So what's this program that you're going to?"

"It's called the House of Hope. It's a program for people who have experienced Domestic Violence or Childhood Sexual abuse. It's an inpatient program. "

"What does inpatient mean?" Sabrina asked.

"It means that it's not a program where you work on yourself for two hours and then go to a different housing unit. There is an entire housing unit designated to this program. And I will live on the housing unit until I complete the program."

Andrea still hadn't touched her tray of food. "So you're planning to leave one program and go to another one?" "Yes," I shot back.

"Well, that's silly. I would have at least enjoyed general population before going into another program."

"What's there to enjoy?" I asked, as I stared at her for an answer.

Silence.

"What's really silly is that when I came back from graduation yesterday, someone told me that they saw you by the closet kissing Raina?"

"You shouldn't believe everything you hear."

"I didn't say that I believed them. But maybe I should?" "Seriously, GiGi?

I looked up and saw Mrs. Henry walking through the pod door. My concentration immediately shifted and I was so happy to see her face. She was greeted at the door by Officer Cedric who then gave her a routine pat search and flipped through her binders and papers.

I heard an array of pleasantries greet her. She walked over to my table and with haste in her voice she said, "Hurry Ms. Greene, we have a bunch of material to cover today."

I excused myself from the table and walked upstairs to my cell to get my folder for support group. It was on the top of my box and easy to locate.

The room where group was typically held was about the size of three cells combined, which was usually stuffed with twenty- six participants from the pod. But today, it was only Mrs. Henry and I. I walked in and closed the door behind me. The room was brightly lit and had two windows that offered a perfect view of the general population yard. Many times we would gaze off watching the general population inmates play basketball. The room consisted of a dry-erase board, one major table with many chairs and white walls that were covered with papers we completed throughout our group sessions.

"Hey, Mrs. Henry. I didn't think that you would come this early."

"Yeah, I headed over here as soon as count was cleared. We have a lot of work to do before you're released to G.P. I've been thinking about you and you have a lot of codependent traits," she said as she arranged her long black dreads in a bun. Gray hairs were sprinkled all throughout her head.

"Thank you for coming."

"So, you've told me a lot about yourself, court, your crime, and county jail. You haven't directly come out and told me everything. But as a facilitator and peer advisor it's my job to pay attention. You've answered different questions throughout these past months, you've done and said different things outside of the group setting. I have mentally stored this information and I really want you to see what I see."

"Let's start with your name. Your name is Giselle. And I could see the uneasiness and disapproval within you every time someone calls you GiGi. But, you don't say anything. As much as you dislike what you are being called, you allow people to call you this."

"Going back to when you were in the county. You explained your attorney was telling you to take the plea agreement for a minimum of five years. You told me that deep down you wanted to go to trial. Going to trial may not have led to a better outcome. But, the fact that you went along with what your attorney said and withheld such important information about wanting to go to trial is quite codependent and problematic. Your life was on the line in that situation and in my opinion you just went with the flow."

"During your sentencing hearing, your judge asked if you had anything to say. In my opinion you didn't speak up for fear of being judged. Minutes after you were sentenced, I can relate to what you were feeling. I know the feeling of standing before a judge and being sentenced. Let's not forget that I have a life sentence. But in that moment, instead of caring for yourself and your emotions, your main focus was your aunt's emotions, which to me seems like codependent behavior. I'm not saying any of these things for you to feel bad about yourself. I just want you to see the severity of what's going on here. You said you stayed in your cell a lot while in county. Was that out of fear of being rejected?"

"No."

"Okay. That's one of the few times that you've given me a yes or a no answer. You use a lot of words that show your uncertainty. Most times you say I guess or it doesn't matter. Those words of uncertainty are examples of Dysfunctional Communication. This also shows difficulty with making decisions for yourself or identifying with your feelings. These are all aspects of codependency, Ms. Greene. I want you to start paying attention to these things within yourself. Are you ready to move along?"

"Yes."

"Okay. Although I've given you examples of where I see codependency, I don't want to label you as codependent. If I do so, I would be doing you an injustice. I'm guessing that people may have put labels on you in the past, and that might not have been a good feeling. I want to give you the opportunity to make this decision on your own. I would like us to read this excerpt taken from Understanding Codependency, which outlines a series of questions. These questions are for someone to ask themselves in trying to make the distinction between whether or not they are codependent. Here, read them aloud."

"Having difficulty making decisions in a relationship? Having difficulty identifying your feelings? Having difficulty communicating in a relationship?

Valuing the approval of others more than valuing yourself? Lacking trust in yourself and having poor self-esteem? Having fears of abandonment or an obsessive need for approval? Having an unhealthy dependence on relationships, even at your own cost? Having an exaggerated sense of responsibility for the actions of others?"

"I don't want you to answer those questions now. Ponder on them later while you have free time, possibly in your cell when you are alone."

"Okay." I've already labelled myself as codependent. "So, let's go back to what we were talking about the other day. Having a low self-esteem can be accompanied with codependency. Which means feeling inadequate and/or self- conscious and trying to hide these feelings by appearing confident. Some people with a low self-esteem feel unlovable. Therefore, they tend to cling to people who show them little hints of love. Or they misinterpret small kind gestures as love. Low self- esteem can drive someone to one of two extremes or both extremes as a result of the other — perfectionism or carelessness."

"Perfection is not attainable. But, in their minds, if things are perfect then they won't feel bad about themselves. This actually has the opposite effect. When things don't turn out to be perfect, as they would like, this person will then beat themselves up. They tend to have difficulty admitting their mistakes because they want to appear perfect. It's a self-destructive behavior. Consequently, this will further lower self-esteem and cause someone to take the other extreme which is carelessness, in which they will judge what they say, think and do as not good enough. They may have difficulty making decisions, getting started, meeting deadlines, and completing projects. This can be done vice versa where someone who is codependent with a low self-esteem will go from carelessness to perfectionism."

"Many codependent people have a passive or passive-aggressive communication style."

"What is a passive communication style?"

"In regards to the way someone communicates, there are a few different categories. But, someone does not have to fall under any of these categories. Or people can bounce between different categories. The categories are passive, passive-aggressive, aggressive, and assertive. I will go over them briefly. I wish we had more time together for me to go more in depth. However, I want you to have a broad understanding before you leave this program."

"The passive communicator has difficulty expressing their thoughts, feelings, and ideas. Therefore, they appear compliant and submissive. This person will talk very little and agree to things that internally they don't agree with. Someone who is passive-aggressive will appear to be passive. They will verbally agree to things and then act out internally, indirectly, or sarcastically. An example of passive-aggressive communication would be someone verbally agreeing to drive you somewhere. But during the ride, they are saying sarcastic remarks like, 'this route will completely throw me off track; driving you here is going to make me late for work.' This person's facial expressions may also be contradicting to what they verbally agree to do."

"The aggressive communicator will say things in a harsh manner. They tend to talk over others and utilize put-downs. They communicate in a way that violates others. I like to refer to them as 'Know-it-alls.'"

"An assertive communication style is the most effective. This communicator will verbalize what they want, feel, and need without aiming to harm others. This person tends to have good relationships because they can set healthy boundaries and they are usually happy with outcomes because they are willing to hear what someone else wants and come up with a compromise."

"Cool. I get it."

"Many codependent people have a passive or passive-aggressive communication style. They're tremendously loyal causing them to remain in damaging situations for too long."

"Uhhmmm."

"What was that? "

"Sorry, I didn't say anything."

"They give up their truth to gain the approval of others, compromising their own values and integrity to avoid rejection or anger. They will put aside their own interests in order to do what others want and are hypervigilant regarding the feelings of others and take on those feelings."

"What do you mean by *take on those feelings*?"

"I will give you an example in the context of prison. Someone may have an upbeat personality and are usually happy and playful during common room and around the housing unit. But, their 'cellie' may be a negative and pessimistic person. So, the passive codependent will then shift their mood while in the cell to take on the feelings of their cellie."

"The passive codependent will have trouble identifying their feelings or they will minimize, deny, or alter the way they are feeling. They will hide their pain in many ways such as anger, humor, or isolation."

"Do you think that you are codependent?"

"I used to be very codependent and it led me to a life sentence. I used to just go with the flow. I followed my friends to a party one day. I really wanted to go home because something didn't feel right. But, I went with them anyways. The events that took place that night at the party resulted in a double homicide. I didn't pull the trigger nor did I know what was going to happen. My codependent ways handed me a life sentence without the possibility of parole for two murders and conspiracy to murder. I was twenty-five when I first came here. The jail didn't have fences yet. We were allowed to wear regular clothes and men were also housed on this campus. Goes to show you, that was a long time ago."

"Wow."

"Codependents perceive themselves as unselfish and dedicated to the well-being of others. Also, they think they can take care of themselves and the world. They find it difficult to ask for help. They are often attracted to people that are unavailable and they don't tend to recognize this unavailability. I know it may seem like I'm repeating myself. That's because a lot of the codependent traits are similar to one another and some traits are even intertwined or a result of another trait."

"That's fine. I'm taking notes. I really appreciate this."

"I've told you before that codependency has many layers and many interpretations. With that being said, some traits contradict one another. A prime example is these two traits: codependents are embarrassed to receive recognition, praise or gifts; codependents seek recognition and praise to overcome feeling less-than."

I smiled. "That is confusing, Mrs. Henry."

"I was confused too. When my Psychology professor was teaching this, I thought to myself, this man must have truly bribed someone for his degree. Then he went on to explain that codependency is compiled of many compulsive traits. Compulsive behavior can take many forms, depending on the person. For some it might mean over-eating or under-eating. Another person's compulsive behavior may lead to isolating herself/himself or the opposite trait, which would be acting out in an attention-seeking manner. Perfectionism or carelessness are again two opposite compulsive behaviors, all of which signal codependency deep within. A good rule of thumb is that too much of anything is frequently not good."

I heard a soft knock coming from the group room door. I turned around as Officer Cedrick opened the door, "Greene, the House of Hope just called, they said that your bed is ready."

I stood up to give Mrs. Henry a hug. "I will miss you, Mrs. Henry."

"Oh, this is not the end of the journey for us. Now that you are going to G.P., I will see you in the yard."

I exited the room and walked up the stairs to my cell. Trisha was waiting for me at the door.

"Can I help you bring your things downstairs?" Trisha said with a soft and sad voice.

"Sure."

"Give me another hug," she said as she began to cry.

We exited the cell to walk back downstairs. I was trying to conceal my smile as I heard everyone banging on their cell doors. I stopped at Andrea's door when I heard the yelling of her voice.

"You never answered my question. What does this mean for us? Are we together?"

"Yeah, we are."

Chapter Eleven

"Damn shorty, you pretty for a black girl."

"Stop talking to my inmate!" I heard Officer Cedrick yell to the one girl.

"Yo, what's my wife Sabrina doing in that program? She betta not be acting the fuck up."

"Stop talking to my inmate, that's a direct order."

As Officer Cedrick and I walked past the big yard, it was heavily populated with general population inmates. It was extremely loud. I could hear people yelling idiotic comments towards me. Officer Cedrick walked very closely beside me as if he were protecting his child. I didn't mind it--I was grateful for the protection. The yard was surrounded by a huge fence with a locked gate. I eyed about five or six officers patrolling the yard. People were braiding hair while others were playing cards. Some played basketball as others circled the track around the yard.

As we walked past the yard, I could see the chapel about a quarter mile to my left. I could see the school building to my far right and other buildings were scattered around the campus. People were straggling towards the school entrance.

Officer Cedrick and I made a sharp right turn.

"Almost there, Greene. Do you think you're ready for general population?" "Yes, I do."

"Well, you were one of the good ones. I'll miss you. Be good out here.... This is it."

He stopped in front of a gray building that resembled a house.

"This is the House of Hope. Go in and tell the officer your name and show them your inmate I.D."

"Bye, Officer Cedrick."

I walked up and pulled the heavy entrance door. The housing unit smelled like a combination of old furniture and someone's moldy basement.

"Hi. I'm Giselle Greene."

"I know who you are, inmate. Follow me this way, you are in cell four."

The officer was a very tall, white man with red hair and reddish freckles.

His tone was unwelcoming and rigid. *I guess that was a part of the job?*

He began to babble as he walked me to my cell.

"When I call count in the mornings, you better be up. If I get to your cell and you're not up, I'm sending you to the hole. Every morning, after count, I come around for sign-ups. You can sign up for a fifteen-minute slot to shower and a fifteen-minute phone call. I don't like horseplay on my unit. If I see it, I'm sending you to the hole. And I betta not catch you fuckin', suckin', or smoking a cigarette. I'll send you straight to the hole. I don't play that shit on my housing unit. What shower time would you like for tomorrow? Today is already filled."

"May I please have a 10:30 a.m. shower?"

"Are you being a smart ass, inmate? Are you being specific as if you thought I would give you a 10:30 p.m. shower when you're locked in for the night at nine o'clock?"

He slammed the door behind me as if I was a caged animal. At this point, feeling like a caged animal was not a unfamiliar feeling, we were reminded daily by some guards we were worthless. I put my two heavy boxes on the cell floor and began to look around. This cell was smaller than the one in the Y.A.O. – was that even possible? The cell was furnished the same way: a bunk bed, toilet, sink, and a desk. The bottom bunk already had the belongings of someone else so I proceeded to put my things on the empty top bunk where a blanket and a set of sheets awaited its new owner. Unlike the other cells I've resided in, this cell had photos all over the wall, I wondered who they belonged to and what meaning they had. As I made the bed, I was frightened by a slamming noise coming from the cell door.

"Oh, sorry. Did I scare you?" There stood a young white girl at the cell window with her brunette hair pulled back into a ponytail, she looked as if she could be my age.

"Nah, I'm good. You didn't scare me."

"You can make ya bed later. Ms. Price told me to come upstairs to invite you down to group. Group just started so you made it here in perfect timing.

I left my things right where they were and followed the girl out the cell, down the hall, down the steps and to the right into a group session that filled a huge living room.

"Oh, I'm Jessica, by the way. Sit next to me."

The materials used in the room were similar to the group room in the Y.A.O. with the dry erase board and completed papers all over the walls. However, this room had army green couches assembled along the walls in the shape of a semi-circle. This room had great big windows that overlooked a farm in the distance. In front of the dry erase board sat a pregnant woman wearing a beautiful smile.

"Hi, Ms. Greene. My name is Mrs. Price. Welcome to the House of Courage. Please have a seat and make yourself comfortable, we were just getting started."

"Thank you." I took a seat on the couch next to Jessica.

"Ms. Greene, this group is called Evolving to Safety. We start each group by warming up. *Warming up* is just another term for check-ins. When it's your turn we ask each person to state their name, tell us how they are doing or something else they'd like to share with us."

"Since you are new, I will go first. My name is Mrs. Price. I am the founder of the House of Courage. I have been running this program for seventeen years. I have a degree in Psychology and a degree in Criminal Justice. My favorite thing about doing Domestic Violence work is watching people regain themselves."

I watched as the ladies went around in a circle introducing themselves. This was different and I enjoyed it. The group was very diverse in ages and race. For a brief moment, I forgot that I was in prison. My eye caught a cat as it walked by a lady's foot. I guess Mrs. Price saw the surprised look on my face because she interrupted the lady that was talking.

"We are the only housing unit in the prison that has cats or any animal. I petitioned for years to have the cats approved. Studies show that cats are a great help and comfort through recovery. Are you allergic?"

"No. But, I really hope that none of them will touch me. And I want to apologize in advance if I freak out as the result of one jumping on me or touching me. I've never been around cats."

"That fine. Let's continue warming up."

I listened closely in an effort to remember everyone's name which would be nearly impossible. I listened to Jessica speak and realized that we had so much in common.

When it was my turn to go, I took a deep breath and began to speak. "Hi. My name is Giselle Green. Please call me Giselle. I am here to learn more about Domestic Violence. I am doing well and looking forward to a visit that I will be having this week or next week."

"When we have someone new to the group we go over the fact that this group is Confidential, meaning anything said in this group will not be repeated. The only thing that should leave this group is the material that you've learned. If you break confidentiality, you will be removed from this program."

"Okay."

"Also, you were accepted to this program because you have experienced one or more of the topics that we will discuss. We encourage each other not to refer to ourselves as victims. Instead, we refer to ourselves and others in the group as survivors. Some people say, I was a victim then, but, now I am a survivor. In my opinion, we were survivors even throughout our experiences because it took survival strategies and techniques to live through the abuse. The term *survivor* feels empowering. There is great significance in owning that term if power has been stolen from you in the past. Also, the term survivor feels hopeful on the healing journey. However, if you feel more comfortable referring to yourself as a victim, we will honor that."

"There is no real beginning to this topic of Domestic Violence. But, it would make sense to start with the definition. *Domestic Violence* is a pattern of behaviors that one person uses to gain power and control over a spouse, intimate partner, or a family member. Many organizations will use variations of this definition and that is completely fine. The important thing to remember is power and control."

"That makes sense. When I did an inpatient program a couple years ago, Domestic Violence was defined as Violence or controlling behavior towards a spouse," said a girl that was seating across the room.

"I've heard that definition. I don't like that definition because violence sometimes won't exist in a Domestic Violent situation. With the word violence in the definition, it is easy for someone to say, that's not my relationship, and continue to endure the abuse. I also dislike the fact that the definition is only inclusive to a spousal relationship. Domestic Violence can happen to people that are dating and to children. Domestic Violence can happen in heterosexual relationships and in LGBTQ relationships or arrangements."

"I feel you."

"Over time, this group will touch on a few different aspects: Domestic

Violence, Child Abuse, and Sexual Assault."

Mrs. Price stood up and began to write on the dry erase board. With her green marker, she wrote 'types of abuse.'

"What do you think are the different types of abuse that show up in Domestic Violence relationships? Shout them out!"

"Sexual."

"Emotional."

"Physical."

 "Verbal," I shouted.

"Financial," I heard Jessica say.

"Perfect. What are some examples of sexual abuse?"

"Rape or forcing someone to have sex with other people."

"Violent sex."

"Forcing someone to watch porn," I said.

"Yes. How about unwanted filming or photography?" Mrs. Price asked as she wrote it on the board.

"Agreed."

"All right. Give me some examples of verbal abuse."

"Put-downs, threats, yelling, degrading comments, name calling, mocking, screaming."

"Wow. Ms. Blagden, you're telling me faster than I can write. You know a lot about this."

"I know a lot because I've lived it. This was my ex-husband's favorite tactic."

"Thanks for sharing that Ms. Blagden, if you'd like to talk privately after group I will be in my office."

"Okay, let's go over emotional abuse," said Mrs. Price.

"Mind games and blaming."

"Disregarding someone's feelings."

"Ridiculing and embarrassing someone,"

"Denying…..False promises."

I looked around, others were looking around for the next person to shout an example. I was hoping that I would have brought paper and a pen to write all of this down. I was blown away by all that I was learning and I hadn't been in group for a full hour.

Mrs. Price began to speak. "This next one is usually overlooked. The type of emotional abuse that I am looking for is silence. The silent treatment is the worst form of emotional abuse because with the silent treatment the abuser leaves the person guessing. The unknown in this context is emotionally damaging." *Oh wow. I never thought of that.*

"What are some examples of physical abuse?"

"Hitting, choking, biting."

"Not allowing your partner to sleep." "Pinching," Jessica shouted.

"Punching and spitting."

"Homicide."

"Stalking."

"Yes, ladies. What about financial abuse?"

"Controlling money or bank accounts."

"Stealing the partner's identity, or misuse of the social security number." "Forcing a partner to have a joint bank account," I said.

"Giving allowances. Or not allowing their partner to get a job."

"Yes. There are so many examples of each kind of abuse, we could go on for hours. I just wanted us to paint a picture of what each type of abuse can look like. Also, some examples will overlap and can be in more than one category. You all are probably wondering, how does this all work? How does a person do all of this to someone without it being obvious that this is abuse?"

"Power and control is gained through the cycle of abuse. It's not always referred to as a cycle. Different programs will illustrate this with different visual terms. But, it's all the same idea. The cycle of abuse has three different stages. The tension stage, the blow-up stage, and the seduction stage. The way I remember this is by using the example that's usually used when teaching someone how to write a story. In writing a story one is taught that there is rising action, a climax, falling action, and a resolution. Except in Domestic Violence situations there's not always an immediate resolution."

"The seduction stage comes before the tension building stage, and again, after the blow-up stage. Many refer to this as the honeymoon stage. In this stage there are a lot of gifts, nice gestures, and romancing. This is when the abuse will put their best foot forward, trying to sweep you off your feet. This period can last for two months, one year, even ten years."

"The tension building stage can include a lot of arguing, signs of possessiveness, and jealousy. Initially, possessiveness and jealously can be misinterpreted as an abuser caring a lot for the survivor. The abuser may utilize many put-downs or even say negative things about your appearance or traits, areas that they once complimented in the seduction stage. Many times an abuser will use their tone of voice, treats, and body language to inflict intimidation and fear. The abuser can become increasingly picky about small things. This is when the survivor may feel like they are walking on eggshells. With the tension building it will seem like the abuser is picking a fight frequently. These days will feel more and more uncomfortable. The Domestic Violence cycle is evolving to the blow-up stage."

"The blow-up stage is where the where the tension comes to a climax. This stage can look like many different things. It could be hitting. It could be the use of a weapon or weapons. This could be rape. This can be pushing. My abuser has pushed me down the stairs, several times."

"How can it be a rape if the abuser is your husband or wife?"

"We will get into the exact definition of rape later. But, unwanted, sexual behavior without consent is rape. It doesn't matter if the individuals are married."

"Good to know."

"The seduction or the honeymoon stage is where the abuser will apologize for their actions. The apology usually blames the survivor for the abuse that occurred. These apologies are also called backward apologies. For example, 'I'm sorry for punching you. That's not something that I would normally do. But, if you weren't pushing my buttons then I wouldn't have done it.' Another example, 'I shouldn't have thrown hot water on you. But, you were talking to that friend that I don't like. You know that makes me jealous.' These backward apologizes are often accompanied by gifts, make-up dates, or make-up sex. These gestures can leave the survivor second guessing themselves, thinking that the abuse is their fault. The cycle can then go back to the tension building stage."

"What keeps the cycle in motion?"

"Can you please tell us? Tell me why I keep going back to this asshole, other than the fact that I love him. I don't even know why I love him. I feel that some of the abuse I endured was my fault because I kept forgiving him?"

"Abuse is not your fault. An abuser makes the decision to abuse. However, there are three things that keep the cycle in motion: fear, love, and hope," said Mrs. Price.

I then interrupted to share, "These three aspects were also taught to me. I keep in mind that every domestic violent situation is perpetuated differently and I am sure there are other aspects that keep the cycle in motion."

"I don't fear my wife?"

"Fear shows itself in many ways. Remember you once said that you purchased a separate cell phone to make calls to your family?" A blonde girl began to question the girl next to her.

"Yeah. I couldn't afford for Glenda to know that I was still in contact with my family. She thinks they hate her--well they do. Plus, her and I made an agreement to not have contact with anyone who was against our relationship."

"So having a hidden cell phone does show that you feared her or what she would do if she knew that you were still in contact with those family members."

"Nah, I only fear God."

"Okay that's enough ladies," Mrs. Price interjected. "The purpose of this is not to make anyone feel bad about themselves."

"I know Mrs. Price, Trina and I had a personal conversation where she asked me to call her out on certain things that I notice from her past relationship with Glenda. Mainly because she's still battling with the decision she made to leave."

"Yeah Mrs. Price, that is true."

Mrs. Price began to speak again, "Fear, love, and hope, keep the cycle going. Many survivors fear their abuser. They fear the thought of leaving, for many reasons, which we will get into later. I feared leaving because my abuser told me that he will kill me if I left. He also told me that no one else would love me the way he does. I loved him. I loved the man and yearned for the person I first met. This brings me to the next aspect – hope.

I hoped that the abuse would stop and I would have the man that I first fell in love with. I later realized that I was being hopeful for something that wouldn't happen."

I heard the sound of a very loud bell coming from the distance. It reminded me of a history lesson in high school where we learned, of a huge bell ringing in town square to announce the time of day, as many people during the olden days did not own personal clocks.

"Okay that's all for today, ladies. We will continue this information in the next group."

I followed everyone out of the group room. I walked toward my cell and realized that Jessica was coming behind me.

"I'm your cellie," she said.

"Okay."

"They about to do count. When count clears you can walk with me to the dining hall. G.P. is not like the Y.A.O. where your trays are brought to the housing unit."

"That group was awesome," I said to Jessica, when we both arrived back to our cell.

"Yeah, it is. It's my third time in this prison and my third time in this program. The cycle of abuse is a hard one to break. I went home with all the information that I learned and felt like I was ready to take on the world. Then, I fell into another abusive relationship. With all the knowledge that I have, I still didn't see the signs."

I was excited to be housed with Jessica. I had not yet become fully acquainted with her, but I could already see that we had a lot in common, which was comforting in itself. As we made small talk, I made my bed and unpacked my belongings. When I removed the books from my grey bin, two unopened letters from Alton fell to the ground. I completely forgot that I received mail from him within the last month. The letters arrived within two weeks of each other and I placed them in my bin, unopened, because I felt that reading the letters would upset me and negatively affect my performance in the program. But today, curiosity led me to open each letter. After reading the letters, I quickly realized that I should not have read them. My emotional state shifted and my thoughts became overwhelmed with all that had occurred throughout the day. I wanted and needed to unwind and process everything and I wanted to do so alone. I climbed to my top bunk and began to write.

Dear Diary,

In one of the letters from Alton, he explains that he cannot wait until I come home so that we could be together. He said that he will not care of the judgements that other people will make because I am his lady and all that he is living for. Alton is outrageously delusional for thinking that I would ever want to be with him. Just the thought of him infuriates me! He is right to think that people would make judgements. What he wants is completely unethical and unacceptable. It's sad what he feels, that I'm all he is living for when I'm living for the day that he is completely removed from my life.

In the other letter from Alton, he states, "Whenever I am with you, I will cherish every moment… You will be my one and only. I just want to give you some serious loving. Please tell me you feel the same? …I have a good feeling it's going to be good. Honestly thinking to make our choice right with God." Serious loving? No, Alton! I definitely don't feel the same. All that you have given me is serious hatred and that's what I feel for you in return. He speaks as if he hopes that we will be in a relationship. He speaks as if he may already think that we are in one. I would never cherish any moment with you. I wish that I could erase the memory of you. What the hell does he mean by saying he wants to make our decision right with God? Our decision? Nothing was ever OURS and nothing will ever be OURS! Alton feels so entitled that he thinks he can make a decision for the both of us and label it OUR decision to make feel that I was included in the decision-making process. When it came to Alton, I was never given choice and always lacked agency. What he needs to do is get himself right with God! I should have followed my initial gut feeling, leaving the letters unopened!

I'm also irritated by the first words I heard today as I entered general population, which were "Damn, shorty you pretty for a black girl." What the hell is that supposed to mean? Definitely a comment, not a compliment that I find the need to address. That comment absolutely shows a great level of ignorance. That comment would never make me respond with any level of respect or interest. It's quite similar to saying, "You're tall for a white person," or "Your English is great for an immigrant." A comment like that usually comes from a place of preconceived stereotype or a prejudice. Telling someone that they are pretty for their race or complexion usually means that you never particularly found that race or complexion attractive. I don't care to change someone's mind about what they find attractive. I just care to say that I will not accept it as a compliment, because it's not! I take it as an endorsement that our society places on white heterosexual female beauty. I have watched and lived in a society that places unrealistic expectations on body image and beauty, defining what they think beauty means. I've internalized these messages, while not speaking up for myself, allowing these messages to define how I navigate this world...

~Me.

Chapter Twelve

I would like to do warm-ups a little differently today. I would like you to reach into my magical jaw and pick a word. Each word represents a particular feeling. Use that word to describe yourself in a current or recent state of mind."

"My name is Angelica. I feel mentally exhausted because I have been writing a letter to my little boy, explaining to him why I'm in prison."

"Lisa. I am suspicious because I think my cellie has been stealing my commissary."

"Naomi. I feel love-struck because today my girlfriend gets out of the hole."

"I'm Jessica. I feel discouraged cause my sister just had her baby and I'm not home to witness it."

As we went around the room doing warm-ups, I admired the skirt that Mrs. Price was wearing. *I admired any attire that wasn't prison clothes and couldn't wait for the day that I would be able to wear my own clothing again.* She wore a bright orange skirt, which was complimented by a cream colored cardigan. The skirt was long and flowy, a spandex material. I wanted to ask if she was having a boy or girl. I decided against it though. Officer Cedrick had told me before that we weren't allowed to know personal information of a prison employee.

The smell of rain seeping through the room was refreshing. Sitting on the couch, I could feel a few rain drops as they sporadically hit my shoulders. It had been raining all morning and the windows in the group room were open. I could hear the rain pounding outside on the concrete. I felt cozy. I felt ready to learn all the information that Mrs. Price would share today.

It was my turn to share with the group, after about nineteen ladies had completed their warm-up. "I feel relieved because I just wrote a letter to my best friend, at home, telling her that I'm in this program."

"Nice, ladies. I hope you all enjoyed me switching things up a bit. Today, I will lecture more than usual. I don't want us to run out of time on this section. Many people ask the question, 'Why doesn't the victim leave?' I purposely didn't say the term survivor because people that don't do Domestic Violence work tend to use the word victim. As we touched on before, fear, love, and hope, keep the cycle going. But, there are many reasons why the survivor doesn't leave. The survivor may not leave due to fear, love, hope, lack of awareness, low self-esteem, children, financial dependence, immigration status, so on."

"I've said before that a survivor may fear their abuser. Fear can be established in many ways. A survivor may even fear life without their abuser. I see eyebrows being raised. Yes, change is a fear for some people. Whether it's a positive or a negative change; fear of the unknown. Some survivors fear leaving because it's the most dangerous time. The likelihood of being killed increases, the likelihood of retaliation towards family, friends, or even fear of the people that offer support to the survivor. See, the survivor is important to the abuser. The survivor is someone for the abuser to control. The survivor provides unconditional love. The survivor endorses the abusers sense of worth and power. Danger rises when the abuser sees that they are possibly losing control."

"If a survivor is in a LGBTQ relationship or arrangement they may stay in the relationship out of fear of being outed, by their abuser, to their families or the community."

"What does 'outed' mean?"

"Some people in the LGBTQ communities may be in the closet about their gender identity or sexual orientation. Some abusers threaten to 'out' the survivor if they leave the relationship. Does anyone have more questions or things that they would like to add in relation to fear being a reason that a survivor may stay?"

I observed many head nods, giving Mrs. Price the confirmation to move forward.

"The other day, we briefly talked about love and hope. I would like to move on to 'lack of awareness' an aspect we haven't yet covered. Lack of awareness is a major barrier that survivors face. Many people stay in abusive relationships because they don't even know that they are being abused. Some people are raped or sexually assaulted and don't know what has been done to them. Or may feel unable to put words to what they have experienced. In some situations, the abuser teaches the survivor what love is. If love is not properly taught or shown to the individual from a young age, the survivor has no foundation to compare their definition of love. In this case, they may stay in the abusive relationship because in their minds, their situation is an accurate definition of love and their situation is perfectly normal. Other survivors may know that they are in an abusive situation, however, they don't know all the resources that are available to them. A lack of awareness and lack of access to resources delays. And for those who know resources are available, they may not know how to access these resources."

"Low self-esteem can keep a survivor from leaving. I have been taught that emotional abuse is the worst kind of abuse because it has the longest effects. If an abuser physically harms a survivor, the scars may heal within a week. The scars from degrading words, name-calling, criticism, comparisons, and put downs can last a lifetime. These scars can lower someone's self-esteem, eliminating the courage or confidence that a survivor may need when deciding to leave their abuser. If an abuser is constantly telling a survivor, 'You're ugly, no one else is going to want you.' Or 'You're worthless, no one will hire you.' These comments may echo, on rewind, in a survivor's memory for years, making it very difficult to leave."

"How many times have you heard the sayings, 'I don't want to leave because I want my child to grow up with two parents?' 'I don't want to leave because I don't want to upset my child.' 'How will I explain this to my children?'"

"Yes. Mrs. Price, I hear these things all the time."

The lady who introduced herself as Lisa was now talking. "That was one of my worries when I was deciding whether or not to leave my abuser. But, I had to tell myself that co-parenting can be successful. And I didn't want to continue raising my child in a relationship where I couldn't completely be myself. My child's father wouldn't even let me practice my own religion. That's not fair to me or my son. My son didn't truly know who Mommy was."

"I just couldn't handle it anymore. My children would witness her beat me at least once a week. I really had to think about whether or not it was okay for them to grow up seeing this--deep down, I knew the answer."

"I would like to interrupt. And say that I am enjoying this group process and appreciate the things that have been shared. However, as a prison employee and head of this program, I am a mandated reporter. Therefore, if you disclose anything that sounds as though any child under 18 has witnessed abuse, I will be forced to make a report. I understand that hearing this information could be hard for some of you ladies because this is so close to home. Some survivors don't leave because their abuser has threatened to use the children as a tool. This could look like many things — turning the child against the other parent to threatening to petition for full custody of the child," said Mrs. Price.

"Financial dependence can also keep a survivor from leaving. When we did the brainstorm on financial abuse, some things that were said included joint bank accounts, allowances, or not allowing the survivor to work. Some survivors may feel that a lack of finances is a barrier to leaving and, in some cases, it is. Some survivors are fortunate to have various outlets of support. I don't think that we mentioned that another tactic of abuse is isolation. Over a period of time, or rather quickly, the abuser may isolate the survivor from friends or family. If a survivor, is on the receiving end of this tactic, the thought of leaving could be overpowered by the difficulty of finding people to turn to."

"Sometimes I wish I had the resources to have a support group for people trying to support a survivor. Due to a lack of knowledge, many people use victim-blaming questions or statements: Why are you allowing this person to do this to you? Why don't you just leave? I won't support you if you stay with this person, or if you decide to go back to this person. These statements actually push the survivor away. These statements often minimize the willingness of the survivor to speak up or limit the amount of information that the survivor will share. These statements may even reiterate the negative messages that the survivor is already hearing from their abuser."

"Immigration status can also be a barrier to leaving an abusive partner. If someone is in the United States of America without being a US national, a US citizen, a resident who is from a country within the Compacts of Free Association, a lawful permanent resident, a green-card holder, a visa holder, or under the visa waiver program, they are considered an undocumented alien. I strongly dislike the term 'alien.' It feels rather distasteful. Undocumented could mean that they don't have proper documentation to be in the US or their documentation could have fallen 'out of status.' If someone is undocumented, an abuser may use this information to their advantage, threatening to have the survivor deported. Or telling a survivor that they cannot receive resources because they are undocumented. There is also another common situation about documentation that a lot people don't talk about. I am going to share a personal situation about a survivor who I worked with about two years ago. I have received her consent to share this story with my groups."

"I was working with a lady who was originally from Trinidad & Tobago. She came to the United States on a student visa. While she was in college, she met someone and started dating. Two years into the relationship she got pregnant, then, soon after they got married. He promised her to file papers through immigration for her to become a permanent resident of the United States. As time progressed, he became abusive. When it was time for her student visa to expire he wouldn't allow her to return to her country to renew the visa, or return to her country to wait for the outcome of the application that they submitted. As a result, this lady became undocumented. This man then used the possibility of the application being granted, as a tool to control and manipulate his wife."

"Wow," I said.

"That's fucked up," Jessica shouted.

"There are many barriers as to why a person does not leave an abusive relationship. Before we dismiss, I would like each of you to begin doing some self-evaluating. When evaluating yourselves, I would like for you to use the phrase, 'who am I?' See you next week, group is dismissed!"

I left group eager to go to the C.O.'s office. I was not pleased to see the same red headed officer sitting in the office. He was sitting in a ragged reclined chair. His legs were stretched out with his black army boots pleasantly resting on the desk as he read the newspaper. *Is this what tax payers are paying for?*

"Excuse me, officer. Yesterday, when you asked me what shower time I wanted, I picked 10:30 not knowing that I would be in group during that time. Is there any way that I may please reschedule my shower time?"

"No, inmate."

"Well, what am I supposed to do?"

"I'm sure the sink in your cell has running water."

I walked away from the C.O.'s officer wanting to be anywhere other than in this prison. The housing unit was only for inmates who were in the program. I could see the hallways clearing out as everyone was going into their cells and closing the door. I did the same. I walked in to see Jessica on the toilet.

"Ma bad girl, I know you probably don't wanna smell my bodily waste. But, I couldn't wait until the next time you were out of the cell. I've been holding this since we started group. Don't worry, I'll flush often so it doesn't bother you."

I chuckled. Jessica passing her bowel movements was the last thing that I was concerned about. I had been in county long enough to get used to it. State prison was a lot better, because in county jail I would have to eat in the same room where my cellie's would pass bowel movements, and vice versa. At least in State prison we could consume our food elsewhere.

"You better hurry up. This prick is gonna announce count time at any moment."

"COUNT TIME…COUNT TIME…"

"See, you would think I'm psychic." We both let out a laugh.

"QUIET ON MY UNIT, IT'S COUNT TIME," the officer yelled again.

Jessica flushed the toilet and joined me at the door for count time.

"Yo, ya pants are still down."

"I know. That's why I'm standing so close to the door. All he could see is my face and my upper body. I'm not done using the bathroom, so I'm not gonna wipe.

We almost out of tissue and we got two more days before they hand out more." "Ya gross girl."

"Trust, one day you may have to do this too."

I watched the officer walk past our cell. I hoped that he wouldn't catch her with her pants down. If he did, there were so many things that he could possibly think. When I could hear him all the way down the hall, I climbed on my bed. It would be about twenty minutes before count would clear.

Dear Diary,

Being in G.P., which is the abbreviation for general population, is really difficult. I feel like a small fish in a big sea. However, this is not my home. I walk this prison campus feeling very alone. I went to church the other day. I looked up into the balcony to see the Y.A.O. Andrea was standing next to Raina. Andrea acted as if she didn't see me. That really hurt. I guess it's naïve of me to think that what we had was something serious. I've been pondering on the last support group that I had with Mrs. Henry. Also, my thoughts have been consumed with the things that I've been learning in Mrs. Price's group sessions. Mrs. Price asked us to write a brief paragraph evaluating ourselves. Here goes my effort:

I never asked myself, "Who am I?" Who am I?
I am the girl that walks along Hair done up--make up on...
The surface says, "I am a happy princess."
But under this mask, I'm a beautiful mess!

So much on my mind,
Why can't I leave it all behind? I try to forget, but it comes
rushing back, the memories of my very first attack. At the
innocent age of eleven,
I was living the opposite of heaven.
Scared to speak up about my abuse.
He controlled my life in every possible way. He still haunts
me to this day.

I am an introvert
I've learned to keep everything in and depend on myself
My favorite line is, "No thanks, I don't need your help!"
Tired of being let-down. So, I became self-sufficient,
As if no one else was around.
I am Codependent.
That is why I've never taken the time to ask myself,
Who am I?
It's people that I love to please. I'll give you the shirt off my
back, and then Freeze.
Going over and above for anyone,
Knowing that I won't get the same in return.
Others, and their needs, were my main concern.
They say that trauma can make or break you.
But what if you're stuck in between, with a slate that's far
from clean?
I'm torn, I'm broken...
But I want to throw away this beautiful mask.
Own my feelings; cry, laugh, and really mean it.
Regain control of my life, in a positive way, and give myself
the best of every day.

I am Giselle Greene and I believe that my life is a gift.
I wish I didn't care what everyone thought. I wanna be me,
whether they like it or not.
Jail has been a hard journey but I have learned,
That my freedom and happiness must be earned.
I am a woman of worth,
You better believe that I'll do my best,
Because the greatest revenge in life is success.

~Me.

"COUNT IS CLEARED LADIES, EXIT YOUR CELLS FOR CHOW."

I jumped off my bunk and hurried to put on my brown state shoes. I was in a hurry to join the lunch line. I was looking forward to walking to lunch with Tasha, one of the girls that was in the program with me. She came to my cell door last night and suggested that we should walk to lunch together. I followed as everyone was exiting the housing unit and forming a line along the fence. I saw Tasha towards the front of the line, waving for me to join her.

"Hey, you."

"Hey. I brought you my extra poncho since I knew that it was raining out here." She handed me a clear plastic poncho. I giggled as I opened the plastic because I had never worn a poncho prior to that moment. But, I was thankful.

"Thank you."

"I didn't want ya beautiful hair to be soaked." I didn't know what to say, so I didn't say anything.

"I've been watching you since you were in the Y.A.O. I use to see you being escorted to school. I think ya absolutely gorgeous."

"Thanks."

"And I heard ya speech at the graduation, I love a girl that's intelligent."

"How long have you been here?"

"Three years. Almost four. And many more to go."

"How old are you?"

"I'm thirty. I hear they call you 'set it off' cause you robbed a bank. Is that true?

"Please don't call me that or ever bring that up again."

"No worries, beautiful. I wouldn't want to upset you."

We walked in the pouring rain for about ten minutes. I could see officers scattered around the prison grounds, holding umbrellas. This would be my second time walking to the dining hall in the rain. Jessica told me that they don't allow inmates to have umbrellas because it could be used as a weapon. I could hear the rest of the ladies from our housing unit, as they walked behind Tasha and I loudly engaging in numerous conversations. Turning the corner to approach the dining hall, I saw C.O.'s running from several directions. I froze. Tasha grabbed me and gave me a tight side hug, "Don't be afraid. It's probably a fight going on. They wouldn't run like that for any other reason."

"STOP RIGHT THERE, INMATES."

Chapter Thirteen

"Why are you sitting on the stool like that?"

"Like what?"

"You're completely dressed. You did ya hair like you're going to prom and you keep rocking like you're on something?"

"Remember I told you that today I will be getting a visit from my Aunt and my best friend?"

"Oh, that's right. Well, you look really nice, if there's even such a thing in here."

I picked up a novel that I had been reading, *Magic in Islam*, trying to keep my mind occupied as I waited to be called for my visit. As soon as I skimmed through the pages to figure out where I had last left off, I heard my door being clicked.

"That has to be the call for you to walk to the visiting room. Enjoy ya visit."

"Thank you."

I walked out of my cell, very anxious and excited, towards the C.O.'s office, where I was told that I was called to the visiting room for a visit. The officer handed me a signed pass, which was verification that I had permission to walk to the visiting room. If I would have been stopped, randomly, on the walkway without a pass, I could possibly receive a misconduct for being in an unauthorized area. I walked so quickly towards the visiting room, it nearly felt like I was jogging.

The visiting room was located in the basement of the Chapel. I arrived at the Chapel and walked down the steps that led to the basement. There was a female officer standing at the door to greet me. We walked into a room that was about the size of a cell. However, the room had a door on both sides. The room was cluttered with white slip on shoes and brown jumpers, which ranged in different sizes. The female officer took my signed pass. I would then be strip-searched and given a jumper along with a pair of slip-ons. While on a visit we were not allowed to wear our two piece uniforms. The purpose of wearing a jumper was to decrease the chances of things being smuggled back into the prison. This also decreased the chances of sexual fondling between an inmate and a visitor. This wasn't my first visit in the state prison, so I was familiar with what would happen next.

"Greene, there are two ladies here to visit you."

"Yep. My aunt and best friend."

"Okay, take your clothes off and hand them to me. What size jumpsuit would you like?"

"Large, please."

The officer began to talk, pausing between each demand. "Okay. Put you head down and run your fingers through your hair, then, let me see inside each ear. Open your mouth as wide as you can, run your two pointer fingers along your gum line, lift your tongue and say ahhh. Lift your arms high and shake your breasts. Turn around, spread your butt cheeks, squat, and cough. Lift each foot and wiggle your toes. Good. Put your jumper on and enjoy your visit."

My best friend was dressed in a tan sweater with dark blue jeans and tan loafers. She smiled. I ran to her and we hugged for about five minutes. It's surprising that I wasn't reprimanded by the C.O. Hugs were supposed to be very brief. My aunt stood beside Amalia in a purple cardigan. We sat down and began to talk.

"We bought you a pizza and a Pepsi. Do you want anything else?" Aunty said.

"No, that's enough. Thank you."

"Amalia, I just sent your letter out. You should be receiving it soon. Thank you for coming. How is school?"

"This year has been challenging, but good. I'm leaving in two weeks to study in Senegal."

"That's awesome."

"What do you do here on your free time?"

"If I'm not in support group, then I'm either in the common room or in my cell writing."

"I didn't get a chance to congratulate you on receiving the Lisa Wagner award."

"Thank you. I'm going to start working in a few days."

"Doing what?"

"I am going to be on the HVAC crew."

Aunty intervened. "What does the HVAC crew do?"

"The acronym stands for heating, ventilation, and air conditioning. The crew is led by an HVAC technician. There are about six other inmates that are on the crew. Basically the prison functions on the labor of the inmates. There is a crew for almost everything: a painting crew, kitchen crew, plumbing crew, commissary crew, etc. Inmates can work in the infirmary, the admissions office, in the yard or in the exercise room. The purpose of the HVAC crew is to maintain and fix areas related to HVAC on the prison campus. Being on the crew will give me hands on experience. Oh, and I will get paid forty-three cents an hour."

"Forty-three cents?" Amalia asked with a surprised look.

"Yea. That's actually good pay in here. And I will be able to buy things that I need and want on commissary."

"How is your supply of toothpaste and soap?" Aunty asked.

"I'm okay on soap. But, my toothpaste and deodorant are both running low. Oh Aunty, at home there is a photo album. In the album is a picture from when I was eleven years old. In the picture, I am wearing a yellow jumper, can you please mail the picture up here to me."

"Sure. I will try to find it. But, why do you need that picture specifically?"

I ignored her, intentionally.

The visit was filled with a lot of joking and laughter. We reminisced and got caught up with what had been going on with each of us individually. We ate food from the vending machine, and took many pictures from the photo machine. We made more precious memories despite being in a prison visiting room. Most importantly, I felt love and care while in their presence.

After the visit, I went back to the housing unit, anxious to write in my diary.

Dear Diary,

On this day, two years ago, my life took a turn. It was a muggy spring day, like it is today. I woke up in my living room and watched my aunt leave for work. It was 1:30 am when I arrived home from a date in the Poconos the night before. My aunt was upset that I came home so late. Since I had been home on summer break from college, I would always get up to watch her leave for work. This morning was slightly different. I didn't get up say good-bye, nor did I tell her that I loved her. This would be another thing that I would regret. However, within these two years, I have learned so much about myself.

Aunty and my best friend, Amalia, came to visit me today. I don't think that Aunty realizes that today makes the second year since I've left home. I knew that my best friend remembered the events linked to today's date. But neither of us brought it up, because of all the emotions and memories of that day. Maybe they have found some comfort today knowing that I'm not out of it nor am I completely okay. But, I'm managing. I really miss them and I can't wait until I'm released.

Support group starts in ten minutes. I am glad that I made in back in time for group. I'm very interested in the information that will be covered today.

~Me

Today we will talk about child sexual abuse, which is one of the many forms of child abuse. Child sexual abuse is any sexual act done to a child. In an article published by the LegalMatch, Peter Clarke, explains Statutory Rape. By federal law it is illegal for someone to engage in any sexual act with any person who is between the age of twelve and sixteen if they are at least four years younger than you. The age of sexual legal consent varies from state to state. The age of consent has ranged from ten to eighteen. Some states, such as California and New York, set an age at which all sexual intercourse is considered statutory rape. For example, a state might set the age of consent at eighteen. In this hypothetical state, two seventeen-year old's who had consensual sex could both theoretically be convicted of statuary rape.

Other states imply a different method which, like the federal statue, takes into account the relative ages of both people. In these states, such as Texas, the age of consent is determined by age differentials of the two persons and limited by a minimum age. For example, a state might set a minimum age of fourteen, but limit consent to partners who are within three years of their age. This would allow a sixteen-year-old to lawfully have sex with a fourteen-year-old, but make it criminal for an eighteen-year-old to have sex with that same fourteen-year-old. "Does everyone understand how consent is given?"

"Yes. Basically, a child cannot give consent. And the legal adolescent age of consent varies from state to state."

"Correct. Also, even though the term in called statuary rape, generally someone would not use the term rape when describing what was done to a child. Instead, the term molestation is used. Molestation is the crime of sexual acts with children up to the age of eighteen, including touching of private parts, exposure of genitalia, taking of pornographic pictures, rape, inducement of sexual acts with the molester or with other children, and the variations of these acts. Molestation also applies to incest by a relative under the age of eighteen, and any unwanted sexual acts with adults short of rape. The terms childhood sexual abuse, molestation, and rape are all used interchangeably. It is important not to correct a survivor's language when they are explaining the abuse that was done to them. Each person defines their own truth and has the choice of using whatever term feels best for them. Someone should only be corrected if they are asking you to so.

Let's talk more about different examples of child sexual abuse and what this looks like. Child sexual abuse can include, but is not limited to, having a child do sexual acts to themselves, other children, or adults. Exposing a naked child, talking to a child in a sexual manner. Forcing or allowing a child to view pornography, or forcing a child to watch sexual acts."

"It's important to know that offenders can be anyone — any gender identity, any sexual orientation, any relation to the child or lack of relation to the child. In terms of child sexual abuse, ninety percent of children know their offender. These offenders can be adult family members, adults outside the family who are known and trusted, or other older children."

"It boggles my mind that someone would do this to a child."

"I agree. Later, we will watch a video of incarcerated sex-offenders. They basically tell us how they set up their victim. It's alarming to watch, yet, insightful. I will review the things that they mention in the video, then we will all watch it together."

"In the video, the perpetrators have explained that they find a child who they have easy access to. *Remember: the vast majority of survivors know their offender.*"

"They find a child that will respond to their advances, that will either keep the secret or and/or won't be believed if they tell. They even said that children who are people-pleaser or children who lie are great targets."

"They provide something that is missing in the child's life. This may be anything from monetary items, attention, or emotional support."

"They establish trust with the child and other adults that care for the child. Offenders say that they look for weaknesses in family defenses, or families that have a lot going on, and/or attention is diverted away from the child for a number of reasons. Families that are experiencing trauma like addiction, divorce, illness, etc., are easy targets."

"They often show pornography to the child to normalize the idea of sexual behavior."

"They will play games with the child that are designed to get the child used to touch. This also provides the offender an 'accidental' way of touching the child. Some games include, but aren't limited to, tickling, playing house, and wrestling."

"They isolate the child. This does not mean total isolation. It just means that the offender isolates the child long enough to abuse them." "I don't understand why the child just won't tell anyone?"

When Jessica asked that question, I wanted to slap her and say, "For the same reason why you didn't leave you abuser."

But the question was quickly answered by Mrs. Price. "There are many reasons why they don't tell. While I tell you these reasons, I want you to picture an innocent six-year-old child. Visualize why all of the reasons for not telling, make perfect sense."

"Children may not tell out of guilt or shame. They can feel guilty thinking that they caused the abuse, or they feel shame as a result of the abuse. They may not tell out of love and/or fear. Keeping in mind that a child could be taught to love their abuser. The abuser may very likely be their parent, sibling or immediate family member. They may fear speaking up will get this individual in trouble. Some children don't speak up because they think they have told in others ways, and some children don't tell because they can't tell. A child who hasn't learned to speak yet, can't tell. A child with a mental disability may not be able to tell as well."

"This is fucking sick. I can't listen to this shit."

"That's completely fine, Tasha. You may excuse yourself from the group today if this information is too difficult. I encourage you to take care of yourself if this information is bringing up unpleasant feelings and emotions for you. Let's do a brief check in. Does everyone want me to continue or is this information too difficult to sit with?"

"Nah, continue. We need to learn this."

"Please continue, Mrs. Price."

These words rolled out of my mouth before I even realized that I was speaking out oud. I needed Mrs. Price to continue. But I could also understand how this information could be very difficult for someone to sit through. Also, I didn't think that Mrs. Price did a thoughtful job of asking such a question in a larger group which excluded the voice of those who possibly didn't answer. I'm sure if someone didn't want her to continue they might not have felt comfortable to say that in front of everyone.

"Okay, before I continue I want everyone to take a moment to escape this place. Oh hold on, not really escape, if any officer heard me say that, I would probably lose my job." We chuckled. "On a serious note, I was us to each mentally escape to a place. Think of a place that makes you happy, calm, creative, or relaxed, and take yourselves there. If it's the beach, picture your feet sinking into warm sand. Feel the grains of sand between your toes. Hear the sound of the ocean crashing against the rocks. Hear the seagulls squawking. Feel the rays of the sun caressing your body. Or picture yourself at the gym. They say that the feelings after a good work-out could be relaxing. Exercise has the ability to change someone's mood in a positive way. Picture yourself running on the treadmill, to the sound of your favorite song, pounding through your headphones. *Feel the runner's high.* I will allow a few moments for you to mentally escape to where ever you'd rather be, this activity is an example of using various grounding techniques."

* * *

"If a child does not verbally disclose that they are being abused, there are other signs that can point to the abuse. However, these signs can be present in a child who is, in fact, not being abused. Unusual behaviors of a child can be a sign of abuse is going on. Some examples are- constant nightmares, outburst, isolation from a child that's usually social, scared to be alone, or dislikes in hobbies that they once enjoyed, etc. Another sign is sexual knowledge beyond what's age appropriate, or persistent sexual play. Another sign, which is usually overlooked, is how the child acts around the abuser. Are they showing signs of fear around someone that that they previously loved being around? Are they telling you that they don't want to go to a certain person's house anymore?"

"It takes a lot of courage for a child to tell you that they are being sexually abused. I want you all to know what to do if a child discloses this information to you. The law is that any adult who suspects or is told that a child is being physically or sexually abused is required to report this abuse to law enforcement."

"Fuck that. I'm not reporting anything to law enforcement. I wouldn't do it then and I wouldn't do it now. I'm here on a life sentence 'cause my husband molested our son, a little boy. I killed that man, and I have no regrets." Angelica spoke up with great anger.

Mrs. Price intervened, "I understand that as a parent it could be hard hearing that this was done to your child. I get it. But, the decision to kill his father was a selfish decision. Overreacting causes your child to undergo many traumas. Your son was raped, that's trauma. He told you and you overreacted, that's trauma. You killed his father, that's trauma. And now you're doing a life sentence, that's trauma. You are not physically there to comfort him and help him to heal through the initial trauma, that's trauma."

"I hear you. But, I don't feel that the justice system would have served justice. Three years' imprisonment is not enough when he caused trauma that could possibly haunt my son for the rest of his life."

"The responsibility of an adult is to report the abuse. If a child tells you that they were abused, do not overreact. Believe the child and tell the child it's not their fault. Tell the child you are sorry you didn't know sooner about the abuse and that they are very brave for telling you. Do not question the child any further. Do not confront the abuser."

"Why shouldn't you question the child more? Wouldn't you want to know as much as you can?" I asked Mrs. Price.

"Good question. You don't want to question the child more because the ultimate goal is to have the child give a statement which will lead to a prosecution of the offender. They want the child's statement to be as authentic as possible. If you ask questions, your questions may influence the child's recollection of what happened. Or your questions may give the child terminology that they wouldn't normally use."

"Got it. I never thought of that."

"In regards to child sexual abuse, we have one small section left. I can tell that you all are hungry and losing energy. I'm asking you all to hang on a bit longer with me. I want to touch base on, what we can do to protect these innocent children. Starting at young age, teach your children the correct names of their body parts. Imagine if you taught your child that their vagina was called a purse. If this child is raped and gives a statement saying in from of judge saying, 'This person sexually assaulted me when they touched my purse.' Incorrect terminology could be problematic and decrease convictions."

"Teach children about safe and unsafe touches. Safe touches are touches that make a child feel happy, healthy, cared for, and safe. Safe touches may be pleasurable or painful. Hugs, peck kisses, and high-fives are some examples of pleasurable touches. A flu shot is an example of a safe yet painful touch."

"Unsafe touches are touches that are unhealthy or uncomfortable for a child, and hurt their body or feelings. Examples of unsafe touches are grabbing, hitting, French kissing, fondling, penetrating, etc. Sexual touches of any kind are unsafe touches. Carefully select the people that are authorized to wash your child's private areas. Communication with your child is one of the best ways to combat child sexual abuse."

*　　*　　*

"Jessica, why are you crying?" I asked in a nervous voice. Since my time of being in the cell with her, I had never witnessed her crying. I didn't know if she wanted me to stay on my bunk; not acknowledging her tears, or if she wanted my support.

"I am just having one of those days where I'm constantly thinking of my current situation. I will be here basically for the rest of my life."

"What do you mean by that?"

"Well, they gave me sixty-five years for shooting my abuser. I'm already twenty-three so I will be about eighty-eight years old by the time I'm up to see parole; if I survive until then."

"I'm so sorry to hear that."

"Yea. I shot my abuser in his leg when he brought his friends over to gang rape me. I over-heard him talking about it, on the phone, the night before it happened. I couldn't believe that he would do something so cruel. He's abused me for years, but not to that extent. I didn't believe that his plan was true until I saw his friends show up that day. All seven of them were planning to rape me. They took me into the basement, of my own home and when my boyfriend began his first advance, I was able to get a hold of his gun. I shot him several times in his leg and ran. While I was in the county jail, I learned that the shooting had immobilized him for the rest of his life. My lawyer and I argued self-defense.

However, my sentence is evidence that we did not win the case.

Since the sentencing of the case, I been reading different things on rape. I rented a cassette from the library the other day. There was a support group on cassette in which they describe different types of rapist."

"Different types of rapist?"

"Yes! I was intrigued. They said that there is a Power Assertive rapist. This type of rape is usually premeditated and involves rape fantasies. This type of rapist uses force and threats to gain control of their victim. This rapist usually feels inadequate and has deep insecurities.

They talked about the Anger Retaliation rapist. This type of rape is more impulsive. This rapist generally uses more physical force than necessary to overpower their victim which means the victim often has physical trauma to many areas of the body. There is often the use of abusive language as this rapist often uses rape to pay back perceived wrongs against them from society. Their victims will often match the description of a person or a certain group of people in which they feel have done an injustice to them. For example, if a rapist's first love was someone of blonde hair and blue eyes and this person hurt them and destroyed their self-esteem, all of their rape victims would probably fit the description of having blonde hair and blue eyes.

There is the Power Reassurance or Opportunity rapist. These rapists often take advantage of an opportunity to commit the rape. These rapes often happen in conjunction with a crime. If an individual went into a house to commit burglary and they see that there is only one person, unarmed, in the house, they may use the opportunity to commit a rape in addition to the burglary.

I was intrigued to learn more about the Anger Excitement/Sadistic rapist. These rapes are calculated and pre-planned. The rape often includes ritualistic behaviors such as bondage or torture. This rapist often switches between being degrading and nice. The rape often occurs over an extended duration of time and the victim suffers from many areas of physical trauma and are often murdered. The rape is usually symbolic with destruction and elimination."

"Oh wow. That's a lot."

"Yea. I just do the research as a way of building a better understanding of what was done to me."

"I'm sorry that you're going through this and I thank you for sharing your story. I'm always here to talk." *I wonder what kind of rape was done to me?* I enjoyed the conversation, but didn't want to get caught up in that information. I could see how that information could take a survivor to a mental place of self-blame and doubt, thinking that the way they looked influenced their abuse. I feel that the most important thing to remember is that rape is always cause by the need for power and control.

Chapter Fourteen

I left the strip room and entered the visiting room. I nervously raised my head to see my brother, his girlfriend, and my four nephews sitting in the visiting room. I froze. I could feel the sweat gathering in my palms. I could

hear and feel my heartrate increase, as if I was gasping for air. In the distance, I made eye contact with my nephews. I heard different voices saying Aunty. I could see their lips moving with the sound, which confirmed that they were referring to me. Words could never explain my excitement and overwhelming joy in that moment. This meant that they actually knew who I was.

The fact that they knew my relation to them was shocking. Of the four of my nephews, I only expected the first-born to remember who I was, which wasn't even a valid expectation, it was a hope. I had been a part of his life when I was about thirteen and living in Massachusetts. My other three handsome nephews were born after I had moved to Pennsylvania with Aunty. Over a period of years, I had only seen them a few times.

With the courage to lift my feet, I began to walk towards my family. I gave everyone a hug. I hugged my brother, Damien, last, because his hug would be the tightest and longest of them all. When I felt my brother's embrace, I began to cry. Through the hug, it felt like we were communicating feelings of anger, confusion, and love. I hoped that things were positively working out in his life. I hoped that he had forgiven me.

Throughout the visit, my brother asked me questions about my daily routine. I somewhat felt restricted when describing my prison experience, mainly because I wasn't sure if he told my nephews the truth about where I was. At this point, my oldest nephew wasn't even ten years old. I remember my brother purchasing snacks for us from the vending machine. Towards the end of the visit, we went to the photo booth to take pictures. It was difficult, yet fun, as all seven of us tried to cramp into the picture.

After about an hour and a half, I heard the C.O. call my last name to announce the conclusion of my visit. I watched as my nephews raced up the stairs, to the exit. I saw them waving good-bye. I heard side chatter, amongst themselves, the cheerfulness and innocence of their voices. I felt a sense of gratitude that they had driven so many hours to see me. The visit left me feeling high on happiness, a feeling that I knew would last for a while. I also felt sadness that they were growing up in this very cruel world. Inwardly, I hoped that they would never be in a prison uniform, like the one I was wearing. I also felt sadness because I knew that there was so much between my brother and I that was left unsaid.

When I got back to the housing unit, I knew that I only have approximately five minutes before my one-on-one meeting with Mrs. Price.

"I saw that you signed up for a one-on-one session."

"Yes, Mrs. Price. I really need to talk. I've been thinking of the things that were done to me. In one instance, I can't figure if I was raped or sexually assaulted. In another instance, I can't figure out if I was being raped or molested. I don't know the difference between all of these words."

"That's perfectly understandable. It's easy to get these terms confused. The terms sexual assault vs. rape is in our curriculum and we will be discussing them in great detail next week. And molestation is what we talked about the other day in reference to these acts being done to children. Would it be helpful for you me to review the terms sexual assault and rape now, or would you rather wait until the group setting?

"I don't mind waiting. In that case, can you tell me more about the showcase that I heard the other ladies taking about."

"Oh, are you referring to 'Take Back the Night?'"

"Yes."

"In 1980, Laura Laderer wrote a book called *Take Back the Night*. After the book was released the Vancover Rape Relief was the first program to hold a 'Take Back the Night' march. For the past thirty years, this event has been happening all over the world. It's always during the month of October and usually takes place after the Clothesline project."

"Nice."

"Yes. Here at the prison we do not do 'Take Back the Night,' the way it was initially done, because we do not own the rights to the idea of the initial project. What we do is a reenactment of 'Take Back the Night,' keeping the broad idea of taking back ownership of what an abuser has taken from you. An example is, a few years ago, a girl took back the night a stranger raped her in front of her children. She took back the memories of the green lamp that she stared at while she was trying to mentally escape what was being done to her. She stated that when she is released from this prison, she planned to purposely buy a green lamp and place the lamp in her room. Facing the lamp each day without allowing the memories to any longer have a negative hold on her life, was her way of Taking Back the Night. The symbolism of talking something back, doesn't always mean that it completely disappears and never affects you again. Healing doesn't happen overnight. It's a conscious thing that you have to keep working on."

"I hear you. For the showcase, I want to take back my voice."

"Okay. Well then I think it will be nice if you also do the introduction to the show, welcoming everyone who's in the audience."

"I think that would be good for me. Who is coming?"

"Everyone in the program, other facilitators, teachers, C.O.'s, and prison staff."

"Okay. I also want to talk about the fact that I'm codependent."

"Why would you label yourself codependent?"

"It's important to me to give myself that label. The label gives me foundation to heal. I think of it like a medical diagnosis. If someone is told that they have a specific disease, knowing the diagnosis gives them the foundation or starting point to move forward. In knowing the diagnosis, one can learn about the disease, then take steps towards healing or minimizing the symptoms. That's the way I feel about codependency."

"That's powerful."

"Knowing what codependency looks like, I could to make small goals to counteract it."

When the session with Mrs. Price and I was over, I went straight into the common room. Fifty Cent's *Many Men* was playing on the common room television. I walked over to the table that was located in the center of the room.

"What's this game ya'll always playing?"

"It's called pinochle! I didn't learn how to play this game until I came to prison. Mainly in state prison. Many people in county don't play pinochle cause a lot of people that come to county, don't stay long. And it not a popular game on the streets."

"Oh. Okay. How do you play?"

"Well, it's a little complicated at first. Pinochle can be played many ways but we often play with two or four players. The deck consists of eighty cards, containing *A, K, Q, J* in each of the four suits, and with four identical copies of each card. This deck can be formed by mixing together two normal Pinochle decks, having thrown out the nines, or from four regular fifty-two card decks from which you throw out all the numerals two to nine. Each person gets twenty cards. After the hand is dealt, each person adds us their points and places a bid. The person or team that takes the highest bid gets to choose the trump suite for that round. But before I even teach you how to play, I would have to tell you how many points each card is worth."

"That sounds like a lot. It sounds like more of a project than a game."

"It's a lot but, when you get the hang of it, it's fun. Two years ago when I was upstate, I was in the cell with an older, really knowledgeable lady. She was German. I do remember her telling me that she really disliked when people played this game without knowing the history of it. She explained to me what it meant and I will never forget it."

"The game of Pinochle was brought to the Americas by German immigrants. The immigrants attempted to pronounce the French word *binochle*, but it came out sounding like pinochle. The game of Pinochle was originally structured from the old world game of *bezique*. The modern two-handed version of Pinochle is a striking knock-off of Bezique. Today's three-handed Auction Pinochle is a derivation of Bezique combined with the German game of 'Skat.' During World War I, anti-German sentiment ran high and the town of Syracuse, New York, went as far as outlawing the game of Pinochle. She said that is one of the main reasons why she loves playing the game. It's like she was staying true to her culture and rebellion against the oppression. I play pinochle because it challenges my mind, but also 'cause it reminds me of her. Feel me?"

"Get a piece of paper so I can tell you what each card means," Angelica jumped in.

"Cool."

As I was leaving the common room to get paper from my cell. I saw about seven C.O.'s rushing into our housing unit. They were wearing white gloves and carried trash bags.

"LOCK IT IN, LADIES.....LOCKDOWN!"

My walk picked up speed. When I got into my cell, I saw Jessica rampaging through her mail.

"I gotta throw this shit away." She said so quickly it sounded like she was out of breath.

"What do you have?"

"Letters from an ex-inmate."

"Oh my God, what am I gonna do with my diary, Jessica. I can't afford for them to get their hands on it."

"Throw it away."

"I can't throw it away. It's really important to me."

"Aight, I have a big manila envelope. You can put ya diary in there and seal it up. Put an address on the front of the envelope. If they ask you about it, tell them it's mail that you are planning to mail out. They shouldn't open a sealed envelope."

"Thank you so much."

"Yea. But, those envelopes are expensive. If I give it you, ya gonna have to order me a new one."

"That's fine. I really need it."

"Oh, and put a real address, just in case they force you to mail it on the spot, ya stuff won't get lost in the mail."

I began to put my diary in the envelope and address they envelope to Aunty's address. I really hoped that the plan would work. I needed it to work. I watched Jessica as she ripped up over fifty letters, flushing the toilet to get rid of the evidence. I stood at the door to let her know when our cell was going to be next. I heard toilets flushing all throughout the unit. Others were also busy trying to get rid of their contraband.

"We're luck out cell is located in the middle of the hallway," Jessica began to say. "If we were located on either end of the hallway then they would have started with our cell first and we wouldn't have had a chance to hide anything."

"I know. I really hate these lockdowns."

"Get used to them. They happen about once a month out here in G.P, and they started this one later in the day, that means no shower for us today."

"Jessica, our cell is next."

Two female officers approached our cell door.

"Step to the back of the cell, ladies."

They stripped us down as usual. This would be my second strip search in one day. As degrading as it felt, it was becoming less traumatizing to me.

They searched our cell. They disassembled the room in less than ten minutes.

The sheets and blankets were on the ground. The mattresses were flipped. They went through our boxes. To my surprise and relief, they found the sealed envelope and didn't even look at it twice or question me about it. This was the first cell search that I saw one of the C.O.s run her finger around the inside ledge of the toilet. I was very disgusted and wondered if she had done that in the other cells prior to coming into our cell and touching all of or belongings. I really wanted to wash everything in the cell but I knew that wasn't possible. So I just tried to dwell on my feelings of gratitude that my diary was not found. While putting everything in back in place, I engaged in small talk with Jessica. I was enormously exhausted, both mentally and physically. I wanted to go straight to bed but, I was so thankful to have my diary, I decided to open it, reread a couple of entries and write a poem. I had made it this far, two years down and three more to go. *Hopefully.*

Dear Diary,

Thinking of what got me through two years of this sentence. I haven't felt suicidal in about one year. I have been doing well. Working on myself and learning many things. I'm still having the nightmares. I'm still receiving frequent letters from Alton. I've been battling with my religion, mainly because I don't understand why a God who loves me would have allowed so many bad things to happen to me. Then again, it's God that I've been calling on to provide me with some sanity behind these walls. There is a song that I often hum to myself at night. The song is called "Reflection." It's by a Jamaican artist named Jah Cure. In celebration of making it through two years, I want to write a poem that correlates with his song.

<u>Prison Walls</u>
Behind these prison walls, I sit and reflect. See, when you
commit a crime, the hurt is like a ripple effect.

I lay at night, and think of all the people I've hurt.
My family......My Victims from the bank
When I picture their crying faces, I cry too. But, my tears
don't symbolize weakness, they symbolize my strength.

When you get locked up, your family; They do the time
that you do.
Not your crew!
I thought my dozens of friends would be down for this ride,
But only two friends and my family,
have remained by my side.

God, to you I'm calling.

I know you'll answer at the right time.
You are my every breath, my every rhyme. Hear my call,
cause without you; I just might fall.

I see my way,
And I don't want to go astray.
Those that are hurting,
They miss the girl that they once knew. But only I could see
the signs, that girl is left behind.
I came here a girl,
And grew into a woman.
Maybe their strength would come,
If they could see, what this experience has done to me.
I wish I could turn back the hands of time.
But, I will remain strong, 'Cause I've learned from my wrong.
Behind these prison walls, I sit and reflect. See, when you
commit a crime, the hurt is like a ripple effect.

If I didn't walk into the bank on that day, those ladies
wouldn't have been victimized; With their sense of security
taken away.
Funds from the Victim's Compensation Act.
Could never repay them for unwanted hypervigilance,

Behind these prison walls, I sit and reflect.
The faith in me,
Shall set me free.
Reflections.

-Me.

Chapter Fifteen

October of 2012
State Prison

"Sexual assault is a general term that includes any forced or unwanted sexual activity. Sexual assault includes any forced or unwanted touching, grouping, or fondling of an intimate part of the body such as breast, buttocks, or genitals."

"Rape is unwanted and unlawful sexual intercourse or any other sexual penetration of the vagina, anus, or mouth of another person, with or without force, by a sex organ, other body part, or foreign object."

"I really appreciate this definition because the definition of rape, which was used by the courts a couple of years ago was very problematic. The old definition did not include the fact that any object could be used. It also didn't include the fact that this could occur without force. Are you all following these two concepts?"

"I get it. Someone could be raped by not giving consent. However, the rape can be done not using force."

"Exactly. We will watch a video about a lady who was being raped over the course of two days. She said that while the perpetrator was raping her, he was going back and forth between complimenting her and saying degrading things to her. She explains being so exhausted from fighting back and, about twenty hours into the rape, she lay there and cooperated with what this man was doing to her. She said at that point, she feared that if didn't cooperate she would have lost her life. In the video she also says that she is confused whether or not the perpetrator was in the wrong because she cooperated."

"I want you all to know that cooperation is not consent. Also, sexual assault and rape are both about the abuser gaining power and control. These actions are not influenced by sexual desire. I would like to switch gears and discuss one of the many forms of healing. I have always viewed anger as an interesting yet effective approach to healing.

"I read an interesting book by written by Ellen bass and Laura Davis, *The Courage to Heal*, where they discuss anger as an approach to healing. They explain that most religious or spiritual ideologies teach us to forgive and love. As a result, many survivors have suppressed their anger, turning it inward. But, anger is not a negative emotion and does not have to be suppressed or destructive. Instead, it can be both a healthy response to a violation or a transformative, powerful energy.

You were probably not able to experience, express and act on your outrage when you were being abused. You probably didn't even know that you had the right to feel angry. Instead of being angry with the person or people who abuse you, you may have done a combination of denying or and twisting you anger. You may have even been so immerged in the perspective of your abuser that you lost connection with yourself and your own feelings. If you are unable to focus your anger toward your abuser, that anger will go somewhere else.

Many survivors may be fearful of becoming angry because their past experiences with anger were negative. Some survivors may not understand the difference between anger and violence. They may have experienced anger that was destructive and out of control.

As someone becomes more familiar with experiencing and expressing anger, it can become a healthy part of everyday life. When it's not so bottled up, its stops being a dangerous monster and takes its place as one of many feelings. After reading that book, I began to view anger as a motivational force. If you listen to your anger, if you allow it to be your guide, then it becomes a valuable resource moving you toward positive change.

There is no exact recipe towards healing; there is no right or wrong answer. I know that may sound daunting and discouraging and you're probably thinking, 'Well. Mrs. Price, the purpose of me coming to this program was for you to tell me how to heal.' Healing looks different for everyone. My goal is to share my knowledge with you along with a combination of things that worked for me. But, my most important goal is to meet you wherever you may be along the healing journey, support, and stand by you."

* * *

"Mrs. Price, do you have a moment? I really need to talk now and I don't think that I could sit with these feelings and questions until tomorrow."

"Sure. But, it's going to be count time. Let me tell the officer that I need you in my office so that they can add you to their count."

I sat in Mrs. Price's office, fighting to hold back the tears that were about to explode from my eyes. Mrs. Price was back before I could even figure out what I wanted to say.

"What's on your mind, Ms. Greene?"

Without figuring the proper way to start this conversation, I just started.

There wasn't any proper way to have a conversation like this.

"I was raped. I was molested many times." I watched as Mrs. Price turned to grab a box of tissue from behind her desk. This really triggered my tears. I continued.

"I was raped recently and I was molested before being incarcerated. And the issue that I'm struggling with is that in one of the situations, my body came to a climax. I makes me feel disgusting to admit the fact that I climaxed. It makes me feel like my body must have enjoyed what was being done to me."

"I totally understand how you could be confused by these feelings. Your mind knows that you are being raped. But, your body didn't know that you were being raped. There are spots on your body that respond to touch and stimulation. It's hard for your body to know that the touch you were receiving was an unwanted and unconsented touch. In that moment, your body just knew that a touch in that spot causes arousal. And if that spot is aroused for long enough then that will cause your body to come to a climax. A lot of people climax during or after a rape or a sexual assault. That's doesn't not mean that they enjoyed the act."

"But, it's deeper than that. I feel like I'm promiscuous. In my relationships, I only want the feeling of climaxing. I don't want any emotional connection, with anyone. "

"Everything that you're saying makes sense. Most people tend to be different after a trauma. You were raped. That's definitely a trauma. I've seen people change in many ways after a sexual assault or rape. I've seen people become withdrawn from sexual desire and intimacy or have act out/rebel in sexual ways of always wanting to be active and with different people. It looks like you're doing a little bit of both."

"And I keep having nightmares. I've been suffering in many ways."

"This sounds like you are suffering from PTSD."

"I've read about PTSD before. I'm just not sure that I completely understand the acronym."

"PTSD stands for 'post-traumatic stress disorder,' which is a set of issues that may occur after someone has experienced a terrible, stressful life event. There are two types of PTSD. 'Simple PTSD,' is from a single incident such as a car accident or family death. 'Complex PTSD,' is from repeated incidents such as domestic violence or ongoing childhood abuse. It has a broader range of symptoms, including problems with self-harm, suicide, dissociation, relationships, memory, sexuality, health, anger, shame, guilt, numbness, loss of faith or trust, and feeling damaged."

"I just want the nightmares to stop. I feel weak for having them because I can't control them. I also feel shame when other people wake me from my sleep."

"You are not crazy, weak, or bad! That is why PTSD has been called a normal reaction to abnormal events. PTSD is considered an anxiety disorder because it is marked by an overwhelming feeling of anxiety during or after the trauma. It is definitely possible to heal from it. Having compassion for yourself and your PTSD is a way of taking back your power. A way to start this process is to speak up. You were very brave in sharing this information with me today. I want you to start thinking about your life-line. Remember I stated before that the criteria for graduating this program is by doing your life-line? In this program, doing a life-ling means standing in front of the entire group and sharing your life story from beginning to present. The purpose of that is many people still have their abuse sitting inside them, untold. Letting it all out begins to free you from the burden. Hearing your own self talk can give you perspective on your life that you may have never thought about before. It's a great way to reflect. Hearing a life-line is helpful for others in the group because hearing the life stories of others shows you that you're not alone in the things that you have experience. We are all helping each other heal."

"Yea, I will prepare that since I'm almost done with this program."

"Also, I was thinking about you the other night and the conversation that we had about codependency. I do want you to keep in my mind that Domestic Violence, rape, and sexual assault are not caused because someone who is a survivor is codependent. It's caused because someone chooses to abuse. Someone makes the conscious decision to use a pattern of behavior to gain power and control. I've heard the incorrect assumption before that survivors are codependent people that allow this abuse to happen to them."

"Yea. I know that there is a difference. I've made decisions in my life based on codependent traits that I see within myself. But, the codependency is not why I was abused. The abuse was based on the decisions of someone else."

*   *   *

I would like to welcome everyone to our reenactment of 'Take Back the Night.'
Domestic Violence and/or Sexual abuse can happen to anyone.
There is great urgency in this matter,
Our world is polluted with high numbers of abuse and batter.
Three to four million people are killed each year.
In the books, these people are just another number
A faded face... Just another Domestic Violence case.
The day they passed... Just dates;
Written in files, tucked away in someone's office, While the epidemic continues.

For so long, I thought silence was key.
I was so wrong.
Let's let it all out, the emotions we feel.
That is the only way we can begin to deal,
With the demons that have been locked away for so long, making
us feel like we were in the wrong.

We join together to fight this fight.
My chest is so tight,
But, we will TAKE BACK THE NIGHT,
Until the numbers of abuse come to an all-time low.
Let's speak up; Speak up for ourselves,
 Speak up for those innocent children,
Who can't speak the words of this awful abuse.
Let's tell those stories that are untold.
Today, we are safe.
I believe that through increased awareness,
we can see less of this in our world Do you agree?
Welcome to 'Take Back the Night.'

I heard a loud round of applause from the audience. I felt good
about myself. I looked into the audience and saw no one I knew
on a personal level. There were only C.O.'s and other employees.
The room was covered with painted T-shirts. In the months
leading up to our 'Take Back the Night' reenactment, Mrs. Price
purchased t-shirts for us and encouraged us to paint them in a
way to convey our personal messages or illustrations of abuse
within our lives. Participating in the clothesline project and 'Take
Back the Night,' made me feel like we were celebrating Domestic
Violence with other survivors across the world. I didn't feel
isolated. I didn't feel like I was in prison.

I walked to the side of the stage and gave Jessica a smile, wishing her luck. I was hopeful that all of the ladies would take the stage and begin to regain ownership of their lives, even if only in a small way. I watched as each of the other survivors stepped up to the mic and spoke. I felt that we had prepared for this day for a long time coming. When it was my turn, I put my paper in my pocket and took the stage. I had prepared a written copy of what I wanted to say but then realized that it would be more meaningful if it were unscripted and came from the heart.

"Hi, everyone. I would like to take back my voice. One night many years ago, something awful was done to me. That night, as I lay there shedding tears, I was also shedding my voice. When I lost my voice that day, I didn't know that I wouldn't have it back until now. People tend to take things for granted. Please don't take your voice for granted. You voice is powerful. Without it, I've endured a lot of pain and welcomed a lot of negative things and people into my life. Without my voice, people have taken advantage of me. I've allow people to speak down to me, just because I had no voice to defend myself. For years, I've spoken a bunch of meaningless sound. None of that sound meant anything because it wasn't a true reflection of who I was. When that sound came out, no one took it seriously. That sound had no confidence. That sound had no identity. If that sound had confidence, it would have set boundaries. But, today, I'm taking my voice. Alton, I bet you thought this day would never come. With this voice, I will tell my story, and I will keep telling my story."

Dear Diary,

Tomorrow, I will do my life-line in order to graduate from the house of courage. Coming to this program has been the most important stop along this journey. I finally feel that I have to right tools to start rebuilding my self-esteem. I will tell my entire story the tomorrow.

Preparing for my life-line was difficult because I realized how many memories have been erased from my mind. Forgetting and ignoring were two of my biggest coping mechanism prior to coming here. It felt great to stand in front of the audience today, taking back ownership of my voice. Taking back my voice made me realize that I need to sit my loved ones down and tell them everything. I don't need to carry this load by myself any longer.

-Me.

Chapter Sixteen

I patiently waited for about twenty ladies to fill the seats in the group room. As I waited, I wrote a quote on the dry erase board along with a few other words. Mrs. Henry was also seated in the group room. I requested special permission from Mrs. Price to invite Mrs. Henry because having her there meant a lot to me. To my surprise, Ms. Price approved my request. Mrs. Price was the last one to walk into the group room. When she took her seat, I knew that it was time for me to begin my life-line. I sat on the floor in front of twenty- two attentive faces. Lightly, I tossed my diary on the floor in front of me, and scattered several sheets of paper around me. I placed my bible on my lap, and then placed my chunky mahogany colored right hand on top of the bible, to proclaim my truth. I took a deep breath and began to speak.

"I swear to tell the truth, the whole truth, and nothing but the truth. So, help me God! Due to the events that have occurred in my life, I have become very secretive. I haven't revealed much from my personal life, because I don't trust people. I sit in front of you today with no filter, I am in my truest form.

I need to get a lot off my chest, in an effort to continue my healing process.

As you can see, my diary is open and my papers are scattered across the floor.

Those are belongings that I treasure. When I look at these papers I see beauty. Because within these papers, I'm entirely me.

These things are scattered across the floor to symbolize that my life is a beautiful mess.

I was born on January 5, 1990, as the baby girl of Shannon Austin and Gregory Greene. I was born on a cold winter day in King's County Hospital in Brooklyn, New York. On that day, I was given the name Giselle Omega Morrison. Omega means the beginning and the end; the first and the last. My mom said that she chose this middle name because I was her first daughter and her last child. She did not plan to have any more children after me.

By law, I'm a Brooklyn baby. However, Brooklyn didn't raise me. My mom didn't have much family support in the United States and didn't want me in daycare at such a young age, so she sent me to Jamaica to be in the care of my aunt, Sidney Austin, and grandmother, Silvia Austin. Once in Jamaica, I lived with my aunt, grandmother, brother Damien, and two cousins, Molly and Tamoy. I remember my mom sending us barrels of food and clothing. I remember being a happy baby. But, I was told that I cried for almost any reason and they always had to keep a lock on the yard gates because I loved venture out into the street. Aunty Sidney would dress me in colorful dresses with matching socks and patent-leather shoes. My brother and cousin Molly would walk me to preschool, which was about a half-a mile from our house.

In Jamaica, watching the children walk to school was a beautiful sight to see. Every school wore a different color uniform. Uniforms were the only attire students were allowed to wear to school. The uniform color for my school was pink. My brother and cousin wore brown. Although most families didn't have the best of things, their children were always neat and tidy. I remember the message I observed from this was that education is important.

Each morning, we walked past a busy shopping center and alongside a highway to my school. My teacher's name was Mrs. Black. For a couple of years, she taught me proper English and would beat me for chewing gum. Jamaica was once ruled by the Queen of England so some of the Jamaican teachings and traditions had strong English influence. If you look behind me, on the dry erase board, you will see that under the first quote, I wrote a few different words. I will tell you what those words mean to me. When spelling the word 'color,' I added a 'u' to the spelling. Colour! When telling someone to hurry, I was taught to say, 'Make haste.' When describing a shirt, I was taught to say the word 'blouse.' We wouldn't say that we were sitting on the porch. Instead, we were sitting on the veranda.

I remember a number of Saturday nights, where Aunty Sidney took Tamoy and I to model at the community talent show. I knew that I was beautifully dressed and wasn't wearing my play clothes. Tamoy would sashay across the stage. I lacked courage to walk across the stage nor did I want to. I didn't want to be considered the Display American Baby.'

When I was about five years old, everyone in my Jamaican household received their green cards. This was a privilege because not every individual who applied was approved and granted with traveling permission. This was also a sign that we were about to begin a new chapter in our lives. With all of our important things packed, we left our home, the one in front of the shopping center, and boarded a plane to Boston, Massachusetts. Logan Airport was their first experience of the United States. 'Foreign,' as some people call it. A foreign land, indeed, it was to my loved ones who were used to the West Indies. And contrary enough, it felt like a foreign land to me to. The weather was torturous, a cold December night. My grandfather, Steven Austin, came to pick us up. He then brought us to a beautiful home in Roslindale,

Massachusetts. This home would be our residence for the next almost ten years.

My grandfather was the stage manager at the Boston Symphony Hall. He was a hardworking man. He and I would always watch 'Family Feud.' And when we both established that I liked Chinese food, he would buy it for me all the time. However, he used to tell me that I walked too loudly. I found myself learning to tip-toe when I was around him so that he wouldn't complain.

Within months, everyone in the house was either working or in school and trying to find their place in this new world. My Aunty Sidney had two jobs. She was working as a teller at The Boston Private Bank and waitressing at the Boston Symphony Hall. It wasn't long before she met a guy named Alton. They began dating. I vaguely remember my elementary school days. But, I do remember the weekends. I would play with my next door neighbors or my friends on the next street over. Alton would always take Aunty Sidney on dates, and many times, they would take me along.

Alton was around frequently, almost every day. He was beginning to treat me as if I were his daughter, and I didn't mind it. He would help me with my homework. One of my favorite games to play was school. I would often pretend to be the teacher. I would make lessons and homework to go with the lessons and Alton would do the homework for me to grade it. He sometimes would drive me around in his green van. He taught me all the part of the car — the correct names and how each part functioned. Once, I learned how each part functioned. He would tell me the rules of the road whenever we were driving, what each sign meant, the difference between a double line and a single line, the difference between a yellow line and a white line. Eventually, he put me in the driver's seat and made me drive. I was probably the only one in middle school who knew how to drive. And he had promised to take me to work with him when school was on spring break.

By the time I got to middle school, I realized that I was really smart. But, I also wanted to be athletic. Some afternoons, when my brother would watch me, he would take me to the Mattahunt, an elementary school in the area that had a nice basketball court. I would watch him play basketball. I also saw other girls playing basketball and I wanted to be like them. So I tried out for the school basketball team and made the team. My school bus picked me up about five streets away. One morning while standing at the bus stop, I began to talk to Amalia Avery, who I saw board the bus with me every day. We were also in the same grade and shared a class together. Unbeknownst to us, our initial conversation would be the first of lifelong friendship. At first, middle school was a lot of fun. Until I returned from one particular spring break.

It was a Friday, the end of my spring break from middle school. Work was done for that week and it was payday, so I'd be getting my favorite fast food. I waited in Alton's green van while he purchased scratch tickets at the Fifth Street Friendly Quick Mart, his usual Friday routine. I sat in the passenger seat for what seemed like ten minutes, thinking about everything I could buy with the money I'd earned, and beating my feet in time to the music on the car radio.

I was eleven years old, working my first job as a newspaper distributor, or should I say, newspaper distributor's helper. Alton worked for one of Boston's well established newspaper/magazine distributing companies, and he was paying me under the table to help him deliver the papers. I had made more on this break than I had just a few months ago during Christmas break. I didn't ask any questions, though. Alton had given me two hundred and fifty dollars for that week, and my pockets were fat. I was feeling on top of the world.

I sat back to read the signs on the businesses surrounding the Quick Mart. The signs indicated that we were in Wellesley, Massachusetts. Working for Alton the way I did enabled me to see different parts of Massachusetts. That was a plus. Out of the corner of my eye, I saw Alton coming out of the Quick Mart, so I hurried to turn the music volume back down.

A couple months before, when Alton and I were driving, my favorite song came on. I turned the volume up so I could really hear it, and started bobbing my head to the music.

Alton rubbed his hand slowly up and down my thigh and said, 'Dance for me. Move your waist-line.'

My gut feeling told me that something was wrong about that request. I laughed it off, and told him that I didn't like to dance, then I changed the subject. I told myself that as long as there was no music, he would never ask me to dance. So, after that time, I made up excuses for not wanting to hear any music. Those excuses ranged from not being able to concentrate on filling out the delivery papers, to music making me depressed, because it reminded me of when I used to live with my mom and the good times we shared, to simply having a headache. On that day, I said I didn't want to hear any music because I had a headache.

'I did not win much tonight,' Alton said as he climbed in and slammed the van door shut.

'Maybe next week. Where are we going?'

'Well, we have thirty minutes before we have to pick your Aunty up from work, and we are about forty-five minutes away, so that's where we are rushing to, honey.'

'Okay,' I said.

'What are you and Aunty doing tomorrow?' Alton asked.

'After we go grocery shopping in the morning, she said she would take me to the mall. Hopefully, she lets me use my money for some clothes. Last time, she let me spend all of my pay on clothes. If she lets me do it again, I am so going to get some Nikes. Man, I'll be stylin."

Alton and I entered the freeway towards Auntie's job, and drove the rest of the way in silence. There was something mysterious about him. I glanced at him every so often, trying to figure him out. He stood at about six feet. Extremely dark brown skin. A weird nose — not straight, not round. Short haircut, almost bald. About a solid two hundred pounds. His taste in fashion was uniquely loud. Alton had a thing for bright colors. Lime green, bright yellow, and golden orange. Today, he was dressed in a sky blue sweater, blue jeans, sky blue slip-on shoes, and a sky blue baseball cap.

The streets were busy with corporate commuters. My aunt was one of the smarter ones. Don't drive your car to work in the city and pay sky high fees just to park it. That meant Alton was not only Aunt Sidney's boyfriend, but also her daily chauffeur, letting her leave her car at home to rest in the driveway so she could save money.

As we pulled up in front of Aunty Sidney's job, I felt a sudden rush of excitement. I was always happy to see her at the end of her work day. I would share with her everything I had done, and she would tell me stories from her day. Boston Private Bank was written in gold letters on the glass doors. My aunt stood in front of those doors, looking like the most stylish woman I had ever seen. She had been working as a teller, in that upscale part of the city, for the last six years.

I shifted to the back seat in the van, and Aunty gracefully took the front seat.

'Hey, Alton. What's up, Giselle?' Aunty said in almost the same breath.

Her Jamaican accent was still present.

'What's up? How was work?' Alton shot back.

'Hey, Aunty. How was your day?' I interrupted.

'Good, Baby,' she said to me. 'Alton, don't take me home. I have an appointment at the hair salon tonight. I told Brenda that I would be there by seven.'

'Okay. No problem. Do you want to eat first?'

'No. Just drop me off and you and Giselle can grab something to eat while' I'm getting my hair done. Then you can drop Giselle at the house. Grandma should be home. Then I will call you when I'm done.'

About forty minutes later, we dropped Aunty off at her appointment and Alton told me to move up to the front seat. I didn't like to sit beside him any more than I had to. We stopped at the KFC and got some chicken wings and French fries. I sat gazing up at the night sky as we rode down Blue Hill Avenue. 'Why didn't you turn there?' I said, pointing to the street where my aunty and I lived.

'We're going to my house first.'

'But, Aunty said to take me home. I want to go home. I don't feel good.'

'I just have to get something.'

Alton started patting and massaging my legs, and I lost my appetite. He continued to drive us to his house. Something wasn't right.

'Come in. I can't leave you in the car alone.'

'Why? You leave me alone in the car all the time. I wanna stay here. I don't feel good.'

'I said come in!' He growled at me as though he were angry.

Alton lived on the top floor of an old three-story house. As soon as he opened the door for us, I could smell old urine and garbage. I crept up the stairs behind him, trying not to look at the cracked and broken plaster on the walls, and stepping around places where the tread was half off the stairs, ready to trip someone. A window on the second landing was broken, and it did not look as though anyone had done anything to repair it, though the bars covering it were still cemented into the outside wall. When we got into his apartment, Alton wouldn't let me turn any lights on. He wanted the television on, instead. A Playboy DVD popped up on the screen.

'I don't like this. Can't you show me where the light switch is?'

'Come here.'

My throat went dry. 'I thought you just had to pick something up. I really want to go."

He came toward me, grabbed my hand and put it on the crotch of his pants. His penis was hard. He kissed my lips hard, before I could duck my head. He grabbed me, twisting my arm behind my back till it felt like my shoulder would pop, and forced me back to the bedroom. The entire way there, I fought and screamed, with tears streaming down my face. 'Stop! Please stop!'

He pushed me down on the bed and pinned my hands down. He was so much stronger than me. My legs were still free. I kicked him continuously, but that didn't even slow him down. He said not one word. He would take what he wanted, regardless of the fact that I was trying to tell him in every way I could that I did not want it. He lay his heavy body on top of me so that I was no longer able to kick, and I had to fight just to breathe. It was obvious that he had already won the battle. I could smell the scent of his cologne and hear the moans of the Playmates on the television. I could feel the ripping, and I tried to scream, as he forced his penis into my eleven-year-old vagina. He stroked me as if he had molested me many times before in his dreams. The look of satisfaction on his face turned my stomach. I could not stop crying. I had never felt so much pain. My vagina felt ripped apart. Even after he had got up and was pulling up his pants, I could still feel his heavy body on top of mine and his sweaty hands stroking me.

I couldn't understand why he had done this to me. That night, my innocence died, and in return a desire for revenge was born, which would change my life forever. I went home that night and I didn't tell anyone. I went into my room and cried for hours. When I went back to school, I wasn't the same person."

I interrupted my life-line and grabbed a picture out of my diary, it was the eleven-year-old Giselle who Alton had molested. I was so happy in that picture before my innocence was taken way. In the picture, I wore a bright yellow jumper. I allowed the ladies to pass the picture around the room. I began to talk again.

"The molestation never stopped. By this time, I believe both cousin Molly and my brother Damien were in high school and had part-time jobs. Because they weren't home in the afternoons, many times, Alton would be done with work early and drive to my school to pick me up. I wanted to take the school bus home because I was scared to be alone with him. But, he would park right in front of the school so that it was difficult to act as though I didn't see him. He began molesting me at least once a week. When Alton would come at our house, he would look for opportunities to molest me. He often sat in the kitchen. So I planned my meals around times that other people would be in the kitchen. I tried avoid being left alone with him.

After basketball season, I wanted to stay active in school. And things that occurred after regular school hours. So I joined track and field. This didn't eliminate the molestation, it just decreased its frequency. I was happy that the summer was approaching and I would be sent to Jamaica for a total of two months.

By the start of the next school year, I was on a mission to always be occupied and avoid being home as much as I could. One day at school, I was walking through the hallway and saw a flyer for cheerleading try-outs. This would be the first time that the middle school would be having a cheerleading team. Amalia and I tried out and we both made the team. On nights when we didn't have cheerleading practice, Amalia and I would go to the Dorchester House, which was an afterschool tutoring program. My grandmother would always yell at me and say that I should start coming straight home after school. She would say that there is no good reason for me to be outside in when its dark. I would come home between six and seven o'clock. But, based on daylight savings time, if it was summer, then six o'clock meant darkness.

Raping me was becoming a habit for Alton. Every time that I would fight him back and lose, he would proceed to molest me. Stiffening my legs and my body only worked for a few minutes then I would lose energy. I began leaving body. I didn't know exactly how I was leaving my body. I knew that one time I was in so much pain. I closed my eyes as tightly as I could and mentally brought myself somewhere else. The feeling of leaving my body was surreal. I felt like I was standing over him watching him molest me. I wasn't in any pain, I was numb. So I began to leave my body every time he would molest me. And each time, I went to a different place. The places that I went to was something that I could control. I began to get creative with formulating these fairytale places that I was escaping to. Later on in life I learned that these are called 'out of body experiences.'

The abuse was causing a lot of anger within me. I began taking Tae Kwon Do. Amalia was in the class with me. We were both very competitive. The skill of disciplined fighting and technique became an outlet for my anger. The abuse was also causing a lot of confusion within me.

Sometimes when he would molest me, my vagina would pulsate, and my body would shake or shiver. Although I was in a lot of pain, that feeling felt a little good. And this feeling made me even more sad because I began to second-guess myself. I was constantly crying, and fighting and stiffening my muscles to try to avoid him from raping me. I knew that those feelings didn't feel good. I also knew based on the feeling in my gut and the fact that he made me hide this from my family that what he was doing wasn't right. So why is it that my body sometimes reacted by climaxing? I knew that the word was called climaxing because when he first started raping me, I went to the library to read about what sex was.

I knew that I wanted the feeling of climaxing, I just didn't want the feeling from Alton. So, starting dating my first boyfriend. At this point, I was twelve years old was in the seventh grade. My boyfriend was my age and was already sexually active. I told my best friend, Amalia about my boyfriend, Jeremy. But, I didn't tell her what we were doing.

The next school year, Molly went away to college and Damien went to the military. Aunty Sidney told me that her and I were moving to Pennsylvania. I was really sad about leaving my friends at school, Amalia and Jeremy. But I was also excited because I would be away from Alton and the abuse. Within a few months, we moved to Virginia. We moved to a suburban neighborhood. The house was huge--I had my own room. We had two a few family members already living there. This also felt like a good move because it gave me the opportunity to build relationships with family members that I didn't know.

It was my freshman year of high school and it felt like a fresh start. The school was gigantic with a population of about twelve hundred. My cousin and I were two of the eight colored kids in school. The school curriculum was definitely more advanced than what I had been learning in Boston. By the time I started at this new school, is was too late for me to join the cheerleading team because tryouts were in the summer. So I asked aunty if I could

184

start working and she said yes. There was a McDonalds that was about three miles from my house that agree to hire me if I had consent from my parent or legal guardian and working papers from my school.

When I got the job, Aunty Sidney bought me a bike so that I could get to work. We lived in an area where there was no public transportation. And I was only allowed to work from 3 p.m.-7 p.m. which would be hours that she was still at work. Things were going great in Virginia, until about six months of being there. Alton was visiting every weekend. I was beginning to feel like he moved to Virginia with us. Then every weekend turned into to longer stay of almost every day.

At this point, I became rebellious. I began using the money from my paychecks to sneak to Boston to see my best friend. When I hugged Amalia, I felt comfort. I felt love. She didn't know exactly what was going on with me but she knew that things were bothering me. I'm glad that she didn't pry for information but she offered support just by being there. This would be the first of many secret trips to Boston, and skipping school to do so.

Now when Alton tried to molest me I became more violent. I would try to hit him with things. In hopes of leaving of bruise so that Aunty Sidney or someone would question how the bruise got there. But he was damn dark-skinned and the bruises never showed. There was one time that he tried to molest me on the steps of our Virginia home. I tried to push him down the steps. But, he only stumbled and caught his fall. Things were getting so bad that I tried locking my room door at night. He often times would try to sneak in and molest me in during the night. Aunty Sidney would yell at me for locking my door. She would say, 'You're not an adult and you don't pay bills in here so don't lock your door. What are you hiding in there? Keep the door open so that I could see.' If only she knew what I was really hiding. If only I had the courage to verbally tell her.

During one of my secret trips to Boston, I met a girl named Lyric. She was a lesbian. And I took a liking to her. When I went back to Virginia, we would spend hours on the phone. And I wondered what it would be like to climax from having sex with a female. Would I feel as disgusting? Or would I feel better being able to look at someone who was the complete opposite image of Alton? Lyric would sing me songs over the phone. In my mind, we were dating. This became my new outlet of happiness. About a year after communicating over the phone, I found out that she was in a relationship with another female.

One day while I was working at McDonald's, a new guy started working there. He introduced himself as Triston. He told me that he had seen me before in school. He was handsome and friendly. He was tall, about 6 foot. He was half-black and half-Hispanic. He explained recently moving to the area from New Jersey and his smile kept me talking. Over the course of time, we began dating. We dated for over two years. We had sexual intercourse many times. However, I started to realize a pattern within myself. Leading up to act of intercourse, I hated the thought of foreplay. After I would climax, I would become withdrawn. I didn't like cuddling or being passionate. I absolutely hated kissing and hugging. This created a great distance in the relationship between Triston and I. During the course of two years, I cheated on him many times. All I wanted to do was climax. I didn't want any of the other feelings associated with it. All of those feelings felt negative and uncomfortable for me. Alton was still raping me.

One night I awoke from sleep to see to a black figure standing over me. I squinted my eyes in an effort to shake the fatigue. It was Alton standing over me. He stuffed a sock in my mouth to mask the sounds of me screaming. This was late in the middle of the night and Aunty Sidney was home, a couple doors down, sleeping. He had snuck out of the room without waking her. And the sock was to prevent me from waking her. I remember him dropping his heaving body on me and proceeding to molest me once more. I was near my end, and if I would have had a gun under my pillow, I would have shot him that night.

When he left my room that night, I walked into the bathroom and almost collapsed into the bathtub. I was dripping blood and was in so much pain. I was extremely weak. I remember seeing and feeling his cum all over my vagina and legs. I felt so nauseated, I threw up in the bathtub. I could never forget the smell of his semen. I took a hot shower and could not stop the tears from falling. I went back into the room that night and knew that I had to do something to stop the abuse.

About two months later, I became worried because I had not gotten my menstrual cycle for a long time. Usually, I would get my menstrual cycle every month so I took a pregnancy test and the results were positive. I wanted to confirm that this was true so I went to the Planned Parenthood and asked for a pregnancy test. The test that they administered came back positive too. I went and I told Triston what had happened. I told him the truth about the abuse, from the beginning in Boston to the present. I explained to him what I knew in my heart to be true. I knew that it was Alton's child. Triston and I always wore protection and although protection isn't a guarantee, the last time Triston and I had sex was months prior to the most recent molestation, and the months leading up to the most recent rape, I had received my period. I also hadn't cheated on Triston in months.

I was scared, excited, and angry--all at the same time. I was scared because I didn't know what I was going to do next and I was scared of confronting Alton. I knew now the whole world would see the evidence of what has been happening to me and I would have to worry about being believed. But, I was also angry because a child should never be used as evidence of anything outside of love, and I wasn't sure that I would be able to properly care for a child that looked exactly like Alton. That wouldn't be fair to any innocent child.

About any other month passed and I was still with Triston. He wasn't upset with me because I hadn't done anything wrong. Instead, he was being supportive of me. I even think that he was beginning to entertain the thought of us bringing this child into the world together. Deep down, I was beginning to feel love for a child that was growing within me. I felt that maybe I could do it. I went for an ultrasound and saw the little specimen inside me. I told myself that I would name the baby Sky, whether it was a boy or girl. I would name them Sky because they would be my world. And I would do everything in my power to protect them from the evils of this world.

One day Alton tried to molest me again. Instead of physically fighting him, this time I opted to fight with my words. I told him that I was pregnant and that I would tell the world what he had done to me. And there would be no way that he would be able to get away with it anymore. I remember the exact day of the week and date of the month that he took me to Planned Parenthood and forced me to get an abortion. I bled for about four days. I knew that, once and for all, I would put an end to this shit.

In two months, I would be graduating from high school and going off to college. I purposely planned to live on campus because that would be my final escape. When I made it to college, Alton began stalking my college campus. He would text my cell phone saying things like, 'I see your dorm room light on. I know you're in there. Why haven't you been picking up my calls?' I began to spiral into a downward depression. I began drinking and I was drinking myself into oblivion. I was dating a sophomore at my college but I was fearful of telling him what was going on. I didn't want people to think that I was crazy.

When I was in the county jail, I thought that I was safe from sexual abuse until I was raped, by a complete stranger. Now that I am here in state prison, I am trying to heal. I am physically away from both of them. However, Alton still haunts me through mail. He doesn't think that he has done anything wrong. He says he can't wait for me to come home so that we can get married. He says that he deserves to marry the woman that he raised."

Chapter Seventeen

"Can I please give you a hug?"

"Of course." Mrs. Henry and I embraced in the yard, hoping that the officers wouldn't see us and reprimand us for it.

"I really enjoyed hearing your life story. The content wasn't enjoyable but, it was powerful to see you take charge of that room and speak the truth about things that you've been hiding. I saw a lot of growth from the Giselle that was speaking. You weren't the little girl that I met in the Y.A.O."

"Thank you. After I graduated, Mrs. Price asked me to stay and be a graduate in the program. So I will be doing further studies and helping out on the unit."

"That's an awesome opportunity. But in the midst of being a graduate, I don't want you to lose focus of you. Remember, codependency is something that you have to keep working at. Please don't focus too much on the program and the other ladies that you begin losing focus of your recovery."

"I hear you."

"Since hearing your life-line, I wanted to point out more Codependent areas. I suggest this as a way for you to keep reflecting and giving yourself answers."

"Sure. Tell me."

"When you talked about being a kid and being told that you walked too loudly, you said that you began tip toeing around the house."

"Yeah. That's true."

"Do you see how this was another instance of people-pleasing?"

"It was. But, now that you bring that up, the decision I made to tiptoe, also makes me remember the groups I had with Mrs. Price on Domestic Violence. Tip-toeing reminds me of the phrase, 'walking on egg shells'. Survivors often use the term walking on egg shells because of being anxious of nervous of doing something wrong that will upset their abuser."

"I've heard the phrase before. Towards the end of your life-line, you explained that, when you were in college, you didn't want to tell anyone that Alton was stalking you because you didn't want people thinking you were crazy."

"I didn't want people to think that I was crazy. Looking back, I know that's the aspect of codependency that speaks to caring too much what others think."

"I also sense that, because of your abuse, you may experience problems with intimacy. I'm not referring to sex, although sexual dysfunction often is a reflection of an intimacy problem. I'm talking about being open and close at the same time, with someone in an intimate relationship. Because of the shame and weak boundaries, you might fear that you'll be judged, rejected, or left. On the other hand, you may fear being smothered in a relationship. You might deny your need for closeness and feel that your partner wants too much of your time; your partner complains that you're unavailable."

"You're on the right track with that point. I do have intimacy problems. I've been dating Jasmine now for nine months. After every time that we have sex, I become withdrawn. Sometimes I think the reasoning is because, internally, I'm struggling with the negative messages I had been taught as a child, through culture and through religion, about homosexuality. But, I also know that the withdrawal is not because I'm not attached to her. I feel more comfortable having sexual relations with a female than I do with a male. I even feel more connected through talking and spending time together. It's all confusing but, the main problem is that I do have a problem with intimacy."

"That's hard. I'm going to show you how easy it can be to misinterpret codependency and Domestic Violence as being the same. They are not. Nor are they results of each other. So, based on Domestic Violence and sexual abuse, the problems that you have with intimacy can be a result of you being traumatized by the events leading up to now. In regards to codependency, you are showing traits of avoidance patterns, which means avoiding emotional, physical, or sexual intimacy as a way to maintain distance. You suppress feelings or needs to avoid feeling vulnerable. You pull people toward you but, when they get close, you push them away. You also use sexual attention to gain approval and acceptance. I see you suffering from both codependency and sexual abuse. It sucks that you are going through both but, don't tangle them up. You did not get molested and raped because you are codependent. You are codependent and you are a survivor of sexual abuse. In healing, it's important to make that distinction and not blame either on each other. If you blamed them on each other, that would lead you to believe that you were at fault for what was done to you and that's not true."

"I wish I could take you home with me in my pocket. I will be up to see the parole board soon. I hope that they release me but I will be sad leaving you behind."

"You're not leaving me behind if you promise to go home and use all the tools that I taught you. Go home and shine."

"I will, Mrs. Henry."

"Starting now, think about the things that you enjoy doing. Think about what makes Giselle happy. Being Codependent, I'm sure that you've lost 'you' along the way but, this point in your recovery is not a bad place to be. Rebuilding yourself is the fun part. You can rebuild yourself to be anything you've always wanted or dreamed of being."

"Well yard is about to end but, this is not the end for us. Let's walk towards the gate. I have a 3:30 phone call."

I rushed back to my unit to have a call with Aunty Sidney. I told her that I needed to have a serious conversation with her when she comes up for the next visit. I can't keep this information about my abuse from my family any longer. I don't have to. I've learned the language to talk about what I was experiencing--not that the lack of proper language should stop someone from speaking up. I've gained knowledge that eliminates the thoughts of seconding-guessing what I was going through. I wanted Aunty Sidney and I to think of how things will be when I go home. I needed Alton to know that his presence is not welcome wherever I reside.

Dear Diary,

I do know that my family loves me. But, I also know that I'm very confused as to what love actually looks like — mature, intimate love. Today, as I was walking back from yard, I began to look back at my relationships. It was then that I realized that I keep carrying this misinterpretation of love into all of my relationships. Thinking back to the group session on Domestic Violence, I've allowed Theresa to control me. She would talk to me as if I was dirt on the bottom of her shoe. Whenever we would make-up, she blamed her actions on her temper. Within my years of being behind bars, I have dibbled and dabbled in relationships, seeking love and accepting anything in return. I have given freely of my body thinking that love is achieved through sexual desire. There is something very wrong with this picture. I have to leave these cycles and these patterns behind the gates of this prison.

LOVE? Love left me hurt, misled, and confused.

Love? Love left me hurt, misled, and confused. I hate the damn word. Love never loved me back. Love left me feeling empty, alone, suffocated, stressed and many times... depressed. The love that I see others with, Don't seem to feel like this. I see genuine smiles, laughter, favors — not just in one direction but mutually. They say love is patient, love is kind. He was patient as he lured me in, he was kind when he bought me baby dolls and wrapped them as gifts. Love is affection, sexual desire, even admiration. He admired my childish desire to care for others. Love is warm attachment, enthusiasm and devotion. He was attached to his sexual thoughts of me. He was enthused by the thrill of molesting me continuously. He was devoted to gaining power and control to validate his own insecurities. Love can be illustrated through fatherly concern. He raised me to one day live a life of promiscuity. Love? Love left me hurt, misled, and confused. I hate the damn word. Love never loved me back. I am a misleading image. An illusion. I want people to perceive me as someone that could actually love them. I hold a misinterpreted demeanor. I love others the way I want to be loved but, that in itself, is an inaccurate idea. The truth is, I don't even know what love is. I've given loosely of my body and materialistic things. Indirectly, that's how I was taught to love. Then reality is revealed. I don't know how to give of my heart. Deep down I know I have a huge heart, with a lot of love to give. I just don't know how to live freely from these bars that I've built, built around my interior, trapped, feeling insecure and inferior.

Love? Love left me hurt, misled, and confused. I hate the damn word. Love never loved me back. Looking for love, I seduced Triston. He was drawn to my work ethic and my independent nature. Mature... that I was definitely was, I had no choice but to be. I taught him how to drive. Kissed him and had sexual relations on a winter night. For his love I strived. Love? Love left me hurt, misled, and confused. I hate the damn word. Love never loved me back.

My dearest Andrea, seduced her with my long jet black pretty hair, my thick yet athletic-built body and my coyness to the homosexual life. I showered her with materialistic things as I was eager to learn more about the female body. She was my African queen. I was her Cleopatra. I ruled over her body like it was sacred land. We embraced the entire rainbow. I showered her with vivid colors and fluid vibrations of love making. Blue and greens, to her clitoris I brought life and liberation. Red and orange, giving her passion and lust.

I made her fluids flow like the waterfalls of Niagara. Sex addicts... We fed each other's sexual needs as we caved deeper into the downward spiral of promiscuity.

Theresa was seduced by my smile and intrigued by my aura. I was young, sweet, and passive. From years ago when I built the bars around my interior. I lost the ability to speak up for myself. So she talked me anyway she felt. I didn't care, I blamed it on her temper.

When things were bad, they were really bad. And when things were good, she often told me that I was charming. She called me her good luck charm. I needed her to want me, the way I walked, the way I talked. I needed for her to stay, but I knew eventually she'd go. I sexed her body till she begged for more. I made love to her mind but couldn't connect with her soul, because my heart... she realized, she would never be able to hold.

Love? Love left me hurt, misled, and confused. I hate the damn word. Love never loved me back. Jasmine, that's when I began to realize what I thought I wanted in a lover. It was time to somehow pull myself out this downward spiral. My passion for literature drew her in like a bee to nectar. But, that's just a Capricorn's nature? I washed, cooked, and cleaned and held back all my sexual fantasies. This was a new leaf for me. Excited that with this experience, true love is what I would really see. Instead, she was a sexual being suffering from promiscuity, just like me. Love? Love left me hurt, misled, and confused. I hate the damn word. Love never loved me back.

-Me

"Not all wounds heal. Not all scars show, sometimes you can't always see the pain someone feels." ~ Cheryl Sullivan

Aunty Sidney came up to the prison to visit me. It had only been three days since our conversation, in which I told her that I had some serious concerns to share.

When I exited the strip room and quickly glanced the visiting room, I saw her and Molly seated near the back of the room, near the door where visitors entered and exited. Although our eyes had met for less than a minute, I was driven to the conclusion that she looked different. Aunty was losing more and more weight. It was evident that the experience of my incarceration was taking its toll on her. Today, as they sat and waited for me, her facial expression carried an unfamiliar sense of seriousness. She was also wearing a cream-colored sweater and pale palettes had not been a usual choice for Aunty.

When I sat in the open seat next to Aunty, I wasted no time in proceeding to the conversation that I had planned to initiate. I anticipated the level of discomfort and difficulty that this conversation would incite. I had prepared mental bullet points and played with words that I thought may be the most effective for all of us. I considered the major differences which existed in me telling my story to Aunty and Molly. These were my family members--individuals that would be able to place memory, face, and location recognition, and their personal interactions in context of what I would share. Also, when I shared my story with strangers, I was able to talk in a way that allowed me to be selective as to whether I would accept and answer questions. With Molly and Aunty Sidney, there would be a different form of dialogue, a form that I wasn't sure I was ready for but, I knew how important this conversation would be to my growth and safety.

Surprisingly, the duration of the conversation was much shorter than I guessed it would, and I wasn't sure if I was happy with that fact. I explained to them the entire timeline of the sexual abuse. I started with the first time in Boston and ended in Virginia. I included the instances of stalking during college, and the inappropriate letters that I was still receiving. I explained to Aunty the reasoning behind why I would always try to lock my room door. I told her that that was my efforts to keep myself safe.

I, intentionally, withheld the gory details and the pregnancy that was aborted. I didn't deem those details necessary to share, as the situation was already painful enough. Aunty and Molly listened, asked very few questions, and told me that they were sorry and that they were sorry to hear of what happened. They also stated that upon my arrival home, they would do everything within their power to keep me safe.

Aunty stated that her first action would be to return home, call Alton and tell him that his belongings would be waiting for him in the garage for him to retrieve. She went on to say that she would tell him that she had been made aware of the truth and that he was no longer welcomed in our home, or anywhere around us.

I think I may have been pleased with her and Molly's reaction. We did not cry. We sat in silence, in empathy, and in thought. God felt present in that conversation.

Chapter Eighteen

January of 2014
State Prison

Dear Diary,

An abuser gains the trust of a child and also tries to gain the trust of the people involved in that child's life. For years I loved him because he felt like family and I clung to the memories that we shared before the abuse began. I also loved him for the input that he had in my life and all the things he taught me. Naively, I kept battling with myself that he loved me back--he's just sick. My family and friends really adored him. My mom would call him from miles away, thanking him for being so monumental in life. They placed him on a pedestal. How was I, a child, supposed to have the courage to speak up against all the praises he was receiving? I was fearful that I wouldn't be believed and also fearful that someone in my family would possibly kill him for what was done to me and I would have to live with that guilt. The first time I felt comfortable to talk about this was in a prison where no one knew me and I didn't care if they judged me.

I'm not familiar with a lot of cartoon, movies, or board games that many people engaged in during childhood. I had to grow up rather quickly, teaching myself survival skills necessary to endure the abuse. I think that's the reason why now, as an adult, I often revert to baby talk and child play, yearning for a connection to innocence that was lost throughout those years. I knew that writing Alton a letter was something that needed to be done, but it wouldn't be easy.

~Me.

Dear Alton,

I would begin this letter with the common pleasantries of hoping that your well or actually taking the time to ask how you are doing. But, I don't care about your current state of being. This letter is to inform you that I have figured out what molestation means. Sit down and make some time for a few questions. Remember when I trusted you? Remember my beautiful innocent smile before you molested me? Remember the first time you molested me? Remember the tears and the screams as I begged you to stop? Remember when you molested me in Boston? Remember when you would pick me up from school to molest me? Remember the look of fear in my eyes? Do you remember me flinching whenever you would come near? Remember when I pushed you down the stairs? Remember when you made me abort the baby that was a product of you raping me? Do you remember all the things you said you would do to me if I told anyone? Well, I dare you.

Your actions caused me to grow up with so much confusion. I loved you because you were like the father that I never had. But any father in their right mind wouldn't do what you did to anyone. After you started raping me, you changed the image that I had of you. I began hating you. I trusted you and you took advantage of that. Due to your actions, I have developed complex PTSD, Post- traumatic stress disorder. I don't remember much from my adolescent life, nor do I know how to properly identify my feelings. My feelings were turned off years ago when you began molesting me. I mentally escaped my body so many times that disassociation became second-nature to me. Every time I smell the scent of Curve for Men, I am reminded of you.

It's insane that I put myself through that mental and physical pain just to keep you from being dead or in jail, especially when many nights I thought of killing you myself. I've lived my life for many years trying to please everyone around me. This character defect is deeply rooted within me. I've lived my life trying to please everyone around me even if pleasing everyone has meant harming myself. I've been a closed mouth and a closed book for years. I don't say how I truly feel and I act like everything is okay. I've been stuffing things for years and its tearing me up inside. I want to grow, heal, and move forward. Holding this pain has been hindering my growth.

I want to assertively speak my mind and express my feelings. I'm twenty- three years old and the thought of love and intimacy makes me sick to my stomach. What scares me the most is that you don't see anything wrong with this picture. It's sick that you think I would come home and marry you. It's sick that you keep referring to your son as my child. I hope that poor little boy won't grow up to be anything like you. Your own daughter wants nothing to do with you. For many years I've wondered why. I wonder if you molested her too. I wonder if you've abused anyone else during your fifty plus years of being on this earth.

It's very true that you played a part in raising me. I hope that you're proud of the woman that you raised, proud that I grew up with courage tell the world about everything you've done. The *madness ends here. I'm scared of what I would do if I were to see you again. I hope these words will haunt you, haunt you enough to never touch or violate anyone ever again. When the world finds out what you've done to me, I don't want you dead, as death would be the easy way out. I want you to live, traumatized by the fact that the world now knows who you truly are.*

Above all, I forgive you. Because forgiveness is a hero's walk. Forgiveness is not about you. It's about me. You no longer have control over my life. I am taking back everything that you stole from me. I will continue to speak my truth.

-Signed,

-No longer your object

I ended the letter and walked to the common room for movie night. We could be watching *Ted*. Although I was Jessica was my cellie and I saw her basically all day long, I still decided to take a seat next to her in the common room. I leaned over to her and told her that I had brought us snacks for the movie. With that gesture I wanted her to know that I appreciated her.

"Hey, I'm sorry I've been so on edge and cranky with you in the cell."

"Girl, don't worry about it."

"My mind has been preoccupied with the fact that I'm going in front of the parole board soon. I'm nervous. The hearing can go either way."

"I definitely hear that. No need to apologize but I would appreciate it if you braided my hair tonight."

I chuckled. "Got it. You and I have a hair appointment at 8:30." We both laughed.

"Yo, you have a ladybug crawling on you." I looked over to my arm that Jessica was staring at. I stood up to shake the ladybug from my sleeve.

Jessica screamed, "No."

"I really dislike bugs."

"No, leave it there and let it crawl on you. Ladybugs are good luck. They say that when one lands on you, you're supposed to count the number of black dots that they have. The dots symbolize the number of months that will pass before your wish comes true. Ladybugs also symbolize protection because their red shell protects them from predators. How many dots do you see?" "Five."

*   *   *

"It seems I had it all!" I said with my heart pounding, as I sat in front of the parole board. Two heavy-set men sat in front of me. I sat in a room in the administration building of the prison. It was the most important building on the campus. In this building was the control room, which held the cameras, constantly monitored by a few officers, as they looked over the entire prison. This building also held the mail room, the superintendent's office, and the offices of all the other upper heads. The room in which my parole hearing was being held looked like an interrogation room. This room resembled the interrogation rooms like the ones you would see on shows like, *CSI* or the *First 48*. There was a long white table in the middle of the room. There were two men sitting in front of me on the other side of the table. One white man, one black man, both middle-aged and heavy built. I had a manila envelope in front of me with all the awards and certification I had received during my incarceration. I wanted them to be convinced that I did deserve to go home. On the table was a stack of brown file folders. My guess was that they had many hearings scheduled for that day. I was nervous, not only because of the details related to my crime, but because the girl that was interviewed before me exited the room in tears. We were about two minutes into the hearing and, by the tone of their voices, this hearing wasn't going well.

January 27, 2014, the day that I had been looking forward to for the past five years. The parole hearing seemed to be going downhill quickly, very quickly. I wore my loosely-fitted state issued brown uniform. I felt my body heavy against the chair, palms sweating. The dark -skinned man began to speak again, "After reviewing your files, I have no intention of granting you parole. People like you really irritate me. You were in college, you seemed to have a wonderful family, and you threw that all away. There's people out there who would have risked their life for the opportunities that you had. I just don't understand."

I was risking my life. "Sir, please let me explain."

"I would rather parole a drug addict than someone like you."

"Sir, just because I wasn't a drug addict, does that mean I wasn't sick? I didn't choose to use drugs to mask my problems. Instead, I masked my problems with a smile. Pretending that everything was okay. I was in a downward spiral

of depression and suicidal thoughts. It seems I had it all. But, none of that had any meaning when I was fighting every day to find the will to get out of bed. I spent more time telling myself that my life was worth living than I spend trying to enjoy the opportunity of secondary education."

"Okay," he said as if he was annoyed and this interview room was the last place that he wanted to be. "Tell me about your crime."

"I am here for bank robbery. An old friend of mine and her boyfriend decided to rob a bank. She picked me up from my house that morning and she drove us to the bank. We circled the bank a couple of times trying to build the courage to go inside. Eventually, she pulled up in front of the bank. Her boyfriend and I were supposed to go inside. The plan was that she would be waiting outside for us in her car. When the car came to a full stop, I ran out of the car and towards the bank. I was a few steps from the bank door and I heard no commotion behind me. I turned around to notice that her boyfriend had not jumped out of the car with me."

"Hold on, hold on, hold on…. Cut the bullshit. If you want to have any chance of being paroled. Give me the raw truth; the entire story from beginning to end. No filter, and don't you dare leave out any details."

Suddenly, I felt a ray of hope. I sat straight up in my seat. I thought to myself, *this is my moment. It's either now or never. I've worked too hard to throw this moment away.*

Chapter Nineteen

"What's that noise?"

"They just shoved mail under the door." Jessica replied. "Can you please see what it is, I don't feel like climbing off this bunk. Plus, it's probably for you."

I watched as Jessica took about five steps to the cell door.

"It's not for me, it has your name on it. Here."

I grabbed a hold of the two envelopes that Jessica handed me; one sealed, one unsealed. I looked at the letter which was sealed. Mail that we received was never sealed because the mail room opened all incoming mail and inspected it before we would receive it. I opened the letter. I saw a Department of Corrections logo on the top of the letter. I began to read it.

"Jessica, this is my letter from the board of parole."

"Oh my God, read it out loud."

AS RECORDED ON MARCH 18, 2014, BOARD OF PROBATION AND PAROLE RENDERED THE FOLLOWING DECISION IN YOUR CASE. FOLLOWING AN INTERVIEW WITH YOU, AND A REVIEW OF YOUR FILE, AND HAVING CONSIDERED ALL TERRANCEERS REQUIRED PURSUANT TO THE BOARD OF PROBATION AND PAROLE, IN THE EXERCISE OF ITS DISCRETION, HAS DETERMINED AS THIS TIME THAT, YOU ARE GRANTED PAROLE ON OR AFTER MAY 2, 2014. THE REASONS FOR THE BOARDS DECISION INCLUDES THE FOLLOWING:

I dropped the letter on my bed and began to jump and cry tears of joy. I was going to be released after five years of my sentence. I was so overwhelmed with gratitude and happiness. The system did work in my favor. As cliché as its sounds, I felt rehabilitated and ready for whatever curve ball may have been thrown my way on the rest of my journey.

"Oh my God. I'm so happy for you."

As I hopped and jumped around the room, I began to babble away.

"Okay so this means that I have to send a form home to get my home plan approved. Then they're going to call me to take a release sample urine."

"Yep."

"And a release picture. I have to look really nice for this picture."

"Yep."

"And I have to ask Aunty Sidney to please bring me a release outfit."

"Yep."

"Actually, I don't want a release outfit. I will leave here in my brown gym pants and my brown t-shirt. Oh my God. Thank you, God. I have to make a plan A and plan B about my goal for the first six months. I have to make a bucket list."

"How do you think it's going to feel to sleep in your bed again and see your family?"

"It's gonna feel amazing. I'm probably going to still get up at six every morning, thinking that it's count time."

We both chuckled. I climbed back on my bunk, and began to read the mail from the opened envelope. It was a letter from Alton. He stated that he received the letter I sent him and was now hoping to be the father figure that I use to perceive him to be. This man continues to validate the fact that I think he is sick and delusional. Does he honestly think that in my eyes, he could go from being a pedophile, my abuser, back to the image of a father figure? I am forgiving, but I am no longer naïve, nor was I willing to allow him to affect my mood or good news.

I took out my letter pad, sat on the metal table and began to overlook the scenery that was visible from my window. From my window, I could see green grass, a tall wired fence, and a farm with two, sometimes three, cows that I often enjoyed viewing. The cow, patient and selfless, like myself, symbolized femininity, nurturing, and grounding. I never appreciated the beauty of a cow until I first sat at this window. I grounded myself in the moment, and began to write.

Dear Toya,

I am writing you a letter that I wish you could read. I don't know where life has taken you, but I hope that all is well on your end. I wish that our friendship wasn't compromised these past five years. I wish that things were different and we had not lost each other. I miss you and I often think of the good times that we shared. I have learned that it takes two strong individuals to make a decision that would compromise their friendship or their future. I hope that I will see you again someday.

My loved ones think that you betrayed me by leaving me at the bank that day. They think that you abandoned me, and they strongly dislike you. There is more to our story than they know, more than they've dared to ask. In their eyes you are the devil and I the follower, without notion of free will and common sense. But, we know better than that.

You knew that I was in a deep depression. I warned you that I was going to kill Alton if he tried to molest me once more, and I knew that him trying was only a matter of time. He was driving circles around my college campus almost weekly, making his presence known and reminding me of his dominance. Had I killed him, I would have gone to jail for a life sentence. You were the only one that knew about my suicidal plans. I didn't want to live anymore. The nightmares were keeping me up. I still get the nightmares but now they're not as bad.

I also contemplated running away, far away, without telling anyone, but I didn't feel that running away was enough to keep me safe. I would have lost contact with my family. They would have thought I was killed, while Alton would have found me. I couldn't live with myself knowing that I put my family through that pain.

On the day of the robbery, I was supposed to stand outside of the bank and await arrest, as we planned. Instead, I ran. During these years you may have wondered why--why I second guessed our decision. At that moment, I realized that you can't escape a prison by voluntarily going into another one. I ran because I wanted to be free, free of Alton, free from the abuse. Our plan worked. Do you know how the handcuffs felt on my skin? The coldness of the cuffs penetrated my soul and set me free. You can't run away from who you are or your pain, you can't ignore it, you can't hide from it. Until someone faces their pain, they remain a prisoner of themselves.

I thought that a jail sentence would be my answer but I never imagined paying such a price. I hoped that the sentence would keep me safe from Alton and still allow me to see my family--I was wrong. I lost people that I cared about, I became worthless in their eyes, and Alton still found ways to contact me. When I got to State prison, I got more than I had bargained for, yet, it helped me. Here, I learned to openly talk about abuse and I saw that I am not alone. For the first time, I did not feel lonely. I didn't know that there were others out there experiencing almost the same things I was. It was behind bars that I opened up to strangers and they believed me.

They helped me become who I am today, and I now like the person I am! Most importantly, I've learned to trust my gut feeling.

This letter is to let you know that I am safe and to thank you for following through with your half of the plan. No one else may ever understand but that is completely fine with me. I have escaped the prison in which I was livin, and now I will be released from this physical prison where I'm staying. If you saw me today, would you recognize the woman in me? Or would you see the child that I used to be? Would I recognize you? I've learned that life (?) is not a destination, it's a journey.

-ME

*   *   *

May of 2014
State Prison

I opened my eyes. I was alert and ready to start the day, as this would be my last day in the state prison. I laid on my bed, staring at the celling. I looked down at the bottom bunk and my cellie was still sound asleep, snoring loudly as usual. While my life was going to change today, hers would continue to be the same, punished by a system that was supposed to protect her, all for defending herself. I can't help but wonder how many other women around the world are suffering her fate, screaming their pain into ears of those who don't want to listen, and having invisible faces in a self-centered world. I don't want her to wake up yet--I want her to continue dreaming of a better place. I want to delay the pain of her realizing that today we forever part ways. I wish for a moment I had super powers to make her small enough to fit in my pocket and give her the freedom to see the beauty of the world, now through our reformed eyes.

The cell was dimly lit by the sun that was trying to rise. It was early morning and not yet count time. My body felt lighter, like I could grow wings and fly to Sky. It was my last morning following a predetermined routine; the sounding of the obnoxious bell ringing and then immediately the count time being announced. Yet, despite the euphoria of what was to come, I still felt an uncomfortable feeling, an uneasiness to move my limbs, like when I laid for the first time on the mattress that day in county jail. Except, that morning I was able to reflect on the last five years: they felt like an eternity to never end, yet those too passed. I have talked and dreamt about this day for all those years. I have cried endless tears hoping the arrival of this morning. Today, that time has come! I had seen many 'bunk and junks' and had often imagined what it would feel like when my name was called to do the same. The housing unit was silent and still, a state that I often didn't take the time to enjoy because I usually slept until the sound of the morning bell. But this morning, my body couldn't sleep anymore. I was preoccupied with thoughts and bursting with emotions. I felt proud, optimistic, and vulnerable, all at the same time.

I was proud of myself for making it through the five years. I was proud of myself for doing the time and not allowing the time to do me--a frequently used prison phrase. I was proud for being strong enough to want to go and face a world that will seek to define me, for the rest of my life, by these walls and these cold, iron bars. I am more than that--more than who they define me to be, want me to be! Today, I can truly say that I knew the meaning of those words. I didn't allow the time to further diminish me and my self-esteem or change me into someone I wasn't, nor wanted to be. I didn't lose my self within these walls--instead, I discovered it! The feeling was bittersweet, caused both by pain and suffering and stolen moments of happiness and peace. I was proud of myself for making the most of my resources. I was proud that I felt rehabilitated. Although the judicial system has their version of what rehabilitation is supposed to look like, I knew what it felt like for me. I was also proud of my loved ones. those who served the prison sentence alongside me.

I felt optimistic for the road that lay ahead, the next chapter. I felt optimistic about accomplishing all the things that I placed on my bucket list, all the things that I set out to do. I knew that when it came to making a life for myself, many of doors would close in my face. But, if I remembered to persevere and remain persistent, I knew that a door would finally open for me and someone would be willing to give me a chance, would want to hear my story and see my tears, and see a part of themselves in me. I felt optimistic for that moment, because I knew I was never going to be alone in the world--someone, somewhere, had been through a similar kind of hell. I had long prepared for this exact moment: I had rehearsed and studied interview skills and advocating for myself, day in and day out. I wanted to be ready for the obstacles that would be thrown my way. Also, I felt optimistic towards rebuilding relationships with my loved ones and strangers that could turn into close friends.

The idea of rebuilding relationships with my loved ones made me feel vulnerable. Although vulnerability wasn't a comfortable or pleasurable feeling, it was a feeling that I was willing to embrace since being away from my loved ones made me appreciate their presence so much more. I felt nervous and vulnerable to meet my parole officer as well. That would be another person that I would have to prove myself to. Would this person really have my best interest at heart? Would they be a source of support or shame? I knew that every time I went in for an interview, I would be asked about my criminal history. I was prepared to tell the truth about my conviction, but I anticipated that doing so would leave me feeling invisible, almost every time. When filing out applications, if I had to check a box that stated I had a felony, the eyes perusing the application would be prone to stereotyping me, even as they advertise being a company of equal employment opportunity.

The mattress under me felt harder than normal. Was this because I knew it was my last day laying on it? I wondered who would lay here next. I sat up on my bunk and observed that, within a matter of minutes, the sun had risen, shining light into the cell. The shelf that held my cosmetic and hygiene products was cleared. My toothbrush and toothpaste were on the top of my locker, for me to brush my teeth this morning. All of my family photos were removed from my locker. I looked over to the door at my grey chest and brown record box, which contained my important belongings, things that I would carry with me through the prison gates. I wore a brown t-shirt and old tattered brown shorts. I had minimal prison attire in my possession. I had given my belongings away to friends that still had time to serve. It was state prison regulation that all state issued uniforms had to be returned to the admissions office prior to leaving the prison. I had returned my uniforms last night, except one, which was saved for me to wear to the chow hall this morning. This final uniform would be retuned at the prison gate. When I handed the clothing over to the admissions officer, I knew that the label with my prison identification number would simply be removed and the clothing reissued to another inmate. I wondered who would wear them next. I wondered if our stories would be similar—beyond just sharing a pair of prison pants. It wasn't long of a wait until count time was announced. I climbed from my bunk and walked towards the door. My cellie awoke from her sleep to a half empty cell reminding her of truths that I did not dare to speak: that today would be the day of my release. I knew the feelings that my roommate was experiencing, for during my incarceration, I had witnessed many people leave.

After count time, I watched as my cellie signed up for a shower and phone time. I did not join her at the door for sign-ups. We waited for count to clear, which didn't seem to take much time because we were in conversation about the outcome she wished was granted in regard to her case appeal. We talked about staying in contact. She asked me to write her a letter explaining my first day of being home with my family. I tried to suppress my feelings of excitement. When our housing unit was called to the chow hall for breakfast, I exited the unit and went to the front of the line. This would be my last opportunity to see people with whom I had established various relationships. Some of these individuals I would never see again. The thought of that broke my heart in a million little pieces, never to be whole again, for each piece would remain inside those walls with the people that were with me through my nightmares and who believed in my dreams and hopes. It is possible to build lifelong relationships in jail, for we become all the same there, naked of prejudice and denied of our freedom, with just each other to derive strength from. At one crucial moment, one realizes that nothing is black and white and that good and evil exists in everyone, with different events triggering different emotions. As such, one learns to forgive and, with our human imperfection, one learns love. That is how life-long relationships are born.

I walked towards the chow hall observing all the different housing units that I was housed in throughout the five years. I thought of all the memories I had made and the lessons I promised myself not to forget. Many people remember that today would be my release date and all of those people made an effort to wish me farewell. It was a Wednesday morning and the breakfast that was served was the same as every Wednesday--scrambled eggs, toast, and grape jelly--my favorite. Breakfast was one of the things that I appreciated most about Wednesdays in the state prison. I had always liked eggs, even when I was at home. However, I didn't often make the time to prepare this meal for myself. This was something that I planned to change in the future.

After breakfast, I walked back to my housing and paced back and forth in my cell for about fifteen minutes. Not only did I pace the cell, but the fifteen minutes was also occupied by two bowl movements: diarrhea. Nine o'clock on the dot, my name was called. Aunty was right on time, just like she said she would be! It was great that I wasn't waiting for a long time because I felt overwhelmed with anxiety, joy, nervousness, and a bunch of other feelings that I was unable to put into words.

When my name was called, my heart sunk, almost rolling down to my stomach and I felt sudden tears rolling down my face. I choked up as I walked to the officer's office to confirm what I thought the call meant. "Yes Greene… Packed it up. Your escort is on the way to take you to the administration building." I walked back to my cell, which was about two doors away. I hugged my cellmate and looked around the cell. The image of the room would be embedded in my memory for the rest of my life. I assumed that others overheard that exchange of words between the officer and myself because that moment was proceeded by loud banging on the cell doors. I heard shouts and well wishes and farewells. This was their way of celebrating with me. I felt grateful. I felt loved and my time had arrived!

I picked up my grey bin and record box, which were extremely heavy, but I was so excited that the weight did not bother me. I guess it's probable that happiness could prompt someone into experiences of having superpowers. I exited the housing unit and recognized a female officer, who looked familiar, waiting for me. Although I didn't know her name, I was sure I had seen this officer before. We walked side by side towards the administration building. I imagined myself doing this walk several times before. Every time I watched someone leave, I would fantasize about my moment of release. It was like I had practiced this walk except, at this given moment, the walk felt like nothing I had rehearsed or experienced before.

I felt a sense of rebirth. I felt fresh and prepared for my brand-new start. In a few moments, I would be driving away from this place, a free woman, with my Aunty and Molly, never to come back again. I knew that I would ask Aunty Sidney to play my favorite C.D., a family favorite that Aunty Sidney used to play, almost every Saturday, as she cleaned the house. At this point I had left my state shoes behind and I was walking in my shower shoes. Walking the campus in shower shoes was forbidden, which was a painful rule for me since I loved sandals, and this was the closest thing to them. The fact that I was able to break this rule was another affirmation that I would be a free woman in a matter of minutes-- a pair of shower shoes had never felt that good!

The big, beautiful, American flag was swaying from the pole in the center of the campus. This image confirmed that we had arrived at the administration building. We walked up the front steps, into the building, and inside, where I was asked to sign the final documents. This part of the process was completed in less than five minutes, and the same officer then walked back through the same door. I stood at the top of the steps and looked straight ahead. Past the flag pole, I could see the big, powerful electric green gate that separated me from the outside world. Within a hundred feet and less than five minutes away, someone would be authorized to open that green gate for my release. I took a deep breath, I held my head high, and began to walk. It was my turn to move forward, but I could not help but look back. Everything in my surroundings had been the same for the last five years. Yet, since coming out of the walls of isolation, I was not the same. I had changed. I had grown!

As I walked towards my freedom, every step was paired by a question or thought. How would I react when I felt Aunty's embrace? Would I transition well back into society? Would I make boundaries and work towards always holding them? Would the people that didn't support me through the years want to embrace me? Would they smile at me and wish me all the best, now that I survived my worst without them? While in captivity, did you reach out to me? Did you open your hand to hold mine in yours and tell me that I was not alone, that everything was going to be OK? I watched as the green gate opened, sliding on it hinges and loudly screeching. At that moment Fluvanna Correctional had one fewer inmate. I could hear the green gate slamming behind my back. I had escaped abuse and prison. On May 14, 2014, that chapter of my life ended and I, the author this time, began to write a new one…

Reclaiming SMITH

Preface II

Dear Reader,

I am continuously living in gratitude for the support that has been graciously offered to me and my platform. *Diary of a Codependent* was initially published in October 2016, and during that book launch, I made a promise to the audience of my platform that I would reenroll in college to pursue a bachelor's degree in business with a concentration in non-profit management. I have made good on that promise and I am approximately one year away from completing the degree. Since we last spoke, I have endured many hardships and heartaches, and experienced what feels like a *growth spurt*.

My platform is invisible without your support and I am yearning to stay in conversation with you. With this release, my hope is to offer an update of the events that have transpired. Giselle Greene has been using her voice and today, she presents to you as me, the author, Kishana Smith, no longer depicted in character. The previous publication of this novel was captured through a fictional lens, based on a true story. This strategic planning was put forth to protect and uphold the confidentiality of many individuals, all of whom will remain in character. Giselle Greene has evolved and now presents as Kishana Smith; this edition is *Reclaiming Smith*, owning my platform, KSmithMission, offering my readers nonfiction content, grounded in honesty and vulnerability for growth. I truly hope that you enjoy!

– aTypeSmitty

Boston

"For what is hidden will eventually be brought into the open, and
every secret will be brought into light."
Mark 4:22

Yellow and white balloons lined the living room and the
entrance to the kitchen at Aunty Sidney's house. It was
evident that she and Molly had thoroughly prepared for
my return home. Aunty's house, *my home*, felt like a foreign place.
Aunty had celebrated me during my darkest times and, at that
very moment, it was with her and only a few other individuals that
I wanted to share this celebration. I had completed five long years
in Fluvanna and felt grounded in the fact that Aunty had never
forsaken me. I didn't care to see or talk to many individuals, and
absolutely shunned the thought of celebrating with anyone that
hadn't been present throughout those years. As strange as I felt, I
wanted to smile, show appreciation, and eat cake--so I did.

The first night was filled with gratitude, a feeling that I was
sure would remain for years to come. While walking in gratitude,
though, I was also met with the realization that many things
had changed, both within the house and in society. One of my
first tasks after having cake was to take a much-needed shower.
I wanted to wash Fluvanna off me. I wanted to scrub away the
agony and afflictions that I knew were embedded in the crevices
of my skin but no amount of soap and water would wash away the
lessons produced by the pain. These lessons would remain in my
gut and in my heart.

I went to the basement, where my clothes were being stored, and excitedly rummaged through my clothing, which once felt familiar. I giggled in exhilaration when I found items that I had forgotten. I came across a range of things, from bell bottoms and revealing dresses to apple-bottom jeans and tube tops, which no longer felt like *me*. From watching television upstate, I had grown aware that many of my clothing items were long outdated. Also, prior to my incarceration, I had used a T-Mobile Sidekick cell phone and a social platform called MySpace. Now, society had evolved to as smartphones and Facebook. My mind was resistant to the news of these changes, and I felt embarrassed to be out-of-date.

In Aunty's three-bedroom house, I would share a room with Molly, and I was elated by that arrangement. Molly's crude humor and stern demeanor would prove to be helpful during my transition. Within three days of my release, I had gathered the monies that had been gifted to me by Aunty as a jump-start to my reentry. I decided to use those monies to renew my state ID, for a valid form of identification. And without time to waste, I took myself and that ID to each store and place of business in the shopping center that was located about fifteen minutes from our house. As celebratory as the time felt, I did not want to celebrate for long. I resisted the thought of complacency and knew that I had to make good on the promises that I had made to myself. I couldn't afford to forget the dark times and knew that this was my time to shine and that proving myself to society would not be easy. I would have to hit the pavement, daily, and put in extra work to make my plans manifest.

My first weekend of freedom was enhanced by a surprise visit from Amalia, Damien, and my nephews. They had again sacrificed hours of commuting to visit me. Seeing their faces and embracing them, in my own driveway versus the strip room, was a feeling that I cannot quite put into words. I was reminded that I had the additional support that would be needed to face the challenges that would arise in the next few chapters. They were still rooting for me to succeed. That weekend, I had many monumental conversations. My brother hastily pushed for us to be alone and he asked thoughtful questions about my experiences. Amalia and I connected through conversations at a nearby park. As we spoke, I enjoyed the visual of children playing with one another and their parents, and a lacrosse team practicing in the distance. We reminisced about how the last half-decade tried to shake our foundation. Yet our friendship was sealed once more.

Life on the other side of the fence was refreshingly rewarding, with numerous opportunities for rebuilding connections with my family, enjoying life's daily pleasures, visiting places and people that felt familiar, and finding my place and purpose within my community. Well, the aspect of community, to be completely honest, wasn't quite refreshing, it was extremely difficult. I met my parole officer and was given my instructions for compliance with parole and how much I would owe the state each month. Most of the current terminology and popular aspects of interest felt daunting to me and it was helpful that I no longer felt the need to be accepted or validated by others.

Molly, thankfully, accompanied me to the courthouse because I needed to take action towards a restraining order against Alton, and I felt relieved by her presence and the fact that I was freely able to express my fears to her. Once inside the courtroom, I was directed to a Victim Witness Advocate, who gave me the paperwork needed to apply for the restraining order. My hands trembled in fear as I recollected the intimate details of what Alton had done to me. Within a page and a half of writing space to explain the events, I tried to condense thirteen years of abuse into the affidavit. I would have to prove to a judge, who would know very little about me, that I was fearful of Alton and why having a restraining order against him was necessary to my safety. In a courtroom filled with strangers and unpleasant memories of authority figures, I would be given approximately ten minutes to describe this fear. With each step towards the judge, my feet felt heavy as cement blocks, weighing me down and demanding additional energy. My voice was reclaimed, and ready to speak my truth. After what felt like five minutes into my dialogue with the judge, I was interrupted and granted a temporary restraining order and told that I would need to return in ten business days for a hearing that Alton would possibly attend.

Exactly a week after my release, I interviewed for a cook position at the neighborhood Applebee's. I wore a white button-down shirt and a navy-blue pencil skirt along with a navy-blue blazer. I presented the way I had been taught by the job-skill programs at Fluvanna. I entered the restaurant in prayer and actively fought against my feelings self-loathing. When asked the dreaded question of whether I had a felony/criminal record, I answered yes and smiled. I wanted to illustrate that I wasn't afraid to tell the truth and as shameful as my situation could be, I was not existing in shame. I engaged with the interviewer in the way I was taught: offer the harsh truth and then conclude with what I had learned or how I had evolved. At the end of a thirty-minute interview, she offered me the job!

For the next sixth months, I walked to and from work and the varying weather conditions did not feel bothersome. Aunty and Molly offered rides when their schedules allowed. As a line cook at Applebee's, I worked for ten dollars an hour. Many individuals complained, respectfully so, that the pay was not considered a reasonable living wage. As they spoke, I was often reminded of the forty-three cents a day that I earned while on the HVAC crew at Fluvanna and knew that with ten dollars an hour I would work to regain my stability. I worked long-hour days, picking up extra shifts whenever possible, and thoroughly enjoyed opening and closing shifts because I knew that although the restaurant closed at 1 a.m., the tasks that needed to be completed to close for the day could take hours, and I craved any additional hour.

I was determined to not walk to work for long. Therefore, I saved eighty percent of my paychecks to go towards a vehicle. On days that I didn't work, which were few, I enjoyed activities like the movies and the nearby amusement park. I loved the thrill of a roller-coaster slowly driving up to its peak, my heartbeat racing and feet dangling. Once it was at its highest point, internally I would scold myself against ever partaking in such an activity again. Then the unexpected drop would remind me of why I loved the risk. I also spent heaps of time at the pool and at the mall, where I would observe the ways in which individuals interacted with one another. When home, I watched Netflix and became introduced to the popular series *Orange Is the New Black,* where I was entertained by Piper and Uzo, and inspired by Laverne and her openness about her truth. I must admit that the plot and scenery did offer true parallels with, and interpretations of, the prison system. But if we had tried to overtake Fluvanna, the way they did at their facility, many more inmates would have been killed.

My mom called regularly, and my dad called once. I had purchased a calling card and attempted, many times, to call him. Each try was unsuccessfully met by the realization that I did not have an accurate and working number for him and my heart sank deeper with each attempt. Today was different, though, he called me. When I answered the house phone and recognized his voice, my heart danced, and I felt the same joy that would come over me as a child when I would receive his yearly calls. I was eager to tell him how much I missed him. I wanted to know how he was doing and to share with him how things had been with me. I hoped that we would laugh and have loads to talk about, since it had been years since we last spoke. Against my hopes, though, he didn't ask about me or express any pleasure at being on the call. Without being asked, I shared that I was working as a cook and hoping to purchase a car. He asked me how much money I had saved and shared that he would be hoping for some help towards buying a new motorcycle. He asked for three thousand dollars, to be exact. The contents of that call clouded my world for days like heavy clouds in the sky, waiting to release their rainfall. My drive, fueled by my anger, led me to finance a Chrysler 200 one month later.

My short-term goals had been accomplished and I was ready to move into my longer-term goals and my bucket list. The next two items on each list: publish the diary that I had held sacred for years, and attend a reggae concert. During these months, I was beginning to create new connections. At Applebee's, I connected with another line cook, Veronica, a hardworking student from Mexico, who offered me training, great conversations, and soon a fulfilling friendship. Veronica was a few years older than me and appreciated many of the leisure activities that I enjoyed.

One day, I received a call from a childhood friend named Jade. She and I reminisced about our days together in middle school and the years we spent apart. She shared with me the thoughts that she experienced when she heard the news of my incarceration. She stated that she wrote many letters to me but never had the courage to mail them, out of fear that she would say the wrong things. Jade shared the letters with me that day and the duration of our call was approximately four hours.

Working at Applebee's felt like a great jump-start, but I knew that the wage would not allow me the amount of funds needed to put my plans in motion, so I began submitting applications at several supermarkets, movies theaters, HVAC companies, and clothing stores. Each application was either ignored or met with rejection. One supermarket stated that they were specifically looking for individuals to work as cashiers and that they couldn't hire me for that position because it handled money and I held a criminal record of bank robbery. I smiled at the white lady who delivered this news. She was not hurting me--she was actually doing me a favor. I trusted that the job wasn't offered to me because there was a better plan in store for me.

Over the next few months, I enjoyed long conversations with Jade. She made several trips to Virginia and clearly expressed her interest in me. Molly and I were also growing closer. I wasn't sure, though, if this closeness was a result of our personalities meshing or the fact that I brought home food from Applebee's at the end of every shift. I often smiled when I thought of how vulgar she was and how we frequently joked that maybe "shaking it" on the pole for some extra cash didn't sound too bad.

Privately, I searched for publishing companies and jobs specific to the domestic-violence field. Surprisingly, I found that the region only had one domestic-violence shelter, which was underused. In many small towns, like where we lived, acknowledging domestic violence was quite taboo, and many people hid these experiences under their rugs and packed them away in boxes that wouldn't be opened for years. I feel confident that abuse was happening in our town. But no one dared to speak about it.

I drew the conclusion that Virginia wasn't for me and dreaded what that meant for the dynamic between Aunty, Molly, and me. I knew that they would be heartbroken by news of my leaving, especially given the fact that I had only been home for a bit over six months.

The conversation with Aunty and Molly was as painful as I envisioned it would be, filled with many tears, anger, and confusion. My body quivered at the thought of hurting them. I knew that hurting them wasn't a part of my intention but this was a calculated risk that I felt confident in making. I wanted and needed to see all that the world had to offer. I wanted and needed to give the world all that I had.

My last day at Applebee's included a farewell party that was planned by Veronica. We didn't get to enjoy much of what she assembled I had long grown accustomed to goodbyes. That day in particular at Applebee's was extremely busy. As soon as we opened at 11, there was an immediate rush. I never truly understood how that worked: *How was it possible that twenty to thirty people could enter the restaurant within minutes of its doors opening? Where did they all come from? What were the odds?*

"Fifty opened, crew! Fifty opened," the shift supervisor came back to the kitchen and yelled.

I appreciated the orderliness that occurred at this specific Applebee's. At least one supervisor was always present and visible in the dining area of the restaurant. Amongst the array of responsibilities that entailed, they often took estimates of how many customers were in the restaurant. *Fifty opened,* was their way of letting us know the current number of menus that were visibly opened, which helped us to prepare our estimates of how many popular items to start cooking, visually survey our cooking areas for additional items needed, and to call for additional help if individuals were on smoke breaks or other duties.

"Seventy opened, crew. Seventy opened!"

Business was booming at Applebee's. The grills were fired up, and Veronica increased the volume on her portable speaker. Romeo Santos' "Odio," featuring Drake, flooded the kitchen--she and I were ready to rock it. *They didn't exaggerate when they said we were signing up for fast-paced work.* But Veronica and I worked the shift by our rules and I certainly knew that I was going to miss her.

It was a Monday morning when I hugged my Aunty and Molly farewell. I had packed my car the night before and all my belongings filled the trunk and the front and back seats of the car. The activity of packing my car the night before had been done within two hours. I didn't own many belongings and therefore didn't have much to pack. I would move to Boston in one trip.

That Monday morning, I watched Aunty prepare for work, the way I usually did when I was home. We talked, joked, and ate breakfast together. I told her of my fears associated with moving. I explained to her that I might have appeared guarded, stubborn, or ready to move away, but these were my coping mechanisms to keep me from breaking down. The truth was, I was missing them already and my stomach was nauseous at the thought of moving, yet again, to another unfamiliar place where I would be forced to start over. Additionally, I was furious at the courts for sending me, by mail, information stating that they were unable to locate Alton and therefore they had not served him the restraining order. I was walking around for months thinking that a restraining order was in place to protect me when, in actuality, the courts had failed me again. Luckily, I had depended on my faith in my higher power to be my primary source of protection. There was *work* to be done and I was heading to Boston to take my place in the movement.

"I am going to miss you," Aunty Sidney said softly as she embraced me. "I know that you are going to do great in Boston-- you are more than able. As hard as it is for me to watch you go, it's time for you to truly spread your wings. Go ahead and fly."

Damien graciously opened his doors to me. My new presence in South Boston felt purposeful. I had a great view of the beach, parks, the highway, and a long-distance view of the skyscrapers located in the downtown area of the city. Jade was also present to greet me and helped to unload my car of my belongings. Damien gave me a house key and parking instructions for the area, and outlined the days designated for street-cleaning.

Jade explained the things located in the vicinity and the societal norms of the area. She reminded me that I would now have to operate under a greater level of awareness, and that it was no longer safe for me to leave my car doors open or forget my cell phone on the car mount or my purse on the front seat. We laughed at my free-hearted spirit that Virginia nurtured. Then she gifted me with a huge box, wrapped in shiny purple wrapping paper. Inside the box was another box, wrapped in shiny gold wrapping paper. I smiled and giggled in enthusiasm as I opened the second box and found two tickets: *Reggae in the Park*.

I stood in pride as we sang Jamaica's national anthem to open the concert. I swayed my green-black-and-gold flag to the tempo of the song. Soon, Beres Hammond would enter the stage in Boston's Franklin Park Zoo. Jade explained to me that the city would often clear the animals from the zoo to rent the space for major concerts. The park was transformed to an atmosphere consisting of a distinct Caribbean vibe. I spotted the flags of at least six different countries. I could smell jerk chicken on the grill. I also saw that some folks were consuming ackee and saltfish, patties, and chicken soup and I was reminded of my younger days spent in Jamaica. I was attending my first reggae concert in the US and knew that I didn't want it to be my last. I enjoyed my time with Jade and was thankful for the gift.

The Monday after the concert marked one week since my arrival to Boston. I had submitted several job applications. In the interim, though, I had begun driving for Uber. I felt thankful to the millennials for demanding and implementing systems of smarter transportation. I reasoned with myself that driving for Uber would allow me to gain income while also relearning the city that I'd once known. Ultimately, though, there were many small defeats. On my second day of the job, I picked up a group of college students and when the ride was over, I checked my car to find that someone had stuck chewed gum on the seat of my brand-new car. I was angry and frustrated that the gum did not completely come out of the seat's surface.

Surprisingly, that day, I received a phone call from a publishing company. The person shared that they had received my email and heard my voice messages about wanting a consultation. She shared excitement about my project and stated that I should send them an excerpt of my manuscript. This news trumped the earlier defeat of that day.

They say that when it rains, it pours and the rainwater was on a constant downpour and flooding in my life. The next month was consumed with me accepting three part-time jobs and signing a contract to publish my book. In the meantime, news traveled quickly to Jamaica that I had been dating a female. My dad called me on a Friday evening to confirm the news. He made it very clear that the confirmation was the only reason he had called. This call would be the first one since our conversation one year prior, when he asked his felony-possessing twenty-four-year-old daughter, who had been six months' shy of being a newly released convict, for three thousand dollars. During this conversation, once he received his confirmation, he responded.

"You are a disgrace to my last name, and you should fall off the face of the earth," he said.

I was overtaken by shock. Once again, my father would abandon me, and this time it wouldn't be a mysterious disappearance. He was telling me that he wanted me dead because he couldn't accept that he had fathered someone that was now identifying as something other than what he wanted. I couldn't respond to him in that moment. I went numb.

The three jobs were a perfect distraction for the pain that I was unable to put into words. Within a few months, my first book would be published, *Diary of a Codependent*, and I would not allow anything or anyone to disrupt my focused vision. Each morning, I awoke in gratitude and in fury with bones had become adapted to holding the nuances of both. My days were long, as I woke up at 5 each morning and turned in to bed at about 1 or 2 a.m. each night. I worked long hours and edited many chapters, while also beginning to network with others within the field. I called Aunty every two days and hung out with Jade whenever it was possible. Jade demonstrated huge amounts of patience.

Amalia and Damien continuously proved to be great supports. I had built a team and stood firm in the support that was offered to me. Living with my brother and nephews felt rewarding and strange. My nephews still hadn't known me very well, nor had I known them. Miraculously, living with them and working led me to earn and save approximately fifteen thousand dollars. My book deal was paid in full, I had rented a venue, purchased intrigue details for the day, and I was ready to launch my first book.

Aunty and Molly were seated in the audience on my big day. My team had assembled the event, just the way we planned. Jade was located at the front of my stage to manage my PowerPoint, and Amalia and Veronica were behind stage, with me, where we prepped and prayed. I then entered the stage. I walked to the middle of the stage. My body knew that I was physically there, but my brain had not fully registered the thought that it was the day of my book launch--the two were still disconnected.

My books had arrived two days prior to the launch event. I knew that many individuals were traveling from afar to support me and I was overwhelmed by the fact that I'd opened the book and found that there were still many corrections to be made. Veronica and I had spent hours the night before trying to figure out how I would handle the fact that I was not pleased with the product. But the launch happened because it had to. And I smiled throughout the day because I was in awe of the support.

The minutes, hours, and days after the book launch were bleak. I was overcome by what many would call a *vulnerability hangover.* I withdrew into my shell and lamented over all that had transpired. There was the realization that I had shared my deepest and darkest moments with my audience and I felt raw and exposed. These feelings lasted for months, which progressed into two years of my own personal deep depression. Depression drifts through our community. Depression is real. The truth is, I may have self-medicated more frequently than I am happy to admit. What was supposed to be a huge accomplishment and a celebratory moment, I experienced as a traumatic event.

Dear Diary,

Perfectionism has had a hold on me. It has been weighting my shoulders like fresh animal skin on sticks, shifting from shoulder to shoulder. Perfectionism has stolen many things from me. This weight bears heavy and my sad days are loud...loud, like my screaming thoughts. I am traumatized. There are typos in the book; --I should have paid more attention to detail. I should have promoted my platform more effectively. These thoughts, they scream. I worked three jobs and slept approximately two hours a night while editing and barely eating and I should feel proud that I am watching my dreams come true. I am fueling my orders, my purpose. The people who showed up came because they wanted to support me. They bore witness to my story, as we honored and celebrated Domestic Violence

Awareness Month. We acknowledged that the voices of many survivors have been in hiding, in mourning.

Perfectionism has had a grip on me for twenty-eight years. Perfectionism has heightened my anxieties towards social media. I haven't even opened the event album or willingly promoted or distributed any books since the launch event.

Since the launch of *Diary of a Codependent*, I've received some pushback on my term of codependency and its use.

The term codependency was first introduced to the movement as a product of research and study specific to interpersonal relationships in families of alcoholics. Codependency was used as a clinical term, narrowly defined as a relationship in which one person physically or psychologically enabled the behaviors of the other person who struggled with substance misuse. The person not addicted to a substance would often be controlled by the addicted person's behaviors. Codependency often emerged from typical behaviors like being compassionate, trying to be helpful, or offering a variety of support. But when these behaviors become extremes and engage in enabling behaviors, it's said that the person is then promoting the sickness, in both themselves and the addicted person.

Throughout the years, as the term gained popularity it still encompassed behaviors associated with substance misuse, but expanded to include people in relationships with chronically or mentally ill individuals, and the fact that codependency could form within a person from a dysfunctional family dynamic. For a wide range of reasons, this expansion caused great controversy within the movement.

When this term began to float through the domestic-violence field, individuals felt concerned that the term was being misused. Domestic violence is rooted in a pattern of actions where one person tries to gain and maintain power and control over another, a pattern that occurs without the presence of consent. Codependency, however, is rooted in enablement. Many feared that survivors of domestic violence may misinterpret the two terms and incorrectly place blame on themselves for aspects of the abuse they endured.

Nonetheless, the most common theme of codependency is the fact that it's a learned behavior, formed from an unhealthy dynamic, resulting in extreme excessive reliance on other people for approval and a sense of identity.

I love my family and they've always done their best with what they personally knew and what was available. But what they *knew* wasn't always correct, and *much* wasn't always available. Therefore, I must be forthright in saying that my primary days were in fact dysfunctional and I am a product of a dysfunctional family dynamic, as many of us are. At a very young age, I learned to please, overcompensate, and tiptoe. I had learned codependency and was living in its ideals years before Alton violated me. Codependency and the sexual abuse I endured are separate. They were manifesting as parallels. Importantly, I was not abused because I am codependent, and I was not codependent because of the abuse.

When I was able to put a label to my learned behaviors, I held less confusion about myself and felt empowered with the knowledge of explanation. Once I acquired this information, like having the label of a diagnosis, I felt equipped to work towards change.

I claim the label of Codependency, and I claim its effects, one of which has been perfectionism. It is with the claiming of these terms that I am standing in understanding and feeling empowered to continue through this journey of healing. I uphold the term's history and the knowledge of those that existed in the field before me. But I know what the term means to me and I will remain unapologetic in my use of it. Swimming in this gigantic lake of depression, I've often felt defeated by the criticism of others, and perfectionism has wanted me to change my book's title and content. However, I am accepting the controversy, which has fed my drive in *Reclaiming SMITH*.

– a TypeSmitty

Good, Better, Best

"It is up to each of us to set the priorities and to do the things that
make our soil good and our harvest plentiful."
Dallin H. Oaks

Dear Diary,

I've been learning to seek counsel before making huge
decisions. Although this road to self-discovery has had
many bumps and unexpected turns, I am enjoying the
journey and this newly evolved person that I am meeting, a
greater maturity within myself, which I truly like. I have been
in hiding, breaking down and rebuilding. This part of me that
I am meeting, I like them. On this beautiful spring day, I am
reclaiming my thoughts. I am pouring into this platform. This
work is my *Honesty*, which I am giving back to society. *Would
this mean I'm rehabilitated?* But I've also been filling this
huge void with things unpleasing. Today, I'm not ashamed to
admit that.

Each day, I'm continuing to learn how to use my voice.
Learning how to speak up but remembering to stop and
reflect to stay humble. *Does that explain why I'm usually
more silent and soft-spoken, and slow to give my opinion?*
Although my opinion is usually screaming in my mind,
analyzing, strategizing, empathizing, grounded in my
disciplined background. My input screams in my head,

deafening! But I'm slow to speak. I anticipate you have experienced this silence that is loud.

I am thankful for the ability to write, to place my pen to this paper, at this ordained and carefully planned moment. Wow, this person that is in blossom, she's sassy. I've grown a special kind of love for my hands. My hands are usually in great amounts of pain. Yet my hands bring me such joy--they are my service, and they feed my art, my contribution. The hands are a reminder of suffering. I am learning to appreciate the NOW as I wait for the best, which is yet to come.

— a Type Smitty

Throughout this journey and the chapters of my life, I have walked in faith, many times, imperfect. I have internally recited quotations of the wise, principles and teachings of prophets, which have offered me inspiration and hope. Faith and positive self-talk, for me, have been amongst the main ingredients resulting in many victories. At times when I have faced defeats, which have been many, I have been able to restore my energy through the ideology of "Good, Better, Best."

They say that if one teaches their children how to live, the child will remember those teachings all through life. I have felt this statement in practice within my own life. It was many years ago that I heard the phrase "God, Better, Best." Frequently, my family uttered this saying, and somewhere along my path, this ideology has become a part of me and has offered a helpful perspective within difficult situations.

At Fluvanna, I encountered several situations that I labeled as unfair, unfavorable, and discouraging. During the first two years of incarceration, I wallowed in thoughts of negativity, blame, self-loathing, and hatred. In preparation for my graduation and entry into the general population, I knew that I needed to make a mental shift. Internally, I knew that the self-destructive thinking that I had been experiencing would have kept me in a downward spiral and my time in captivity would have been in vain. Because of the shift in my thinking, many things took a positive change for me. It was during my incarceration that I located this phrase, "Good, Better, Best," within my being and I've operated whole-heartedly by its meaning ever since.

I've long lived by the phrase, which was shared with me during my youth. It has felt vital to make an internal note that, once I had access to accurate resources, I would explore the ownership of the term and seek the author's intended meaning. My search led to the originator of the phrase, Dallin H. Oaks, who spoke these words from a religious lens. His intention states that not all acts are good ones and an individual should continuously strive to do better, and better will then develop into its best.

Placing this ideology into perspective for my own life, I have unintentionally stumbled, experienced defea,t and loss. Yet I have been able to, intentionally, regain my balance and experience people, places, and things that have felt better than what I had before falling. Through my own perspective of not only *acts* but an inclusion of labor, positive thinking, and anticipation of results, I have been able to appreciate the present while waiting for the future, and the best is yet to come.

When I was temporarily residing at Fluvanna and confined to a six-by-eight cell, the words of Officer Cedrick echoed in my mind. He firmly believed that if an inmate could not properly care for such a small-dimensioned cell, how would that person properly care for and maintain a bigger space? This echo led me to clean and care for my cell by means of sticking sanitary napkins to the palm of my hands to sweep and mop the cell floor, a technique used by many inmates. I made my bed and wiped the metal desk, daily. My *cellie* and I would rotate the task of cleaning our toilet. As temporary as the situation was, I considered my cell to be a safe haven, my own personal space within a facility where I had control over very little. I took pride in having a clean space, which soon contributed to my mental health. This space was *good*, for the time being.

Working on the HVAC crew was challenging. I was the only "feminine-identified" individual on the crew and was treated as such. I was never the first, second, or even third pick when it came to being selected for a difficult task. The crew was led by a kind and knowledgeable HVAC technician who had been in the field for years. We were placed on specific crews based on our personal interests and the crew's availability for new workers. I was eager to learn the fundamentals of HVAC and acquire hands-on training. But the leading technician often uttered or mumbled confusing snippets of directions and I often felt that he forgot we were apprentices, working and striving to learn for forty-three cents a day. I appreciated even the dysfunctions of this experience because I knew that good would come.

At Applebee's, I cooked on a fast-paced line and learned a wide range of recipes, food-safety information, and plate displays. I learned how to open and close a restaurant and sometimes floated to help the dishwasher. My clothes were often smothered in food, grease, and dirty water. One Friday, during the dinner rush, we had to rapidly make an order of potatoes. I reached into the microwave to remove the container of cooked and bubbling potatoes. Accidently, another cook bumped into me and the steaming-hot water emptied, scorching my entire left shoulder. Veronica ran over to console me. The burn, about the size of a golf ball, immediately removed my top layer of skin. Aunty Sidney was not happy to hear this news or pleased to witness me endure an extremely painful healing process. The opportunities that sprang from my employment at Applebee's were *good* but I knew that I wanted something more. My energies felt *better* suited towards areas in which I possessed great passion and purpose.

The *better* that I had envisioned was waiting for me in Boston. Within a year of taking the risk to relocate, I secured a job caretaking for an amazing individual, which also enabled me with the time and opportunity to volunteer at a domestic-violence organization.

In Fluvanna, I bounced from one six-by-eight to another, whenever the prison saw fit, and I had very little say in when and where I was being relocated. I knew that wasn't my home but rather my temporary place of residency. When released from Fluvanna, I happily shared a room with Molly in Aunty Sidney's house. I was overjoyed by the opportunity to share this closeness with Molly. Moving to Boston included the arrangement of sharing space with my brother and four nephews, which wasn't always a comfortable situation. This, however, was better than Fluvanna and I knew that although this wasn't the most ideal situation, I was being trusted to care for the space I did share with them. I lived in pride of the small space, because whether temporary or not, it was still my current space. Each day, I reminded myself to actively shun the thought of complacency. Two months after the book launch, I knew that I was ready for the next step. I would strive for the next step to be a bit *better* than my current one.

Amalia, Jade, and I decided that we would rent a house and split the cost among us. I was excited for what this chapter would read. We found a house in Quincy, a small and historical city located about twenty minutes south of Boston. This new house would be our home for the next two years. The neighborhood was quiet and reminded me of Virginia. Aunty and Molly visited plenty and I felt blessed that all three of our families continued to mesh. The unity of the house symbolized, to me, the coming together of three young professionals, grounded in faith, love, and support. We continually rooted for one another and I adored the fact that they too shunned complacency.

One day, I proceeded to exit the house for my drive in to work. The landlord was seated on the front lawn chair and said to me, "Amalia?"

I responded, "Nope, I'm not Amalia. I am Kishana." I was surprised by her confusion because she and I had interacted many times before.

"Oh, I'm looking for Amalia, not you," she said. But what was even more shocking was the action that accompanied her words. She lifted her left hand and shooed me, as if to nonverbally tell me that she was done talking and that my time of communicating with her had expired.

In that moment, it was the love of God that ordered my steps to my car. I felt completely dismissed and belittled by the interaction. And the fact that she was a white lady and I was who I am didn't make things any more bearable.

Dear Diary,

Today the landlord called Amalia and shared with her that she needed my name removed from the mailbox because she didn't know that I was a resident of the home. We were all shocked by this news because all three of us were on the lease. We then learned that because the lease was being managed by the broker, the landlord had never thoroughly reviewed it. And now I was having to pay for her lack of attention to detail.

The landlord and I had interacted many times before but the landlord explained that she thought that Amalia and I were the same person. Amalia did, in fact, remove my name from the mailbox. Ignorance prevailed that day.

I can understand that Amalia was trying to appease the landlord in the interim of us all figuring this out. However, returning home and seeing that my name was removed from the mailbox was traumatic.

Traumatized from fear of displacement, while also being ridiculed by a white woman, I began to pack! My mind and body quickly reverted to survival mode. This was the first time that I had recognized this pattern of behavior, or made this kind of connection--my trauma was manifesting in ways that felt familiar, yet foreign. The pattern of having to move was taking its mental toll on me. In my past I'd been told at least twenty times, "Smith, pack it up; bunk and junk." The prison system labeled my property as junk, a sense of ridicule back then, as well. But my possessions were valuable and meaningful. And so, I learned to live with my belongings organized, in preparation of hearing this news, at any given random and sporadic moment. With no hesitation, I packed my things.

The pain in my hands was progressively getting worse, hurting more frequently and escalating in levels of pain. I had gone to several doctors and paid heaping amounts of co-pays in an effort to have a proper diagnosis. After seven years of fighting this battle of what was beginning to feel like an invisible disability, I had reached no solution.

I prayed long and hard when I was preparing for my pen-to-this-paper process. I began to write small. I then began to realize that there was nothing small about what I was thinking and therefore nothing small about what I was writing.

Then, I didn't feel that my "now" was small. The "now" was important; it was big, it was huge. Then, the "now" was in preparation for the "next," the bigger, the best. Each phase, each chapter, and each piece were important parts to the puzzle.

I opened my email and found a special invitation to participate in the upcoming series of TED talks: *Stories That Inspire*. I realized that this invitation was perfectly timed because I was unapologetically enjoying the big, while waiting for bigger. *Good, better, best* replayed in my heart, as I *Reclaimed SMITH*.

– aTypeSmitty

Sigma Kappa Psi

"Watch me grow!"
Emrika Smalls

She sat contently on a thin mahogany branch and her aura demanded my attention. My eyes were drawn to her and intrigued by her stunning powdered-pink feathers, which seemed delicately assembled in a fan-like pattern, each circular layer neatly in coordination. Her feathers appeared smooth and soft like velvet. What seemed like her birthmark or orange spot was gorgeously placed behind her head and slightly behind her right ear. This vibrant spot reminded me of liberation and grace. I felt struck by her beauty and continued to observe the intricate white details against her gray-colored claws. She was a rare and unique creation of God. It was evident that she was beautifully and fearfully made.

Absent thought and hesitation, I gently reached out my hands to touch her feathers. She quickly and precisely jumped away, communicating to me that my touch was unwanted and unwelcome. Her reaction made it clear that I had decided without having consent; I was wrong for doing so.

The legal caretaker of Sassy began to share a few special details regarding Sassy's background. He stated that she was originally from Puerto Rico and that she was a recovering alcoholic. He went on to explain that Sassy's prior caregiver was an alcoholic and often gave alcoholic beverages to Sassy. He stated that Sassy's recovery was difficult. But she was now well. I experienced Sassy's demeanor as reserved yet stern. She embraced and wore her confidence. I stepped back to admire her guardedness and her wings, which grew long past the torso of her body. I thought of her ability to spread her strong wings and soar towards the sky. She knew obstacles and adversity. Yet she had overcome. She had owned her truth; her name is Sassy.

The beginning of a new year, for many, symbolized a fresh start. Veronica once shared with me that she aimed to plan trips and vacations for the beginning months of the calendar year because she had observed that, in her experience of doing so, she was able to start the year in either self-care or adventure. This year, we planned our vacation from this perspective. It was January, the start of my twenty-eighth year, and I was in Miami Beach with Jade, Amalia and Damien, and Jade's best friend, Chasity. I was in awe of meeting Sassy, spending time with my loved ones, and working through the strategic planning process for my platform.

I tried several water sports, for the first time. The banana boat was my favorite. The person who operated the boat drove us about four miles offshore and began to accelerate quickly, then pause, and continue this pattern throughout the ride. At one point, the driver sped up and then took a very sharp right turn. Chasity and I went flying off the side of the yellow blow-up banana boat and into the open sea. With my head and mouth covered in salt water, I realized that my left hand was still holding on to the side of the boat. I'm not sure where the muscle strength or energy came from, but I swung my right arm over to grasp hold of the edge, having both hands to support my weight. As I held on, I could feel the waves of the sea slapping against my body. The resistance was becoming unbearable and I could hear Jade and Amalia screaming to the driver that he needed to stop. Damien reached over the side of the boat and was able to grab me back on board. Relieved to be back on board safely, I turned to look into the rugged sea that

I had just exited to realize that the bottom half of my swimsuit was lost at sea. The boat then turned in the opposite direction. We were speeding towards bringing Chasity back on board.

Upon returning from Miami, I joked that I had had enough fun to last for the duration of the year. I was ready to get back to work; I would return to my work and platform, anchoring myself in discipline. Partially into the month of March, I was growing fatigued by the random obstacles that were heavily being sprinkled along my path. Deep anger was growing in me at the fact that my father had said such awful things about me. His actions were screaming volumes and, whether he meant the words that were spoken, his actions completely supported the fact that he did not like me, and he absolutely did not love me. He was never truly present in my life and I could count on one hand the small snippets of times that we had seen each other. The instances in which he had proclaimed love for me I could count on the leftover fingers of that same hand. I found myself yearning for him and wanting a relationship. And that, I knew, deep down, would not happen. Burdened and hurt by these thoughts, I continued to navigate my daily responsibilities, wishing that each day didn't require so much energy to get out of bed and face the world.

Dear Diary,

Kishana Bianca Smith, a name that has felt joy, pain, and adversity--a name that I love. Gregory, today, I officially mourn the loss of my relationship with you. Documented. Sometimes I wish that I could erase you from my memory, so it wouldn't hurt so badly. But every time I take a picture, I see you. I can't seem to escape you. I AM SMITH. My oval and slender yet chunky face looks like yours, when I smile and even when I frown. This pain lingers like a summer mist.

But none of it smells good. I don't know why I still await you. I'm ignoring the messages of things that have been clear from the beginning. When I exited the womb, screaming and crying, you were not present. Those tears that I cried that gave the doctors a brief confirmation that my vitals were functioning, also served as a foreshadowing of what was to come.

Dad, did you eat today? Do you have enough money for your cigarettes? I know you're not going to put them down. I don't know why I asked because I would like to think that I don't really care. They say history repeats itself-- *thanks*. If that's the whole truth, I guess I'm doomed.

You've said you don't want me to have this name. Yet, I question myself, *what have you done with the name?*

Gregory, how dare you not want me to have your name? SMITH: Slavery, Hardship, History, Tribulation, and Growth.

Dad, wow! The young girl within me still calls you Dad. The enraged me reminds her that you won't answer. Right now, my platform is experiencing pain and is in need of release, Truth and Vulnerability for Growth. I am Rebelling. I am Reclaiming SMITH.

Gregory, I mourn the loss of my relationship with you. Documented. This name SMITH, are you sure you don't want me to have it? I'm calling you to this window because I wish I could tell you all my aspirations. Gregory, I really don't like you. Dad, I really love you. You gave life to SMITH. Sassy is holding both--both are true.

My pen trembles in the fear of breaking free. My heart that sings aches. My SMITH is growing. I love my SMITH--it was given to me and I won't so freely give it back. Not only am I keeping the name, but I'm planning to get a bit creative with it.

When I was incarcerated, Officer Cedrick called me *Smitty* for short. Given the fact that inmates weren't usually given nicknames, especially from COs, I asked him why he continuously referred to me as Smitty. He stated that calling me Smitty was his way of letting me know that I was a great person and that, although I walked the prison, I was different. "You're all right with me, Smitty," he said that day.

Dad, your birthday is exactly one month away from today, May 29th. I still think of you and celebrate your life on your special day. It was years ago that I last received a birthday call from you, though. I can't even remember the year. I should keep no record of wrongs, *right?* Love is patient. Love is kind.

Today, I mourn the loss of you. May God keep your stomach filled and heart at peace. Possibly, I may see you in an upcoming chapter. While we are apart, I'll be growing. Gregory Smith, I've got news for you. I'm keeping the name and I don't need your consent to do so: Kishana Bianca Smith. Reclaiming SMITH.

– aTypeSmitty

Not wanting to pull myself out of bed, but knowing that I had to, I hit snooze on my alarm clock and lifted my body to an upright position. It was Monday. Within the hour, I was dressed and heading out of the door to work. I decided to take the train on that particular day because I had overheard news of a possible snowstorm. Don't ever place a bet on New England weather because you will likely lose your money--the only thing certain is the uncertain.

I walked into work and addressed the room with a morning greeting. I was taught that greeting the room upon entrance was a sign of respect, a teaching that never departed my being. I took my seat and began to check email. The cracked screen of my iPhone lit up, notifying me that I had a message. When I opened it my body stiffened. It read:

Emma was just killed. She was on her way to work around 7 a.m. when an unknown shooter shot a bullet, which lodged in the side of her neck. She was on life support for two hours. She just passed.

My body went from hardness to confusion. My heart was viciously pumping in my chest. I could feel my blood going from hot to cold and then hot again. My underarms were sweating, hands shaking, my mouth went dry and my eyes began to see blue dots. I was confused. I tried to put words to my mouth to explain to my supervisor that I had to leave for the day. But I couldn't speak. I wrote this message on a piece of white napkin, which she read. She then looked up at me and asked how I was doing. I began to cry.

The ride home was long. It was by chance that I'd ridden the train today. I was relieved by the fact that I would not have to drive--I don't believe that I would have been able to. I watched as the train drove by several stops. My brain was heavy with many thoughts. I began to reach out to the family members of Emma that I had contact with.

I couldn't believe what I had read, and I couldn't believe what the news report had confirmed: Emma was gone. I had seen Emma not even a month before her passing. Emma was one of my close friends, whom I'd met while in the House of Courage. She shared with me that she was also a survivor of domestic violence.

254

She was at least ten years older than me and she often scolded me about the people I had dated. We would drink tea and play cards together. She often showed me pictures of her beautiful daughters and said that she could not wait to be with them. The time we spent together was priceless. We talked about our dreams and hopes. She told me that she would go home and work towards opening a halfway house specific to self-identified female individuals. I joked with her that she would one day be able to call my facility, the SMITH House, whenever she needed to make referrals.

It had been less than a month since I last saw Emma. I went to visit her in Virginia and she was sharing all of her good news with me. She showed me the ring on her beautiful finger and told me that she was engaged to be married. Also, she told me that she had just opened her halfway house. She showed me a picture of her certification from City Hall and we jumped up and down in excitement. *I'm proud of you Emma. The city needs a facility headed by a strong black woman like YOU.*

I spent the next two months at my bedroom window. I was exhausted from pain. I continued to go to work and I tried to function as usual but losing Emma was hard, and my body reminded me of that every day. After work, I would spend the entire evening at the window. I spent time talking to Gregory and Emma. I looked up into the sky, as I often did when I was incarcerated. The sky helped me to feel connected. The sky was universal. I would ask Emma if she was okay and resting well. I asked her what she wanted to see happen, here on earth, with her halfway house. I asked her to give me the strength and joy that I needed to go on. I told her that my dark times were growing plenty and that life on the other side of those gates was constantly filled with battles and I knew she understood me.

At that window, Emma was with me and offered me the same quality of support that she had given me while we were behind bars. Emma told me a few things that day: republish your book, work hard, and have faith that things will be *better* this time. Do that other thing that you have been wanting to do--that would be the *best*. This is your twenty-eighth year so embrace new beginnings and calculated risk. I will be right here, to *watch you grow*. I knew exactly what I needed to do.

Dear Diary,

I have been navigating Boston and I truly enjoy the things that this city has offered me. I love my jobs and the purpose behind them. School has been hard. But I have a strong team of support, which has served to motivate me on difficult days and celebrate with me during positive moments. I enjoy watching the fast-paced nature of the city--people walk quickly as if each on a personal mission.

The one thing I have lacked in this city, though, is a meaningful sense of community. I spend most of my free time with my family and close friends, which has been rewarding. Still, I yearn for a community that could share a similar purpose, a network.

During my college days in Virginia, I enjoyed watching Greek life. I admired the fact that each sorority and fraternity that I encountered operated under shared values, purpose, history, creed, network, and many other things that held them to one another. I watched from afar, and wanted to experience a similar unity. Their pride was evident. However, I never saw a place for myself within any of those existing organizations.

Once I moved to Boston, I secretly hoped that I would find Greek life here. I hoped for a sense of belonging to an organization with shared values and purpose. I desired a similar form of sisterhood but when I began attending online college, Greek life, in the way I had known it, would no longer be an option for me. Sororities and fraternities were born out of college campuses, and I was not physically studying on a campus. Additionally, I didn't see Greek life the way I had experienced it in Virginia. Boston held very little Greek-life presence.

Just because I was attending online college didn't mean that I should be excluded from the possibility of that form of accomplishment. I knew what it was time to do: prepare. I began the research process and scripted the mission, vision, and principles for what would be born. I also spent months writing the creed. I knew that I would select a strong board of directors to lead this creation.

As my deep research process continued, I learned from Wikipedia, "The first fraternity in North America to incorporate most of the elements of modern fraternities was Phi Beta Kappa, founded at the College of William and Mary in 1775. The founding of Phi Beta Kappa followed the earlier establishment of two other secret student societies that had existed at that campus as early as 1750. In 1779 Phi Beta Kappa expanded to include chapters at Harvard and Yale. By the early 19th century, the organization transformed itself into a scholastic honor society and abandoned secrecy. In 1825 Kappa Alpha Society, the oldest extant fraternity to retain its social characteristic, was established at Union College. In 1827, Sigma Phi and Delta Phi were also founded at the same institution, creating the Union Triad. The further birthing of Psi

Upsilon (1833), Chi Psi (1841) and Theta Delta Chi (1847) collectively established Union College as the Mother of Fraternities.

"The development of 'fraternities for women' during this time was a major accomplishment in the way of women's rights and equality. By mere existence these organizations were defying the odds; the founding women were able to advance their organizations despite many factors working against them. The first 'Women's Fraternities' not only had to overcome restrictive social customs, unequal status under the law and the underlying presumption that they were less able than men but at the same time had to deal with the same challenges as fraternities with college administrations. Today, both social and multicultural sororities are present on more than 650 college campuses across the United States and Canada. The National Panhellenic Conference (NPC) serves as the 'umbrella organization' for 26 international sororities."

I grew in confidence of the details regarding the sorority that I would birth. Our mission would be grounded in the ideals of creating access and equity. Our guiding principles would be embodied by the aspects of freedom, perspective, work-life balance, self-care, calculated risk, mentorship, and advancement. Our creed would illustrate that we always stroll with God at the forefront because God has been the purest example of love. God had ordered my steps and my faith has continually offered me protection and guidance. We would also navigate this value with the understanding that each sister may call her God differently. Sassy would also sit at the head of that crown, reminding us that when we encounter difficulties and hardships, hard work and persistence will prevail.

The organization would be grounded in its ancestral roots and history, while also embracing change and advancement. Our organization would be open to nontraditional lifestyles such as online schooling and trade work.

I began to envision the formation of a founding line, which would center on traditionally marginalized individuals and communities, a line that would have confidence in these ideals and enthusiasm in our stroll. This sisterhood would hold a wealth of love, support, and knowledge, striving to intervene and show up for community, in proactive rather than reactive service. This would be an organization that values accountability, growth, truth, discipline, and advancement; Upward, Onward.

I would give birth to Sky, a universal entity, with a passionate founding line, Boston leadership chapter. This meant that soon, I would stroll in unity with my melanin sisters, linked side by side and looking *Upward. Onward.* Sigma Kappa Psi, Incorporated, would be born October 2018. I am free to celebrate its life because I have Reclaimed SMITH.

– aTypeSmitty

Bibliography

Bass, Ellen and Laura Davis. The Courage to Heal: A Guide for Woman Survivors of Child Sexual Abuse: Collins Living. 1988

Beatte, Melody. Codependent No More: Unabridged Recorded Audiobooks. 2006

Clarke, Peter. Statutory Rape: The Age of Consent. Legalmatch.com. 2016

Dallin H. Oaks. (October 2007). Good, Better, Best. The Church of Jesus Christ of Latter- Day Saints: General Conference. Retrieved from https://www.lds.org/general-conference/2007/10/good-better-best?lang=eng

Lancer, Darlene. Symptoms of Codependency: psyhcentral.com. 2016

Najavits, Lisa M. "Seeking Safety;" Gilford Press. 2002

National Education Association. (2017). Cradle to Prison Pipeline Campaign. Retrieved from http://www.nea.org/home/31606.htm

University of Texas at Austin: Texas Institute for Child and Family Wellbeing (Steve Hicks School of Social Work. (2018). 4 Things You Need to Know about the Cradle-to-Prison Pipeline. Retrieved from https://txicfw.socialwork.utexas.edu/4-things-you-need-to-know-about-the-cradle-to-prison-pipeline/

Wikipedia.(July 30, 2018). Fraternities and sororities. Retrieved from http://en.m.wikipedia.org/wiki/Fraternities_and_sororities

"You have the power…know how to use it: Victim Impact Facilitators Manual" "n.d"

About the Author

Kishana found her passion for domestic-violence (DV) work behind the walls of a state prison. Being a survivor of childhood sexual abuse and realizing the prevalence of incarcerated survivors of abuse, Kishana was eager to learn more. This deeply rooted passion led to years of extensive research. After performing a spoken-word piece at a youth talent show, Kishana was offered a job to advise and mentor the youth. She facilitated groups on self-esteem, codependency, creative writing, and anger management. Her work was recognized as effective and inspiring. She was then offered another position to work with impatient and outpatient survivors of DV and sexual abuse. When nineteen-year-old Kishana addressed an audience, her messages driven by experience, passion, and awareness trumped her age.

Inspired to reach audiences of many ages with her work, Kishana moved from Pennsylvania to Boston to become a domestic-violence advocate. If she's not walking the streets of South Boston with her hot tea from Dunkin' Donuts, she's working on a piece of literature to build community awareness around this issue. At the age of twenty-six, Kishana published her first book, *Diary of a Codependent*, which she explained as her second biggest breakthrough along her healing journey. Now, at the age of twenty-eight, this young, vibrant Caribbean-Boston author and activist is revealing her thoughts and strolling into what she now names her *Adulthood*, Reclaiming Smith.

"May people read or hear my work and be inspired; inspired to heal, to support, to educate, or be reminded of the importance of self-care and grounding, in doing 'this work.'"

– Kishana Smith

Codependency Hotline 1-855-315-4766
The National Domestic Violence Hotline 1-800-799-7233
The National Sexual Assault Hotline 1-800-656-HOPE